JAC SIMENSEN

Selma's Dowry

A Love Story

chapter

ONE

Izzy Katz didn't drink much. He'd have a Manhattan, on rare occasions two, and then he was done. Con Sullivan drank wine in place of cocktails, a taste he'd acquired while a guest in the British officers mess in North Africa during WWII. At a neighborhood bar, decent wine wasn't an option, so Con settled for a bottle of Pabst Blue Ribbon. When Izzy was building in South Jersey, which nowadays was most of the time, after paying their workmen on Fridays, Con and Izzy would get together for a drink. Over the past two years this meeting had turned into a ritual that happened more often than not.

Izzy was half way through his Manhattan. "It's a great shame, ya know; Selma's going to waste. She's such a wonderful girl: smart, hard working, loving. Beautiful, she's not, except to me. The only men she hangs around with are this arty-farty professor and his queer friends." Izzy sighed as he sadly shook his nearly bald head from side to side. "You know Selma's thirty now, not much hope for her getting married; breaks my heart."

Con didn't interrupt; Izzy had given this speech a dozen times and would likely do so a dozen more before he gave up trying to marry-off his only daughter.

Izzy was a successful home builder and Con had been Izzy's primary, carpentry subcontractor for thirteen years. They both trusted and respected each other and their business arrangements were always done with a handshake rather than a contract. Con and his wife, Ellie, had been invited to all of the Katz' weddings and bar mitzvahs; they were part of the extended family. Although Con had seen Selma recently, he always remembered her as a child; a chubby, serious little girl with beautiful porcelain white skin, and wire-frame glasses.

"Con, you won't believe it, I finally came up with a solution to her problem. It's so simple I don't know why I didn't think of it before, what our people have been doing for centuries. I'm going to give her a dowry, a big dowry, big enough to attract a decent husband."

Con chuckled under his breath, this was a new addition to the speech. "Izzy, this is nineteen-sixty-three, people don't give dowries anymore. What are you gonna' do, put a classified ad in the paper? 'Husband wanted: marry my daughter and I'll give you lots a money.'"

"Nah, nothin' like that; I'll just put the word around. I'm not thinkin' of a lump sum sort of dowry. I figure I'll give the two of 'em a new house and buy the husband a big car; Caddy, Lincoln, whatever he wants. I'll give him a good paying job, but he won't have to work if he doesn't want. He can go fishin' or golfin', whatever he wants to do, and I'll still pay him. All he has to do is make Selma happy and maybe give me some more grandkids. You think it'll work? There's gottta be a half-decent boy out there who would go for this deal; it's not like Selma's a leper."

Con half-smiled, "Izzy, you just might be onto something. What's Selma think of the idea?"

Izzy shook his head, "I figure I have to find the husband first and get Selma interested. Then, I'll explain the details to her."

"No Izzy. Not a good idea. You need to explain the dowry idea to her before you try and cut a deal with a potential husband, otherwise she's going to feel like you're putting her up for sale. Selma won't like that." Con tapped his beer glass on the bar for emphasis.

Izzy didn't agree, but decided not to argue the point. "Yeah, I guess you're right. Anyway, would ya help put the word around? Anyone who's got an unmarried son, one who's healthy and not stupid, and under thirty-five; they should give me a call. I'll check out the boy and if he's okay, I'll introduce him to Selma; alright?"

"Izzy it's a pretty far-fetched scheme but I'll do what I can to help, I know how much you love that girl."

They clinked glasses.

"Yes I do, I surely do."

———

Con and Ellie Sullivan always dined at home on Friday nights; it was their time to catch up on the week's events. Con came into the kitchen from the garage and was immediately enveloped in a fragrant cloud of spices and garlic. "Whoa, does that smell great."

Ellie put her arms around his neck and kissed him while he squeezed her rear, "Your favorite Friday night meal, linguine with garlic and shrimp."

She removed a large frying pan from the cook top for his inspection. "I finally got the fish man to get me large shrimp with the heads on. He thinks I'm crazy because he has to charge the same per pound with the heads on or off. 'Lady, you really wana pay extra money for shrimp heads? You eat em?'

I didn't even try to explain how the heads add flavor. I just told him that we deep fry the shrimp and eat 'em whole." She put the pan back on the gas. "There's a bottle of Chablis in the fridge; open it before I die of thirst, please."

Con pulled the cork and half filled two glasses, while Ellie poured the shrimp and garlic sauce over the linguine. "Can you bring the wine and my glass? We're in the bar room tonight."

The bar room was an intimate room off the main living area; a comfortable room with a recessed ceiling and crown molding, a chandelier, and parquet flooring. At the end of the room in front of a large bay window stood a small, custom made, slate top bar and three barstools, and in the middle, a round, inlaid antique table and four leather chairs. They usually used the bar room for dinner alone or with their closest friends.

Ellie tossed the spinach salad then served the shrimp and linguine. "So how's old Izzy doing? You two did have your regular Friday board meeting didn't you?"

"Izzy's same as ever. He's still going back and forth about moving to Jersey. Now that Jack's moved into Quail Run it's only a matter of time before he leaves Philly; just he and Selma rattling around in that big old house."

"And how are Jack and Syd doing? Are they gonna stick it out?"

Con broke the head off a shrimp and dropped it in the refuse bowl. "I haven't seen Jack in almost two months and Izzy doesn't bring up the subject of divorce anymore. I talked with Roz, Morty's wife on Tuesday; she said that Jack and Syd are doing just great. Roz said they went to Venice for a week and came back madly in love, like teenagers. Roz is a pretty sharp judge of people so if she says their doing great, they probably are. Actually, Jack called just this morning; I'm meeting him tomorrow to go over some drawings."

Ellie picked up a shrimp and began to peel, "What about Jack's floozy?"

Con shrugged, "I guess she's out of the picture." He took a sip of wine. "So, listen to this, Izzy's got a new twist on finding a husband for Selma. He's going to give a prospective husband a dowry to marry her."

Ellie almost choked on the linguine she was swallowing, "A dowry, you're kidding?"

"I think he's at the end of his rope. He asked me to put the word around; about the dowry, I mean. I told him I would. I know that Angelo has a son about thirty or so who's a mechanic, I don't think he's married. Joe Dunny has a boy in his twenties; I don't know anything about him except that he used to be on TV when he was in high school, a regular on *Bandstand*. I sort of remember Joe saying his boy was in California trying to break into the movies. It would take a pretty unusual guy to be interested in Izzy's scheme; someone really lazy, someone who could handle the stigma of being kept by his wife's father. Not many guys around like that."

Ellie bit her lip, "Let me tell you a sad story and you just might think otherwise. I was going to save this until after dinner but you might as well hear it now. We got a letter from Saint Stephen's today and…"

Con interrupted, "You don't need to tell me, they finally followed through on their threats and threw him out?"

"Exactly."

Con put down his fork. "No surprise, this has been in the making for awhile; ever since sex and booze took over his life."

"I'd sure like to come to his defense, but I can't; fun seems to be the only thing important to him right now. I guess we should be thankful that he's not into crime or drugs." She wrinkled her forehead, "At least I think he doesn't use drugs."

"Connor's drifting around without a rudder but I doubt that he would do anything self destructive. He loves life too much. Somehow that's what this is all about, having fun and ignoring responsibilities—I don't know what to think."

Ellie refilled their glasses. "That's not all, after I read the letter I called his apartment and, surprise, surprise, he was there. I think I woke him up. I asked him what he planned on doing. He said that he got fired from Acme Markets but got his old summer job bartending at Cappy's back. He asked if he could come home for a while; I said that he could. I know I should have asked you first, but I didn't; I said he could come home."

Con reached across the table and took her hand. "You did the right thing. Of course he can come home, he's our son, and I love him. I'd still love him if he was a serial killer and he hasn't done anything that depraved yet. He's been working hard at screwing up his life for the last couple of years, but it is his life. I can't live it for him and neither can you."

Ellie sighed, "It's just a pity to see him squandering the opportunity to get an education and a good job. He's such a bright kid. He can be so charming, and he's honest. I don't think he's ever told me a direct lie, not even when he was little."

Con released her hand and sat back in his chair. "Well it's not time to give up on him; took me a few years to get myself together after the war. Maybe it's genetic. My father roamed around the country for a while when he first came to America, before he settled down. Anyway, when's he coming home?"

"He didn't say, probably when his rent comes due."

Con snorted, "That's exactly when he'll come home."

chapter

TWO

"Papa, I don't need you to do this. I know that you'd do anything to make me happy, but I am happy, I really am. I have lots of interesting friends, I go out weekends and I enjoy my work. I don't need you to go and buy me a husband." Selma continued scraping dishes while she talked.

Izzy sat at the kitchen table finishing his coffee. "It's not natural for a woman to stay single all her life; you'll dry out and get old and cranky. I'll be dead and there won't be anyone to take care of you."

Selma put her hands on her hips. "Papa, you're only sixty, you're not going to die for decades; you're as healthy as a horse. Jacob and Morty and Syd and Roz and the kids all love me, Aunt Sally too. If anything happens to you, they'll help me. I don't need a husband and I don't want you to buy one for me. That's it, the end."

Izzy knew that when Selma said 'The end,' there was nothing to be gained in trying to persuade her further, at least not for a day or two. He changed the subject.

"Jacob says he's got a nice three bedroom Cape in Quail Run he wants us to look at. They're just starting to work on the inside so you can still choose the colors, cabinets, appliances and everything. Whada you think? Wanna look at it? Jacob says it's a corner lot and backs up to preservation land. He's put it on hold until you see it."

Selma took her seat at the table, she sighed. "Last year I said we should stay in the neighborhood, but the neighborhood has changed so much it's almost like we've already moved. Did you see that Mrs. Kovacs closed her store last week? Grandma loaned her money to get started and I've been going there all my life; then poof, just like that, it's gone. Mrs. K said that with her husband dead it was too much for her. Nobody wanted to buy the store; she just sold off her inventory, closed the doors and went to live with her sisters in Allentown."

Izzy filled his coffee cup from the aluminum percolator and motioned with the pot to see if Selma wanted another.

She shook her head, "I guess it's time we moved: seems like all of your business is in Jersey now, it would be better for you. Be nice to be close to Jacob and Syd and the kids. We could have dinner together more often. Morty and Roz would be closer too. With the new bridge, Delaware Township isn't that far from town anymore, I can get to Center City in under an hour or…"

"Cherry Hill," Izzy interrupted. "Its Cherry Hill now not Delaware Township. The town fathers thought that Cherry Hill had more sizzle and so the people voted and now it's Cherry Hill."

Selma laughed, "Quail Run in Cherry Hill; now that's a mouthful of kitsch."

Con was surprised to see Connor's red Corvair in the driveway; he'd come home several days earlier than Con expected. His first thought was that Connor had run out of money, but he scolded himself, "No sarcasm; that's what he's expecting and I'm not going to do it. Be positive." Con noticed that the Chevy was clean with no noticeable dents or scratches. "That's a good sign," he thought.

Connor was slouched at the kitchen table reading the paper. He folded the paper and stood when he saw his father enter from the garage. Con came right up to him and hugged him. Surprised, Connor hugged him back.

"Good to see you son," Con looked him over. "Well, not too much the worse for wear. You look good."

Connor was wearing a short sleeve, blue golf shirt with CAPPY'S embroidered on the pocket; obviously he was back to bartending.

"You look good yourself, Dad." Conner sat.

"Where's your mother?"

"She had to go down to the post office. I just got home from the eight-thirty to four shift."

Con smiled, "Many people come in for a drink at eight-thirty?"

"No eight-thirty to ten is restocking and cleanup from the night before. We don't actually open until ten for a few hard drinking, shot-and-beer locals. The business types start rolling in at eleven-thirty and it's flat out from then until closing. Cappy has a great business going for him."

Con went to the refrigerator and took out an open bottle of white wine, "Glass of wine?"

Connor motioned with his cup. "No thanks, I'm drinking coffee. Funny how working with alcohol all day puts you off drinking; at least for a couple hours."

Con half filled his glass and sat at the table opposite Connor. "So, everything's all finished at school?"

"I packed my stuff in the car last night. Sold the bed and furniture to the new tenant for thirty bucks, about what I paid at Goodwill. I left on good terms with Saint Stephan's. They said that if I passed some night or summer school classes they'd consider my re-entering as a junior next year. With my record I thought that that was pretty decent of 'em."

Con struggled to keep the emotion he was feeling out of his voice. "Is that what you're planning on doing?"

Connor went to the coffee pot for a refill, "I don't know what I wanna do. Working at Cappy's is okay, it'll buy me some time to think things through. Thanks for letting me come home Dad. I really appreciate it."

Jac Simensen

"Son, this is your home as much as it's mine or your mother's. You can always come home, always."

Connor returned to the table and rested his head on his arms. "Dad, I'm sure that you think I'm a total screw up; I couldn't disagree. College just didn't work for me. After the first year I just didn't wanna study or go to class. Lately, I even started to get bored with my social life. Understand, nobody made me screw up, I did it all by myself."

They heard the noise of the garage door opening; Ellie was home.

Con rose and put his hands on Connor's shoulders. "Son, if you want, we can talk later on. Might help if I told you about some things I've screwed up in my life, including not going back to college after the war."

Connor looked down at the table. "Maybe tomorrow? I gotta run over to the mall tonight and get some black chinos for the bar. These are the only pair I own and they're pretty skanky."

"Tomorrow night, then?"

Connor half-heartedly nodded, "Sure."

chapter

THREE

Jack Katz was just finishing a detailed description of his vacation to Venice. "Connie, you gotta take Ellie there. She'll love it and I guarantee it will improve your love life. Syd is like a young nympho now. All I have to do is say something in Italian or pour her some Campari, that's this red Italian liquor, and she heads for the bedroom. I'm telling you, it's worth every cent I paid for that alone."

Jack was the only person who called Con, Connie. Con didn't mind, Jack was like that, he did everything his own way. If anyone corrected him or objected to what he said, Jack would look at them quizzically like they were speaking a language he didn't understand. Jack's real name was Jacob, but only his father and sister called him Jacob, even his wife called him Jack. The name suited him; he was much more a Jack than a Jacob.

Con grinned, "I spent enough time in Italy during the war. I'm sure Venice is wonderful but I think I'll live out the rest of my days in the U.S. I've done all the traveling I want. As for Ellie, there's no need to restart the fire, it gets warmer every year."

Jack laughed, "Your Ellie is quite a girl. I haven't seen her since Morty's David's bar mitzvah. I'll get Syd to call and get us together."

The waitress cleared away the remains of their lunch and brought them coffee. She knew not to hurry Jack even during the busy lunch hour. Jack was a regular, a big tipper who gave all of the steady girls a nice present at Christmas; Olga's Dinner was Jack's second office.

Like his father, Izzy, Jack was a developer and builder. He bought farms and rural land tracts in Southern New Jersey and turned them into communities of well-built, attractive, split-levels, raised ranches, colonials and Cape Cods for the growing middle class. Where after the war, Levitt had built communities of inexpensive, cookie-cutter homes for the returning G.I.s, ten years later, Izzy and Jack Katz, were constructing upscale, semi-custom homes for those same G.I.s, now business owners, professionals, executives and well-paid tradesmen.

Morty Katz, Jack's brother, owned a lighting supply business in nearby Pennsauken. Of course, all of the lighting fixtures in the houses Izzy and Jack built came from Morty's store.

Con and Ellie lived in a house Izzy had built six years ago. Izzy had put in lots of unbilled extras and Con did most of the finish carpentry himself. While of modest size, the house was exceptionally attractive and sited on the best lot in the neighborhood.

Con and Jack were talking about Jack's next development. Jack still had some legal hoops to jump through before he could break ground. Con had a good eye for land use and Jack was showing him the architect's initial usage plans for the land.

Con looked at the spread out drawings. "This is more complex than Quail Run or even Millside Farms. I can't tell from this why they're planning on putting the larger lots up on the hill and why they want to take these trees out. I'll have a look this afternoon and get back to you tomorrow. Where is this place?"

"Blackwood," Jack replied. "It's called…"

Con cut him off, "Sunny Slope Farm."

"Oh, you know it?" Jack looked puzzled.

"That's Ellie's aunt and uncle's old place. Ellie and I had our first date there. The Carter's were very special people who had a run of really bad luck. The son was killed at Pearl Harbor, the father died of a heart attack not long afterward, and then the son in law, who was running the farm, died from lung cancer. That's when they sold out."

Jack shook his head. "Damn, that's sad. Do you think Ellie will be unhappy with me for building there?"

"I know she won't. After the Carter's sold, Ellie's cousin, Flora, took her mother and sons to Vermont where she raises goats and makes cheese. She remarried and last I heard is doing well. She got a good price for the land and is pretty much set for life."

Jack grinned, "Considering what I had to pay the current owner, I'm happy to hear that she did well. Thanks for looking at the property, Connie. By the way, how's young Connor doing at school, things looking any better?"

Con told Jack a brief version of Connor's sad story; Jack kept shaking his head.

The waitress brought the check. "You can take that to the register whenever you're through Mr. Katz, no rush."

Jack smiled at her. "Thanks Margie, we're just finishing." He turned to Con, "I got an idea, might be something to help Connor out and help me as well."

Con was surprised, "Oh, what's that?"

"You know Maryann; she sits the sample house in Quail Run? Yesterday, Maryann told me that she needs to go to Denver to take care of her mother for a while. Seems her mother's been fighting cancer for a few years and is in the final round. She wants to leave as soon as possible but said that she would stick around until I could find someone for her to train. The job doesn't take specific experience. Anybody smart and personable can do it. Maybe Connor would be interested? I can pay him two thirty, two forty a week, probably more than he's getting at the bar."

"That's really kind of you, Jack; I don't know though, I'd worry he'd screw up. You don't need a screw up and neither does he."

Jack picked up the check and stood. "Look Connie, Quail Run is almost sold out; I don't think he could do much damage. Talk to him tonight and if he's interested let me know. Let me know tomorrow, okay?"

They shook hands and Con took the plans and headed for the truck while Jack paid the check.

chapter

FOUR

Selma liked the house. It was a three bedroom Cape with one downstairs bed/bath combo, and two smaller, upstairs bedrooms with a shared bath. She would take the upstairs rooms for herself and give her father the larger, downstairs bedroom. She could see that it wouldn't take much work to combine the two upstairs bedrooms and expand the bath and walk-in closet into the freed up space. Two bedroom houses weren't very marketable, but then Selma planned on living in the house with her father for a long while.

The kitchen was large and bright. The rough plumbing was already in place but she would have it redone to accommodate a center island sink and dishwasher. The dining room would need a chair rail and crown molding. The family room would become her office; the only change it would need to suit her requirements would be a set of French doors opening to a glass and steel conservatory where she would grow herbs. The living room wouldn't need any structural changes at all.

The basement was enormous with a ten foot ceiling and could easily be turned into a cozy living space where they could watch TV, or read, or just get away from each other. A wet bar would be nice, and maybe a small guest room and shower in case they needed to put someone up for the night, she thought. The two car garage had lots of storage room, and the corner lot, as Jacob had said, assured their privacy.

Yes, Selma thought, this house would suit her just fine.

When she told Izzy the changes she would need he just shrugged. "Tell your brother, I'm only the one who has to pay, he does the work."

With her notes in hand, Selma headed back to the model home to look at paint, tile and carpet samples and at catalogs of appliances and plumbing fixtures. On the way home she planned to stop at Morty's showroom and pick out a chandelier for the dining room and ceiling lighting for the rest of the house. Selma could make choices and decisions quickly and she was sure she could have everything decided with only two or three more trips to the house.

Connor had already discovered that the meager income from bartending was destroying his social life. He was working more hours than his former part-time job at Acme Markets, but, including tips, taking home only about seventy percent of his meat cutter's pay. His parents had bought him a car when he started college but made it clear that he was responsible for the maintenance and insurance expenses that went along with it. His parents hadn't asked for any board money and Connor hadn't offered.

He'd been spoiled by having his own apartment for the last year. When he found a woman interested in sleeping with him he simply invited her to his place. Now most of the women he dated still lived at home and most of his prospective sex partners had out grown the high school, back seat experience. That left either a girl with an apartment, (who Connor hadn't met yet,) or a motel, (which was expensive.) His sex life was definitely in decline.

When Con told him about Jack Katz' job, Connor's heart sped up. He quickly figured that the salary would net him enough to rent a decent apartment and restore his independence and libido.

Con wasn't exactly thrilled with the idea of Connor working for Jack; Jack was one of Con's principal employers and also his friend. Connor's track record for dependability and initiative over the last year wasn't stellar. It would cause Con pain all around if Connor screwed up. Con strained to find the words that would alert Connor to his concerns without implying that Connor was a loser; he never found them.

Con had to review the drawings of Sunny Slope Farm with Jack. He thought that perhaps the architects had made a few questionable trade-offs in laying out the land usage plan and Jack needed to hear his concerns before a Monday meeting. Con drove them both to Quail Run in the pickup.

They had only traveled a few hundred yards when Connor brought up the issue on Con's mind. "Dad, I know that the Katz' are the main guys you work for and they're your good friends. I promise you that if I get this job I won't do anything that will damage your relationship. If I can't do the job, I'll tell you right away. Okay?"

Con was surprised by Connor's concern and directness. "I appreciate that. But there's no doubt in my mind that you'll do a great job for Jack. I wouldn't have mentioned it if I thought otherwise. I don't expect that you'll want to be in construction for the rest of your life, but this job will give you some great experience working with families who are making a big decision about spending a large part of their income. It's a lot more than a sales job; it's helping people make choices that are right for them. Jack builds a quality house and stands behind his work so there's no concern about the product."

Connor shifted in his seat, "Do you think Jack meant two thirty or did he mean two forty?"

Con grinned, "Knowing Jack, it probably depends on how impressed he is with you. In the real world, the first thing you have to sell is yourself."

———

Maryann and Selma were making great progress. Nearly half of Maryann's forms and check sheets had been completed; it was rare that she got to work with a decisive buyer. The model house was a 'Carlton,' a four bedroom, four-and-a-half bath colonial with a side facing garage and colorful pavers forming the crescent shaped drive at the front of the house. As was his usual practice, Jack fitted out the model with top of the line plumbing fixtures, appliances, accessories and extras. That made Selma's job easy, she simply wandered from one room to the next, picking and choosing,

"I like that bath tub. Can I get it with gold fittings instead of pewter? That refrigerator is perfect; does it come in almond or just white? This is beautiful carpet. I'd like the exact same thing in the upstairs bedroom."

From time to time Maryann ran off to check the catalogs or call a supplier. She was having fun; it was a pleasure to work with someone who never asked about prices, and they finished in only an hour and a half. Maryann had a sheet of questions she would follow up on when all of the suppliers were available on Monday. She put the forms and papers on her desk and turned to Selma.

"Wow, that's the fastest I've ever specked out a house in my whole career. It's great to work with someone who knows exactly what they want. I'm afraid that I can't help you with the structural changes. You'll have to discuss those with Mr. Katz; I mean your brother. He's scheduled to be here in half an hour to meet with Mr. Sullivan and his son. Do you wanna wait?"

Selma extended her hand, "Thanks Maryann, you've been great to work with. I can see why my father and brother speak so highly of you. I'll go in the kitchen and see what my father's up to. I've got the whole afternoon free so I can wait for Jacob as long as my father's okay with that."

"Thank you Miss Ka…. Selma. I'll let you know as soon as Jack gets here."

———————

Con and Connor entered through the garage. The garage was both the temporary office and show room for Quail Run. Maryann was seated at her desk reviewing the forms she had just completed with Selma. When she saw Con she gave him a big hug and a kiss on the cheek.

"Con Sullivan, where have you been hiding, it's been months."

Con put his hand on her shoulder. "Well Moneypenny I've been on a secret mission to Marlton saving the world from shoddy construction."

Maryann laughed; Con always called her Moneypenny. Connor checked her out. She really did look like *007's* Miss Moneypenny. With long, ash-blond hair and a trim figure she was quite attractive. But at forty-ish she was over the horizon of his personal interest; still, she was quite attractive.

Maryann noticed Connor checking her out and extended her hand, "No doubt about it, you're Connor; quite the handsome combination of both your parents."

Connor took her hand. "Dad's right; you do look like Moneypenny. But much prettier, of course."

Maryann laughed and shook her head. "Like father like son. You Irish rogues are all alike, must run in the blood." The phone was ringing. She motioned them in and went back to her desk.

Con walked to the plot map on the far wall. "Like I said, there aren't many houses left to sell. The red pins are closed or occupied. The blue are under deposit. The green are available. Here's where we are now. Next door used to be a 'Provincetown' model. Provincetown's a Cape and the smallest and least expensive thing Jack builds. Still, it's a quality house and a real bargain for young couples. Provincetown's usually sell out first. Con studied the map, "Looks like they're all sold except maybe this one here." He pointed to an oversize lot on the edge of the plan.

Maryann had finished her phone conversation, "Nope, that one's sold. That's Izzy and Selma's new house. I better put a pin in, might as well make it a red one. Selma's got some great plans. By the time she's through it will probably be more expensive then a Carlton…Izzy and Selma are in the kitchen having coffee, waiting for Jack. If you want to go back and see them, I can start getting this young scamp ready to show houses."

Connor looked puzzled, "But I thought that I was here to interview with Mr. Katz?"

Maryann shrugged, "Jack told me that you'd be here to start training today, I guess that means you're hired."

Connor smiled broadly, "Sounds good to me."

Con headed for the kitchen and Maryann steered Connor back to the wall. "First let's spend a little more time with this plot plan and get you up to speed on what are still available and the features of our different models." Maryann handed Connor a folder of home plans.

Connor turned to Maryann. "I was sorry to hear about your mother's illness. I'll try my best to keep things running smooth until you get back."

She put her hand on his arm. "Thanks for saying that Connor, it's going to be real hard. My mother's always been my best friend as well as my Mom. It's like I'm losing the two people who are closest to me at once." She lowered her voice, "I haven't had a chance to tell Jack this yet, so keep it to yourself; I'm moving back to Colorado for good."

"Maryann, I know that we really don't know each other, but if I can help you in any way, drive you to the airport or anything, know that I'll be happy to help, just ask."

She patted his arm and gave him a shy little smile. Connor thought that she looked even more attractive when she was sad... Maybe forty wasn't too old after all.

"Hey Con, come have some coffee with us." Izzy and Selma were sitting at the kitchen table watching a news program on the counter top TV. Selma stood and held out her hand.

Con ignored her outstretched hand and gave her a hug. "Selma, Selma, look at how pretty you are. I always think of you the way you looked at eight in a white dress with a big red bow and little wire frame glasses, always so serious you were."

Selma gave him a big smile. She had always liked Con Sullivan. "Well, the dress got a little too tight, and I wear contacts now, other than that, I guess I'm still pretty serious."

Con took her hand and slowly twirled her around. "Selma, you look great." And she did; a dark-blue velvet, Empire-waist dress with a fitted bodice accentuated her perfectly proportioned breasts and gave a hint of the great body under its folds. It fell to just four inches above her knee, enough to show off nicely proportioned legs but not too short to be provocative. Her thick hair was pulled back, tied with a blue ribbon and allowed to cascade down her back. She wore an expensive watch and had a gold chain around her neck suspending a single, intensely blue sapphire. She wore no rings or other jewelry and had on only a small amount of makeup, just enough to accentuate her large eyes and full lips.

Con released her hand and turned to Izzy. "So Jack made the sale. Maryann said that you decided to take the last Provincetown; the one on the great lot that borders state conservation land."

Izzy shrugged, "Jacob didn't sell me anything. Selma's the one who decided that it was time to leave the neighborhood."

Selma set her mug down hard. "That's not true Izzy Katz and you know it. We both agreed that the neighborhood has changed so much that there was no reason for us to be there anymore. In fact, you wanted to leave before I did."

Izzy smirked, "I don't know about that. You know that my father moved into that neighborhood when he came here from Germany? I spent my whole life there."

"Papa, you're being an *alter cocker*. Don't listen to him Con he's just fishing for undeserved sympathy."

Con sat next to Izzy. "I grew up in a city neighborhood and I admit it took some adapting when we moved out here. The main thing is the driving: drive to get the paper, drive to get the groceries, to go to the post office, the dentist, doctor; to do anything at all, you drive."

Izzy pushed back in his chair, "I don't think I'm gonna like it out here with all the trees and weeds, I have allergies you know."

Selma stood and put her hands on her hips, "Papa, now you cut this out. I think I'm gonna move here by myself and leave you in the city, alone."

Jack Katz came into the kitchen in time to hear the end of the conversation. "Papa, are you working at being a pain in the ass or is it just one of things that comes naturally with age?" Jack took off his trench coat and hugged Selma. "You look wonderful little sister. Is this old man trying to spoil your fun?"

Selma looked back at Izzy, "It's just his warped sense of humor, don't pay him any attention."

Jack kissed Izzy on the cheek and shook Con's hand. "Thanks for coming over on a Saturday, Con. I ran into Maryann and Connor in the office, they're getting along just fine. Connor hasn't changed; he's still the charmer. That should work well for him in this job since the ladies usually make the buying decisions. Look, we got a lot of stuff to do here and I have to be home by four-thirty. Syd got us invited to some formal charity function at Tavistock Country Club in Haddonfield. Actually, it's not in Haddonfield; the wealthy WASPs there had enough pull to get the politicians to make the golf course and all the houses around it into a separate town. Can you imagine that? Just because they couldn't drink on Sunday in Haddonfield they set up their own town where they can sip martinis all week long. Now that's what I call real power. Syd got to know some of the women there through the charity stuff she does and they invited us. Somehow, I don't think that they know we're Jewish. I mean, Katz does sort of give it away, but I thought that I'd better take along a bottle of Mogen David just to make sure they realize who they've invited." Everyone laughed at the image of Jack and Syd in formal wear with a bottle of kosher wine in hand.

"Connie, let's clear off this table and we can review the drawings here; Papa you stay and help, you're good at this. I think this should only take a half hour, what do you think Connie?"

Con nodded.

"Connie can get back to his Saturday and his pretty wife. Then I need to talk business with Connor for ten minutes. After that little sister, you and Papa and I can go over and figure out how we're going to turn a Cape Cod into the Taj Mahal. Is that okay with everyone?"

Con said, "You might want to start with Selma. I'm going to have to wait for Connor to finish with Maryann. We didn't realize that you wanted him to start training today so we came together."

Jack shrugged, "Connor can start working with Maryann tomorrow, that'll be fine."

Selma stood up. "I have a better idea, Jacob. You and Con look at the plans now then Con can go home and I'll drop Con's son home when you and I are finished at the Cape. I'm going to Morty's to look at lighting fixtures and Merchantville's on my way."

"Good idea," Jack said. "Let me see those drawings Connie."

chapter

FIVE

Connor was impressed. He'd never ridden in a Mercedes before. Not only was it a Mercedes, it was a 190 SL sports car, triple black: black body, black, canvas top, black leather interior. The chrome trim glistened in the afternoon sun, from the large three pointed star that dominated the front grill, to the massive rear bumper. He'd driven an MG a few times and cruised around in a friend's Triumph TR-4, but this was different. The190 SL screamed style, wealth and sex appeal. The flowing lines of the 190 SL's bodywork mimicked the curves of a naked woman lying on her belly on a bed or beach. Connor was impressed.

He looked at Selma, the car suited her perfectly; she was dressed in tasteful, obviously expensive, clothing. Connor's penny loafers, chinos, pale-blue, oxford-cloth, button-down shirt, and tan sport coat were the height of style at St. Stephan's, but, seated next to Selma in the luxury of the Mercedes, his clothing seemed dated.

Selma worked the manual gearbox with grace and precision, the mellow tones of the exhaust, rising and falling as she shifted. The sophisticated interplay of piano and vibes, performed by the Modern Jazz Quartet, spilled into the car from the Blaupunkt radio.

Connor pointed toward the radio, "Jazz at 96.5, my favorite station," he lied. His car radio was always set to WIBG and the top forty rock an' roll hits.

Selma shifted in her seat. "Jazz and classical are about the only things I listen to; everything else seems so noisy."

"Jazz and classical are my favorites as well, but I do listen to folk music and sometimes top 40 hits. You know the kind of music you hear at parties."

With men she didn't know, Selma liked to start out a bit aloof. If she found that she enjoyed their company it was easy to become friendly. If she didn't, she simply turned up the frost.

"Most of the parties I go to are cocktail parties; jazz rather than dance music." It was her turn to lie. Martin, her bi-sexual boyfriend, and his friends tended more towards Jerry-Lee Lewis or Mongo Santamaria than Frank or Ella, and when the grass and hash got passed around, Dylan would likely take center stage.

Connor either missed or ignored the coolness of her remark. "My grandfather had one of those clunky, old fashioned combination radio-phonographs, the type with the giant speaker in front and push buttons for the radio stations and a turntable inside."

Selma nodded, "I know the kind. We had one in our living room until I replaced it with a stereo."

"My grandfather had a huge collection of classical records, 78 RPM: Beethoven, Brahms, Chopin, Mozart, all the biggies. My father was off in Africa and Italy in the Army when I was born, I didn't get to meet him until I was almost three. My mother and I lived with my grandparents and so I was bombarded with classical music from birth, in fact even before birth. When I hear a classical piece on the radio I often recognize the music. As soon as it starts I know what will come next, I can whistle along with it, but I can't tell you the name of the piece or who wrote it. I have this uneducated relationship with classical music. It's like the music is stored up inside my head and when I hear a piece begin, the entire thing just pours out of my memory; kinda strange, huh?"

Selma smiled. Connor noticed that her teeth were all straight and perfectly placed. The fortune Izzy had poured into the orthodontist's pockets hadn't been wasted.

"My father loves to listen to violin music. Until I went to school I thought that all music was for violins. When I heard a piano or singing I kept waiting for the violins to start. I know what you mean; I can hear a violin piece and instinctively know the music but not have any idea who wrote it."

Connor pointed out the turn onto Kings Highway and changed the subject. "So you and your father are moving to Cherry Hill?"

She nodded, "It's going to be a while. I think it'll take three or four months to finish the house. That's a good thing. My family's been in our current house since the mid-forties and while my father and I aren't pack rats, there's still a lot of stuff to sort through and unload. My brother, Morton's room is still the way he left it when he got married. It's going to take some time to get organized. Fortunately, we have a daily, Mrs. Weiss, who's been with us for years. I'll let her make the decisions about what to throw out. She knows the family history better than I do. Except for my father's favorite chair and my grandmother's desk, I've decided to chuck all the furniture and curtains and stuff and start fresh. New furniture for a new house makes sense to me. I have a girl friend who's a decorator; she'll help me make sure things go together. That's not one of my strengths."

"If you don't think I'm being too nosey, what are your strengths?"

She glanced sideways at him, "Considering we just met, that is a bit direct, but since you asked: numbers are my strength."

Connor was puzzled, "Numbers?"

"Numbers," she repeated. "Ever since I was a little kid I've been good with numbers: arithmetic, math and then accounting; I majored in accounting. I always struggled with composition and spelling but found that math just came naturally. It's one of those things. Most people are better with either words or numbers or just average with both, few people excel at both. Think about it; are you better with numbers or words?"

Connor thought for only a second, "No doubt about it, words. I never really had trouble with math but I had to work hard to pass calculus; composition was never a problem."

"So Mr. Sullivan, what are your other strengths?"

Connor half smiled, "I'd say screwing up is my great strength, yes, definitely, screwing up."

Selma down shifted and passed an old Nash Rambler that was smoking badly. "Phew, that stinks. And just what have you screwed up lately?"

"I've been doing a pretty good job screwing up my life. I got myself mentally gunged up last year. I decided to major in fun, but the college wasn't too thrilled with my choice and threw me out in the beginning of my junior year. That was about four weeks ago. I've been tending bar and living with my parents since then."

"Where were you going to school?"

"Saint Stephan's near Wilmington; you know it?"

"Of course, it's an excellent school. You must have had great SATs and grades to get in Saint Stephan's. My sophomore roommate transferred from Saint Stephan's to Temple because she found the academic pace too tough for her."

Connor ran his fingers through his hair. "I did pretty well in high school and the fact that I was a decent football and basketball player helped me get accepted. I did okay through freshman year before I came off the tracks. It wasn't the academics it was just all the stuff going on around me that caused the problems. Anyway, I screwed up with panache."

"So, you've decided to go to work for my brother sitting models?"

Connor laughed, "Is that what it's called, sitting models?"

She nodded.

"What do I call myself, a model sitter? That sounds like the perfect hunting dog. How about, a model minder? No, that sounds like a queer who helps the models change their clothes at fashion shows. I know, I'll be a master of models, I couldn't get a B.A. so I went straight for the masters."

Selma shook her head, "How about if you just say you sell houses at Quail Run?"

He snickered, "How about, I say I sell quail burgers at Quail Run? Madam, would you like your quailburger with cheese? Onions? Tomatoes? Feathers?"

"Okay, enough; for a screw up you're pretty glib."

Connor pointed right, "Take this turn and then the third left onto Comstock Road, in about three miles."

"How long has your family lived in Merchantville?"

"Just about six years. We moved when I was getting ready for high school. The high school in Camden where I was supposed to go was getting rough. I remember some of the kids saying that a good year there was when you had the same number of teeth at the end of the year as you did in the beginning. I went to Merchantville High, it was okay, and we had winning sports teams during my three years… You went to Temple, you said. Rough in that part of Philly, wasn't it?"

She shook her head, "Not really, not when I graduated. I mean the neighborhood's full of poverty and crime now. It wasn't as bad then. You learned real fast how to survive."

"You went to high school in Philly too?"

"Actually, I went to a convent school called Our Lady of the Little Flower, near Valley Forge."

Connor was visibly surprised, "But I thought that you were Jewish, I mean my parents have gone to your family's weddings and bar mitzvahs. You're Catholic?"

"No, no, I'm not Catholic. I guess I'm not much of a Jew either," she paused, "it's a long story."

"We've got time; I don't have to be home till dark."

"It's not that interesting."

"Come on, a Jewish girl at the Lady Flower Convent? That's got to be interesting."

"Little Flower not Lady Flower," She corrected.

"Sorry, Little Flower."

She looked at him sternly. "Connor, do you want to hear the story or not?" He folded his hands in his lap, "I'll be quiet."

Selma down shifted and turned onto Comstock Road. "My grand-mother and grandfather and their two children came to Philadelphia from Germany around the turn of the century. Because of some con-nections, which I won't go into, my grandfather got an excellent job. When he left Germany and sold his farm, he got about $2,000; that's probably about $40,000 in today's money. Since he had a good job he didn't need to spend the money so he gave it to my grandmother and told her to put it to good use. Over the next ten years she learned about investing and grew the money quite a bit. She bought old build-ings and converted them into apartments. She'd pay a builder to reno-vate; make them safe and install basic kitchens and baths. Then she'd rent them cheaply to new immigrants with the condition that the ten-ants had to provide the labor to finish the re-decoration. You know; things like painting, flooring, and cabinetry.

Connor pointed left, "Sorry to interrupt, but you turn here."

Selma looked at him, "You asked for this, have you had enough?"

"I'm fascinated, I really am; can't wait for the part about the Flow-er Convent."

Selma made a face. She realized that he was purposely misquot-ing the name of the convent school and chose to ignore him. "I'll get to the convent in a minute…Because her investments were always very conservative, grandmother made it through the Depression in one piece." She looked at Connor, "Now for the Lady Flower convent school."

He grinned, "I thought that it was Little Flower?"

She returned his grin, "Two can play the game.—Lots of Grand-mother Miriam's tenants were Catholics: Irish, Poles and Italians. The success of grandmother's plan depended on renting to responsible people. So when it came time to select tenants, Grandmother would often turn to the local priest and nuns to help her find the most reli-able people. She developed a particularly close relationship with the Mother Superior whose order was…..." Selma pointed to Connor.

"Our Lady of the Little Flower," He said, syllable by syllable.

She grinned, "Very good, see you are trainable. I'm sure you can guess the outcome. Miriam loaned the convent school money to see them through the Depression. To help cash flow, the school decided to open their doors to non-Catholics. The strategy worked; the school survived and became quietly well known for their classic approach to college prep studies for young women. The school still exists and is well endowed. More than half of the students are non-Catholics. End of story.—Oh, I'm on the Board of Directors of Little Flower."

"That's a great story. You sure have an interesting life."

Selma shrugged, "Not really. I manage the books for my father and brother and look after grandmother's trust fund. Not that interesting."

Connor twisted toward her in the seat, "And what do you do for fun?"

"Connor," Selma frowned, "that's a personal question. I hardly even know you."

"I'm sorry, I was out of line. I didn't mean to embarrass you. Look, you can ask me anything, anything personal and I'll have to give a truthful answer. It'll be my punishment: like, do I pee in the shower, do I have hemorrhoids? Okay, go ahead, ask."

Selma shook her head. "I don't wanna ask you personal questions and I don't need to know about your hemorrhoids."

"Who said I had hemorrhoids?"

"You just said that you did, must be pretty uncomfortable."

Connor took the bait, "I didn't say that I had hemorrhoids, I just said that you could ask me about my hemorrhoids."

"Oh, I'm asking, how long have you had them, the hemorrhoids?" Selma replaced her scowl with a smirk. "I don't believe that I'm driving down the road with a man I only just met having a conversation about his hemorrhoids; Connor, you're a certifiable lunatic."

Connor gave her his biggest smile, "Aw shucks, and I thought I was being charming.—Take the next right onto Iris and then right again on Peony; it'll be the gray house on the corner with the red door."

Selma's jaw dropped in surprise, "Peony, Iris? I remember these streets, I named them!"

"You named them?"

She excitedly bobbed her head, "When Papa built this development he let me come up with the names for the streets and I chose flowers. I've never been here before; I never saw the street signs. This is so exciting, it's like seeing something you created and then put away and forgot."

"If you had to tell people that you lived at seventy-six Peony Place all your life you might not be so excited."

She grinned, "I could have chosen Pansy Place, think about that."

Connor put his hands on his head, "No, no, anything but Pansy Place."

"Can we drive around for a few minutes? I want to see the street signs?"

He nodded.

Selma called out the names of each street they passed. "Sunflower Court, Violet Drive: I named that after our housekeeper." Fortunately for Connor it was a small development and the flower tour lasted only a few minutes.

Selma returned to 76 Peony Place, pulled into the drive and set the parking brake. Connor extended his hand.

"Thanks Selma, it was kind of you to give me a lift. I really enjoyed talking with you; I'm not always this crazy. I think it's the exhilaration of being away from school and getting my first, real job. There's a small chance I could actually turn into an adult; that worries me."

Selma gave him a big smile, "It was different. I hope you enjoy your new job. I'm sure I'll see you again, I have to come back to Quail Run several more times to get things finalized on the house."

Connor exited and came around to the driver's side; Selma rolled down the window. "Thanks again Selma, I'll look for you at the model, maybe we can have another profound and deeply moving conversation…Do you know how to get to Pennsauken from here?"

"I remember the way back to Browning Road; I know how to go from there."

She waved goodbye. As the Mercedes backed into the road Selma called out in a loud voice, "Take care of your hemorrhoids!"

Connor waved and watched the 190 SL disappear, the mellow exhaust notes tracing its path amongst the Peonies and Iris. Connor turned for the house, smiled and said aloud, "Now that's what I call a class act."

chapter

SIX

Ellie heard Connor come in, "Hey, I'm in the pantry." She shouted. He stuck his head in, "Hi Mom, any chance of milk and cookies?"

"How about some wine and cheese?" She gently pinched his cheeks and kissed him on the nose. "How'd you make out with Jack?"

Connor stepped back as she headed for the refrigerator. "I am now an official model sitter or model minder or—Anyway, I got the job and at two forty a week."

She opened the refrigerator door. "Oops, I forgot to put in more white, we'll have to settle for red. Open something from the kitchen rack for me, please. I'm not allowed into the cellar without the master's permission."

Connor chose a bottle of Chianti. He placed the bottle on the counter and opened it with the ease of a professional bartender.

Ellie arranged some crackers and cheese on a plate. "Good choice, that Chianti is excellent," she said. "Two-forty a week's good, I doubt that Maryann gets much more than that and she's worked for Jack for awhile. Jack's a generous man.—Oh, before I forget, Cappy called. He said that he found someone to cover for you tonight and tomorrow. You called him?"

"Yeah, called from the model home. That's good news; I can have a glass of wine with you, then. I arranged to train with Maryann, tomorrow, so it's excellent Cappy found someone. I wouldn't leave him in a lurch; he's been good to me." He went to the cupboard and took out two wine glasses.

"Cappy also said to keep the shirts so that you'll know where to come next time you need a job."

Connor filled their glasses. "I hope that this is the closest I'll come to bartending for the rest of my life."

They clinked glasses, Ellie smiled, "I'll drink to that."

Where did your father go?"

"Don't know. He left the model about one. I thought he was coming home."

Ellie pointed to a stack of mail on the far counter. "Looks like he's been and gone, unless you brought the mail in?"

"Nope, not guilty."

"I think he was planning on going to the wine store in the Pennsauken Mart. He says that the owner will order what he wants and for the best prices. I think he just likes to wander around the Mart, must remind him of when we were really broke and we would walk the Mart for our Saturday night entertainment. He'd carry you around on his shoulders. He was so proud of you in your *Phillies* hat and shirt. You don't remember the Mart do you?"

Connor shook his head.

"It was a fun place to go when they first put it up. It was a long ramshackle building that always looked like it was about to fall down. In the early fifties, it was mostly a farmers market with lots of stands selling produce and meat. Then they brought in people selling clothes and jeans, then hardware, fishing poles, building supplies, appliances, cotton candy, and hotdogs. You name it and the Mart sold it. Most of the things they sold were rejects or last year's model. But you could find some bargains. Once, your father bought a two-speed electric broiler for five dollars. When we got it home he found that it only ran at one temperature, hot. Well, your dad took it back the next weekend and complained that it wasn't two speeds. The salesman took the cord in his hand and gesturing with the plug explained, 'Of course it's two speeds, on and off. Whada ya want for five bucks?' The funny thing is we used that broiler for years, it never burned out.

"Your car's in the garage, did you walk back from Quail Run?"

Connor shook his head and finished chewing a cracker. "Great cheese, really creamy, what is it?"

"It's a French goat cheese; your father bought it at a new deli that opened in Marlton. Hard to imagine a gourmet deli in Marlton, a few years ago there was nothing except cows and pigs out that way. It is good; I'll have to check out the deli sometime."

Connor washed down the cheese and cracker with a sip of wine. "Jack's sister Selma brought me home. She drives this fantastic Mercedes convertible with a four speed. Selma's driving made me think of you, she downshifts and accelerates out of the corners just like you do."

Ellie smiled, "Was Selma looking at houses in Quail Run?"

"She and her father bought a Provincetown, that's a Cape. They're gonna move from Philly in a few months. Selma's making all kinds of changes to the house; moving walls, adding a conservatory. Maryann says when Selma's done it'll probably be the most expensive house in the development."

Ellie nodded. "Jack's been trying to get Izzy to move to Jersey for several years. I'm glad he finally agreed. Con says the neighborhood where Izzy lives now is getting pretty rough, lots of boarded up houses and shops."

"Selma didn't say how she felt about moving, but I think that she was pleased. She seemed to like her new house. The Katz' family must have big bucks."

Ellie twisted her mouth sideways, "They're not rich like the Fords or Rockefellers, but I'm sure that Jack and Izzy, probably Morty too, could all stop working tomorrow and have enough to live well for the rest of their lives."

"Mom, that's rich! Not having to work for the rest of your life? Imagine doing whatever you wanted every single day: go to the beach, fish, call up your friends and have a party, go to Europe or France!

33

And think of the women you'd collect. Mom you're talking paradise on earth! I can't understand why anyone would work if they had the money to play for the rest of their lives."

"You really believe that you could spend the rest of your life like that?"

Connor spread his hands on the table, "Well maybe not the rest of my life, but how about the next thirty years!"

Ellie poured more wine. "What did you think of Selma? I'm curious."

"Selma's different; sophisticated. She's funny; witty. She has amazing porcelain white skin; beautiful hair, and great legs. It's a real shame about her nose; with her family's money you'd think she'd have had a nose job by now. She might even be pretty with a new nose. If I compare Selma with a lot of the women I hung around with at Saint Stephan's, I'd say that she comes out ahead."

Ellie laughed, "You mean she wins by a nose!" They both laughed.

"Mother, that's unkind, shame on you! But very funny," they laughed again.

Ellie shifted in her chair. "Syd Katz called today to invite us to dinner at Quail Run two weeks from today. Syd's Jack's wife, her real name is Sydney. I don't think you've met her, have you?"

Connor shook his head. "I haven't been to one of the Katz' family functions since I was a little kid."

"If you'd met Syd, you'd remember. She's gorgeous; used to be a singer or dancer I can't remember which. Jack met her in New York City. In his younger, wilder days, Jack used to be a major league rogue, probably put even you to shame. After they married, Syd transformed into the perfect mother and hostess and I hear she's doing a good job as wife as well. Anyway, Syd and Jack are giving a surprise dinner party for Izzy and Selma to celebrate their new house. Syd's going to tell Selma and Izzy it's at her house. Actually, it's going to be at Izzy and Selma's new house! Syd's renting furniture and is having a caterer bring in the meal. Should be lots of fun and you're invited too. Jack told Syd that since you're one of the Quail Run family now you should be there. Morty, Izzy's younger son is coming, his wife Roz as well. Morty is dull and serious. He has a dry, sarcastic sense of humor that some people find amusing; I'm not one of them. Roz, on the other hand is just terrific. She's a school social worker and full of genuinely funny stories. So, you're invited. If you don't wanna go, tell me soon so that I can call Syd and decline on your behalf. You should know though, Syd doesn't take turn downs easily."

"No problem Mom, I'd love to go just to meet Syd if for no other reason."

They heard the squeaks and groans of the garage door opening. "That's your father," Ellie said, "Better give him a hand; I have a feeling that he's got more than one case to bring in today."

chapter

SEVEN

Connor quickly discovered that 'Model Sitting' was an appropriate name for his new job; the intellectual content wasn't high. When prospective new customers visited, his first task was to greet them and offer an information pack with the floor plans and prices for the models still available.

Of the nineteen unsold houses, ten were on premium lots and that would add nine hundred to two thousand more to the total price.

Most prospects walked around the model and then left. Looking at model homes on weekends was recreation for some couples.

Since the first house had been built three years ago, Quail Run had acquired a certain cache. It was viewed as a community of doctors, lawyers and other professionals. While it was true that a sizable number of professionals called Quail Run home, most of the houses had been purchased by young families often with two wage earners. This cache had allowed Jack to raise prices four times in three years. A base Carlton on a standard lot now sold for $52,000, nearly 15% more than similar houses in nearby developments.

On Sunday, traffic through the model was light. Connor followed Maryann around listening to her conversations with the few prospective customers. He watched her price options for a snooty couple and later helped a returning buyer choose carpet, tile and wall colors. This wasn't rocket science.

On Monday the model was closed and Maryann had set up appointments for Connor to meet with local bankers and mortgage companies to hear their spiels and collect business cards that he could pass on to his prospects. Connor found the experience tedious. With one exception, the bankers would spout information as if they were delivering a recorded message.

The exception was Maria Tendios. Maria was in her middle thirties, pretty in a chunky sort of way. A diploma from Rutgers University hung on the wall of her office. Although Connor had little business experience, it was obvious to him that as a woman, a Hispanic woman, Maria must be especially capable to have achieved her position, even in a sea of mediocre men. She taught him the basics of home financing in less than a half-hour. Connor liked Maria, but the wedding band on her finger and the pictures of her children on the desk assured that the meeting stayed professional; Connor kept his boyish charm in its holster.

At four, Connor finished his final meeting with Mr. Burrows who was clearly a clone of Messrs. Borden, Castillanos, Carpenter and Plotnic. He headed back to the model to meet with Maryann for their final debriefing session.

Maryann had spent the day at her apartment packing the few things that she would ship to Denver. She was anxious to be on her way home. The last year had been painful.

She had dumped Rico in July…Feeling feverish one day, she left work early to go home and take some aspirin, soak in a hot bath and sleep.

When she entered the house she heard music flowing from the bedroom. The door was ajar; she pushed it open and saw a naked, busty bimbo astride Rico. Her arm was extended in the air, cowboy fashion and between gasps she shouted, "Go boy, give me more, do it, do it!" Maryann watched for several minutes. As the bimbo achieved orgasm and shouted something like, "More, I want more!" Maryann started to clap.

Rico sat up with such force that the bimbo fell backward with her head extending over the end of the bed staring up at Maryann. Maryann closed the door. She found Rico's shirt and trousers on the hall floor next to the bimbo's huge bra and skimpy panties. She bent down and took the wallet from the trousers. There was almost three hundred dollars inside. She shoved the money in her pocket and then his credit cards. Before she threw the wallet across the room, she thought, "What the hell," and took his drivers' license as well.

The bimbo was the first to exit the bedroom. She had pulled on a low cut, tight, pink sweater and a very short skirt, obviously without bra or panties.

She screamed at Maryann, "That lying bastard told me he was divorced!"

Maryann felt the simultaneous need to throw up and relieve herself. She struggled to control both her stomach and her bowels. She saw the ring on the bimbo's right hand. It was the ring Rico had given her on their last anniversary.

"Take that ring off before I get a knife and chop off your finger; it's mine!"

The bimbo sensed that Maryann was deadly serious and quickly twisted the ring from her finger. She tossed it toward Maryann, retrieved her clothes and shoes and ran for the door.

Maryann could taste the acrid vomit rising in her throat; she dashed for the bathroom and made it just in time.

She downed some aspirin and Pepto sat on the toilet for ten minutes, and prayed that Rico had left the house. She washed her face walked to the bedroom and opened the door. The music still played. She looked in, no Rico. His trousers, shirt and shoes were gone and his keys and sunglasses were missing from the bowl on the bar where he always put them. His empty wallet was still where she had thrown it, on the floor by the refrigerator. She spied the emerald ring on the tile floor. She crushed it with her right heel and then twisted back and forth as one might squash a cock-roach. The golden band was flattened and disfigured, the 'emerald' shattered. Maryann laughed, "Just one more of Rico's lies."

She struggled to get two suitcases down from the loft. She threw in all of her clothing that would fit, and filled a large shopping bag with her favorite shoes and another with her make-up and jewelry. She smashed a framed picture of her and Rico and threw it, broken glass and all, onto their bed.

She hauled Rico's four albums of baseball cards to the bathroom, partially filled the tub, poured in a gallon of bleach and dropped in the cards, a handful at a time. Next, she took a kitchen knife and forced the flimsy lock on Rico's desk drawer. There was no money and the check register showed that he had the astounding balance of fifty dollars. Hidden in the back of the drawer were two letters from the bank; they were in default on the mortgage and the bank was threatening foreclosure…Rico was gambling again

Maryann dragged the suitcases and bags to her car and returned to the house. She tossed her house keys into the tub where the baseball cards and bleach had become a brown-grey mush.

She checked into the Quality Inn a few miles from Quail Run and called Jack Katz to tell him that she'd be out sick. Syd answered instead of Jack. Twenty minutes later Syd picked her up and moved her to the Katz' guest room.

With Syd and Jack's help she got a lawyer and an apartment.— Rico didn't give up easily. He showed up at the model to harass her. The second time he came she called the cops who chased him away. A half a mile down the road they hauled him off to jail for DUI. Finally, he left her alone.

The day she filed for divorce, Maryann found out that her mother had less than a year to live. She felt the hand of destiny at work and decided to move back to Denver. She would help her mother complete life as comfortable as possible and then start out fresh. Maybe she could learn from her two failed marriages and avoid the handsome, exciting, soul-less men who attracted her like a moth circling a destructive flame.

Connor found Maryann in the kitchen reading the paper and drinking a Rolling Rock from the bottle. She gave him a big smile and kissed him on the cheek. Connor checked her out. She wore a man's plaid, flannel shirt with the top three buttons undone and the tails tied around her midriff. She was obviously bra-less, and the nipples of her small, upturned breasts were clearly visible through the flannel. Her snug fitting slacks accented her long legs. Her ash blond hair was pulled back in a ponytail and except for a trace of lip-gloss she wore no makeup.

"You look terrific."

Maryann raised her eyebrows, "Wanna beer? There's more in the fridge."

Connor opened the door of the refrigerator and found a twenty-four pack of Rolling Rock mini-bottles; two were missing.

"I haven't seen these pony bottles in a while; they used to be the favorites of a crazy girl I knew in high school. She'd keep a half dozen in her locker and then stuff one in her bra between her boobs and drink it with a straw during study hall. I don't think she ever got caught."

Maryann laughed, "She must have had pretty big boobs to fit a beer in her cleavage."

Connor nodded, "I think she had pretty big everything. Probably all the beer she drank."

"Okay hot shot. How did you make out with the movers and shakers of ol' Cherry Hill?"

Connor groaned, "I know you set this up just to torment me."

He pinched his nose, rolled his eyes into his forehead and in an affected accent said, "Well Mr. Sullivan, we here at Tweedle Dee Bank would like to service all of the financial needs of the wealthy WASPS at Quail Run. We like to think of working with you as a partnership. You sell them the houses and we imprison them in nasty contracts of life-long financial serfdom.—Would you like me to kiss your ass now or later?"

Maryann choked on her beer. "Don't do that Connor. I got some up my nose!" She got a paper towel and dabbed at her mouth and nose. "Let me guess. That was Burroughs or Borden, right?"

"Wrong. That was Plotnic. Burrows has a lisp and Borden is queer. He couldn't take his eyes off my crotch."

"Shame on you Connor! Borden isn't queer. He's got a wife and a bunch of kids. You'll find that he's the most resourceful of the lot when it comes to getting mortgages for young couples without much of a credit history. Really, he's a good guy. How about Maria?"

Connor sipped his beer. "Maria was the highlight of the day. I think I'll send everyone to her."

Maryann shook her head. "No can do. You have to try and spread the business around. Give the customers two or three recommendations. Otherwise they'll complain that they didn't get the best rate and that you're in cahoots with Maria. Sounds foolish, but it happens. It won't matter much at Quail Run with only a few houses to sell, but when you move on to Sunny Slope Farm you're looking at two hundred or more houses. None of these little banks could or would want to take on that many mortgages in one place. Sorry, but you're stuck with Borden and his buddies."

Connor went to the refrigerator for another beer. "Okay, okay. So I have to work with guys who are after my body, what other tortures do you have planned for me?" He tapped her empty Rolling Rock, "Another pony?"

She smiled at him. "Well, just one, they're small."

After an hour Connor was ahead five ponies to four.

There wasn't much more he needed to learn. When a prospect decided to buy a house Connor would fill out a sales agreement and go through the selection check list. Maryann told him that almost all customers ordered the basic house with only a few upgrades and so the process was usually straightforward. If a customer wanted to make structural changes, Connor would call Tony Pinto, Jack's construction foreman. When he had finished with the checklists Connor would call Bernice Jones, Jack's business manager and drop off the completed forms and lists along with the customer's deposit. Bernice did all the costing and math for the upgrades and options. That was about all there was to it; Bernice was a licensed realtor and handled the completion of the sale through closing.

It was after six and Connor was getting hungry. He hadn't eaten since breakfast. He could feel the effect of the beer working through his empty stomach. "I don't know about you boss, but I'm starving. If I keep drinking beer without eating I'm going to fall asleep and you'll have to carry me home."

Maryann stood, "Fat chance buster."

"How about we get a burger at the diner?"

She came closer to him; her belly button was at his eyelevel. He took hold of the tail of her shirt at her midriff. "What happens if I pull this?"

She smiled sweetly. "I pour the rest of this beer over your head for starters."

Connor stood but held onto the shirt. "And then what?"

She took a small step backward. "I need to use the bathroom. Be right back."

He reluctantly let go of her shirt. He was getting sexually stimulated. He couldn't tell if she was interested.

As she reapplied her lip gloss Maryann looked in the mirror and smiled. She was going home in two days and would never see Rico or New Jersey again. Jack had given her an extra five hundred in her check. Syd's realtor friend had agreed to buy her old Chevy for three hundred dollars. She'd have plenty to buy a good used car in Denver, maybe even a new car; she'd never had a new car. Her few belongings were packed. The only thing left was to decide what to do about Connor; he was obviously interested in having sex with her. He was cute, funny, twenty-three and in great physical condition. He would probably be good in bed; at a minimum full of enthusiasm and energy. She hadn't been with a man for weeks, and that a quickie in the back room of her girlfriend Debbie's house while everyone sang Happy Birthday in the living room. She would be leaving and never see Connor again so the likely-hood of complications arising was small. She felt her level of sexual arousal rising. "Oh what the hell," she thought. "I deserve it." She re-tied her shirt tails in a single knot that would easily come apart.

Connor was standing at the kitchen table reading the paper. She stood close to him.

"Connor I just got an idea. Yesterday you said that you were going to start looking for an apartment, right?"

He nodded.

"Well, why don't you take over my place? It's plenty spacious and only three years old. It's furnished and I'm leaving the sheets, towels and pillows; you could move in with a suitcase and toothbrush. It's a hundred forty a month plus utilities, which cost me about another twenty-five. It's only twenty-five to thirty minutes from Quail Run... Interested?"

Connor smiled, "Sounds too good to be true. When can I see the place?"

She looked directly into his eyes, "How about now? We could pick up a pizza on the way and bring a few of these ponies along."

He put both his hands on her shoulders. "Do you always have such great ideas in the bathroom?"

She laughed, "You'd be surprised, you really would be."

———

Maryann drove fast; she seemed to have no regard that Connor was following her. On Kings Highway, in order not to lose her he was forced to follow the big Impala through a light that had just changed to red. The speed limit was forty-five and she was averaging sixty. She had called ahead to a pizzeria that was on the right hand corner of White Horse Pike at Cuthbert Road. If they got separated she said that he should meet her there. He was unfamiliar with the area and so tried to stay with her.

Connor was excited at the prospect of having his own apartment again. With any luck he could move in Friday or Saturday. He turned his thoughts to the slim, ash blond woman in the car ahead. He tried to visualize her as he removed her clothes. One of his erotic, fantasy games was to try and guess the color of a woman's nipples. Maryann's eyes were bright blue. Although her roots weren't showing, he guessed that she applied the ash blond color to what was probably mousey brown hair. Her skin wasn't pale and seemed to retain a bit of the past summer's tan.

"Pink. Definitely pink nipples and pretty small as well." He could feel his penis starting to become stimulated. He had never had sex with a mature woman before.

Maryann turned right onto White Horse Pike and slowed a bit. Connor's thoughts returned to her body. Her pubic hair was probably light brown and very fine; most likely she kept it closely trimmed. He planned how to approach her in bed, what to do first. He wanted her to be satisfied and not think of him as young and inexperienced.

They were approaching an intersection; she veered into the right hand lane. This must be Cuthbert Road, he thought. He tried to calm down; it would be embarrassing to walk into the pizzeria with an obvious erection. The Impala's right turn signal flashed as it approached the intersection. Connor thought that the pizzeria was likely to be in the strip mall just beyond the light.—From that second on, he would remember the train of events with total clarity.

An old pickup truck traveling east, the opposite direction, on White Horse Pike turned quickly into the intersection with Cuthbert Road apparently trying to make a U turn. The load of large plywood sheets in the bed of the truck were leaning precariously and shifted violently as the driver accelerated into the tight turn. Two of the plywood sheets flew from the truck; the driver attempted to brake and lost control. The Impala had just cleared the intersection when the pickup slammed directly into the driver's side. Connor saw Maryann fly across the front bench seat; her head seemed to collide with the passenger side window and then disappear. He braked hard and steered to the right to avoid the Impala. His Corvair came to a stop about six inches from a big Cadillac that was waiting to turn from Cuthbert Road onto White Horse Pike.

The driver of the pickup backed up and attempted to drive away. The truck ran into the curb and a tire blew. Two men leaped from the truck and raced toward the strip mall.

Connor jumped from the Corvair and ran to the Impala which had come to rest after colliding with a mailbox. He tentatively opened the passenger side door. Maryann lay on the seat on her right side, her face toward the floor. A pool of blood had already accumulated beneath her head.

"Maryann, are you alright?" Connor knew that she was not. He turned her head. Her eyes gazed sightless into space. He saw a deep puncture on her right temple; blood flowed freely from the wound. Other than the puncture she seemed uninjured. Her breathing had ceased. Connor couldn't feel a pulse. He screamed, "Somebody get help, call an ambulance!" Connor knew that she was beyond help; she wouldn't be going home to Denver.

The policeman who arrived within five minutes found Connor knelling on the asphalt beside the Impala, stroking Maryann's hair. A crowd had started to gather. The police officer helped Connor stand and moved him away from the car. Connor sat on the curb with his head in his hands. A second police car arrived and after a short conversation with the first officer on the scene, drove toward the pickup. The ambulance arrived. The EMTs examined Maryann in the car and then moved her to a wheeled gurney and into the ambulance. The ambulance sped away, sirens blaring.

The first officer approached Connor who was still slumped on the curb. "I take it you knew her?"

Without taking his hands from his face Connor nodded. "We work together. Her name's Maryann Daag. I was following her in the Corvair." He raised his head and pointed to his car. "We were going to pick up a pizza around the corner."

"Can you stand up?"

Connor slowly pushed himself up from the curb. The officer looked him over. "Are you injured? Did you bang your head?"

"No, I didn't get a scratch. I was lucky and managed to avoid that Caddy."

The officer looked closely at Connor's eyes. "Were you drinking?"

"Just a couple pony bottles after work; not much, the equivalent of two regular sized beers each."

The officer put his hand out. "Can I see some I.D.?" Connor held out his wallet.

"Take your driver's license out, please." The officer looked at the license. "Mr. Sullivan, would you like to go to a hospital to be checked out?"

Connor shook his head. "No. I'm okay."

A third police car arrived and two officers approached; one wore sergeant's stripes.

The first officer turned to the sergeant. "They find the guys in the pickup?"

The sergeant looked at the Impala. "Yeah, they ran to the bar over there in the strip mall."

The first officer grunted. "That's a new one, hiding in a bar."

The sergeant nodded. "Who can figure drunks? Fergie's taken them in. Looks like they stole the plywood from a construction site and were going to sell it to someone in Mt. Ephraim; they got lost along the way. What happened to the driver of the Impala, a woman?"

The first officer turned toward Connor. "Maryann Daag. Mr. Sullivan here was following her in his Corvair. They worked together and were heading to *Oakies* to pick up a pizza when the pickup ran into her Impala. The EMTs said that she hit her head on the lock button on top of the passenger door; it punctured her skull at the temple, killed her instantly. Freak accident."

Connor felt nauseous. He turned toward the curb and threw up what little was in his stomach.

The first officer approached Connor. "Mr. Sullivan would you like to sit in the police car? I have a few more questions for you and then I'll have someone drive you home. He held up the license, this is the address where you live?"

Connor nodded, "If I can call home, my parents will come and drive my car." The officer took Connor's arm. "No problem, I'll patch you through."

Ellie drove Connor and the Corvair home; Con followed in the pickup. Once home, Connor ate some pretzels and drank several glasses of red wine. He told the story of the night's events four times. With each repetition his voice grew flatter and less emotional.

chapter

EIGHT

Syd had pulled it off. The dinner party at Selma and Izzy's new house was a complete surprise. Selma and Izzy arrived at Jack and Syd's house at six-thirty expecting a small family get together.

Jack hugged them both. "Don't take off your coats. I need to take you down to the house for a few minutes. Tony has some questions about those conservatory doors. It'll only take ten minutes."

Izzy started to take his coat off. "You take Selma; she knows where she wants the doors. I don't care where she puts 'em."

"No Papa, I need your help to get this right. You have a better eye for structural change than I do. Come on, we'll come right back and I'll make you your Manhattan first thing."

Flattery usually worked with Izzy; he pulled his coat back on. "Okay, let's get it over with."

They climbed into Jack's Lincoln and drove the few blocks to the Cape. The house was dark. The driveway pavers hadn't been laid so Jack parked on the street and they walked up to the house. Jack's flashlight shone the way to the front door. He pushed open the unlocked door. Selma stepped in first.

Everyone in the house shouted "surprise!" Syd flashed the lights on and off for a few seconds. Jack's children had crayoned a poster, 'WELCOME TO YOUR HOME ANT SELLY AND GRAMPA.' Syd switched on the portable stereo and the room filled with Yiddish Klezmer violin music.

Syd grabbed Izzy and forced him to dance a few steps. "Come on Papa, pretend you're happy!"

Izzy kissed her on the cheek. "It's a wonder you didn't give me a stroke, I'm an old man you know." Izzy had a way of complaining and smiling at the same time. Izzy dearly loved all of the women in his family but Syd held a separate and unique place in his affections. She was beautiful, charming and fun to be with; best of all, she loved Izzy and treated him as if he were the father she never had.

Jack danced with Selma, Ellie with Con and Roz forced Morty into an awkward attempt at shuffling his feet. Connor stood at the make shift bar with the caterer and smiled. Selma wiggled out of her fur jacket and dropped it on the floor. Conner picked up the jacket and placed it atop some boxes the caterer had stacked in the corner.

Selma grabbed Connor's hand. "Come on, everyone has to dance to this music, its Jewish law."

Jack rescued Izzy from Syd and put his arms around both their shoulders.

Connor was an excellent dancer. As the tempo of the violins and clarinets grew faster everyone formed a circle around Connor and Selma and clapped. Connor and Selma were doing what appeared to be a polka with a pinch of 'Zorba the Greek' thrown in. The music ended and they all cheered and embraced.

Jack turned to Izzy. "Okay Papa, let's get you that Manhattan." The caterer had handled Katz family affairs before and was already headed for Izzy with a glass in hand.

Connor released Selma's hand. "Was that a dance or an exercise routine?"

Selma groaned, "The way you dance I'd say it was more like a wrestling match."

"You do that at weddings, right?"

"And Bar Mitzvahs. I think it's much more sophisticated than the chicken dance or bunny hop I've been dragged into at 'goy' weddings."

Connor looked puzzled. "I didn't know they did the bunny hop at gay weddings. I've never been to a gay wedding; didn't know that there was such a thing."

Selma laughed. "I said 'goy' not gay. 'Goy' means non-Jewish, gentile."

Connor scratched his head. "Okay, let's see if I got this straight; you were doing the bunny hop at a non-Jewish, gay wedding; right?"

Selma shook her head and moved toward the bar. "My teachers always told me to avoid conversation with the village idiot...what do you wanna drink?"

"Some red wine would be great or a beer if they don't have wine."

Selma shook hands with the caterer. "Hello Miss Katz, congratulations on your new house."

"It's nice to see you again Charles. I can still taste the marinated salmon you did for Jack and Syd's anniversary party."

"Charles is the best chef in the Delaware Valley." She said to Connor. "Where's Richard tonight?"

"Richard drew the short straw. He's doing an after theatre dinner for a nasty old Queen over in Rittenhouse Square; bunch of rich, old farts making feeble, out-of-date conversation and showing off their pretty young things . She pays us very well and we get lots of referrals from her parties; so we can't say no...Now what can I get for you?"

"Connor and I will both have a glass of red wine."

Charles nodded. "Mr. Sullivan picked out the wines so we have some very fine choices; for the reds, a St. Emilion Grand Cru or a Burgundy, a Pommard."

Selma twisted her lips, "Connor which do you think?"

"Pommard's my father's favorite so that's likely to be really excellent."

She put her hand on the bar, "Pommard it is."

Charles put his thumb and finger to his lips and pulled them away with a light kiss, "Excellent choice. I always have to test the wines," he raised his eyebrows, "to make sure that they're not off, of course, and I can say that the Pommard is a lovely mouthful of fruit."

Selma and Connor clinked glasses; Selma took a small sip and quickly set her glass on the bar as Syd hugged her from behind. "You really were surprised, weren't you? Papa said he didn't have any suspicion at all."

Selma kissed Syd on the cheek. "Surprised is an understatement, I was overwhelmed. Thank you, thank you; you're always so kind to Papa and me."

Selma turned to Connor. "Have you met Connor?"

Syd took Connor's offered hand and kissed him on the cheek as well. "Hello Connor." She turned to Selma. "We met at the Sullivan's last week, the night of Maryann's accident." She turned back to Connor "I'm sorry that those were the circumstances but I'm pleased to see you looking so much brighter."

Connor gave Syd the smile he reserved for beautiful, sexy women. "I don't remember much that happened that night, but I clearly remember meeting you."

Syd returned his smile and patted his hand. "Excuse me you two, I've got to check on dinner, see what Tina's got for desert. Connor, I've seated you between Selma and me so that we can keep the conversation bright and breezy, okay?"

Connor shuffled his feet. "Thanks Syd, I'll practice saying bright and breezy things."

Selma watched Connor's eyes follow Syd's shapely rear across the room. "I need to talk to Roz." She said. "Go talk to my father, he needs someone to talk to."

Connor raised his glass. "Yas'm boss."

Selma hadn't exaggerated, Charles was a superb cook. The *amuse bouche* set the tone for the feast. It was a tiny, two inch round pastry filled with foie gras and topped with half a quail egg and a few grains of caviar. Next was a creamy, flavorful, Italian bean soup; then a small glass of lime sorbet to clear the palate. For the main course: skewers of grilled filet mignon wrapped in bacon to preserve their moistness, with near marble-sized roasted Dutch potatoes, steamed asparagus in a butter-herb sauce. Dessert was a rich Key Lime pie with graham cracker crust garnished with tiny, pale orange colored-limes that were both sweet and tart. Finally coffee and a platter of French cheeses with unpronounceable names appeared. The wines were perfectly matched to the meal; bubbly Italian Prosecco with the bean soup, a mature St. Emilion with the main course and a just off-dry German Riesling with dessert. A fresh bottle of Pommard was set out with the cheese. Everyone ate heartily and enthused over each course. Charles was pleased; it was greatly satisfying to cook for people who appreciated his skill and attention to detail.

The round table facilitated easy conversation. By the end of the meal Connor felt that he had a reasonable take on each of the personalities. Morty had few redeeming qualities. His attempts at humor seemed to always require the embarrassment of someone else at the table, most often his wife or brother. Connor noticed that Morty never picked on Selma; in fact, he rarely even looked in her direction. Connor saw that he chose to pick on more docile targets. Roz, on the other hand was delightful. She told funny stories with the phrasing and delivery of a stand-up comedian. Izzy said little, but it was obvious that he expected to be treated as the honored patriarch…He was.

Besides being physically stunning, Syd was the consummate hostess. During the meal she worked the table to make sure that no one was allowed to remain in the background. She asked questions, requested people's opinions, referenced past family gatherings, told happy, inclusive family stories and attempted to soothe egos dented by Morty's acerbic attempts at humor.

Izzy was the first to leave. Jack drove him back to the house to pick up his car. Selma offered to drive Izzy home but he declined, saying that he was going into town to visit friends the next day and would need his car.

Everyone at the table except Connor and Ellie knew that Izzy would spend the day with Reba. For eight years Reba had been Izzy's lover. She was a Russian Jew, fifty three, twice divorced and with a dead husband behind her as well. Izzy paid the rent for her modest, center city apartment…If Izzy and Reba's love had been a picture it would have been painted in subtle earth tones rather than the bold reds, yellows and greens of youth. Their love was intensely personal, not to be shared with anyone, not even Izzy's family. None of the Katz' spoke of Reba or acknowledged her place in Izzy's life, not even the crass Morty. Selma was the only Katz child to have ever met Reba and that had been an accident.

Selma had always been interested in art and artists. Two years ago in nineteen sixty one, she was co-chair of the Philadelphia Museum of Art Women's Committee. The Committee's spring meeting was focused on Russian painting and in particular on the Museum's Christian Brinton Collection of pre-world war two Russian and Slavic artists. Selma's job was to find an appropriate speaker. Through her friend Martin Cortan, now an associate professor at the University of Pennsylvania, Selma contacted a speaker's agency in New York who specialized in art experts. In only a few days the agency identified Professor Doktor Hudavan Yukor as being available to speak to the Committee on Current Trends in Russian Art. The Professor Doktor would be in Baltimore on Monday to meet with a group of wealthy Russian-American Art collectors. For a hundred dollars and expenses the Professor Doktor would be pleased take the train to Philadelphia on Tuesday, give his lecture to the Women's Committee on Wednesday afternoon and tour the Brinton Collection.

When Selma collected the Professor Doktor at Penn Station on Tuesday at noon it took less than a minute for her to realize that she had a serious problem. Hudavan Yukor's command of the English language was far 'worser' than even Yogi Berra's! She dropped him at his hotel and then dashed to a phone to call the Speaker's Agency.

Yes, they said, it was true that the contract said that the Professor Doktor spoke four languages; it was just that none of them happened to be English. The woman at the agency was most unhelpful. No, they couldn't supply another expert. No, their fee was non-refundable, and yes, the Professor Doktor would just have to give his speech in Russian or Serbo-Croat if they preferred.

Selma called Martin. It took forty-five minutes and three calls to get him on the line, by then she was desperate and furious…It was all Martin's fault, he had recommended the agency. Well, not exactly, Martin countered, Selma had actually talked with Gary Orstrov, the Chair of Slavic Studies and he had given her the recommendation.

Martin could sense that Selma was seriously angry; he came up with a solution. "Let him give the lecture in Russian and we'll have someone translate into English."

"And just where will I find a translator?"

"Relax. I'm sure there's someone in the University fluent in Russian and English who can come to the Museum tomorrow."

Martin told Selma to go home and call him in two hours, he was confident he could find a translator.—The task wasn't as easy as Martin expected, but after four phone calls he had found their man, or rather, their woman. Reba Parson-Jones was a professional translator, a native Russian speaker and well educated in literature and the arts; best of all, Reba was available to do the job.

Selma countered. "How could she be a native Russian speaker with a name like Parson-Jones?"

"Her husband's Welsh?" Martin offered.

The arrangements were made for Selma to collect Reba at her office at eleven and the Professor Doktor from his hotel at eleven-thirty. They would lunch at the Museum Director's private dining room at twelve-thirty and then on to the meeting. Selma swapped her two seat Mercedes for her father's sedan. Izzy grumbled all through breakfast about having to shift the old-fashioned monster all day. "Probably get a hernia," he grouched.

As soon as Selma introduced herself, Reba knew that she was Izzy's daughter; how many Selma Katz' could there be in Philadelphia? When Selma opened the door to Izzy's Cadillac, Reba was unable to suppress a laugh which she tried to turn into a cough. The light went on for Selma when Reba reflexively opened the glove box and took out a pack of tissues.

Selma swiveled in her seat and extended her hand. "You really are our Reba, aren't you?"

Reba smiled broadly. "Well if I'm your Reba then that must make you my Selma?"

Selma took both of Reba's hands and they both laughed until tears ran down their cheeks. Selma spoke first. "What are the odds of meeting like this?"

Reba handed her several tissues. "Perhaps this wasn't an accident; the Gods have a peculiar sense of destiny."

"Or a warped sense of humor," Selma added.

The Professor Doktor's presentation was a triumph. He was the picture of a Russian Art expert; tall and slim with a short, well tended beard and near shoulder length hair. His mangled English comments were greeted with respectful laughter. After agreeing to take on the translation, Reba had thoroughly researched the Professor Doktor. Her introduction covered not only his degrees, honors, appointments and world reputation; she also focused on the seminal role he had played in developing young Slavic artists following the carnage of the war. She described how he had `used his own modest resources to support an unknown female painter who would eventually be recognized as Czechoslovakia's greatest post war artist. She explained that the Professor Doktor would be giving his presentation in Czech rather than Russian as his quiet way of protesting the censorship of the arts by the Soviet leadership. His presentation was powerful with considerable emotion. Reba's translation was accurate but tilted toward the sensibilities of the mostly female audience. By the end of the question and answer session, several of the Women's Committee members were prepared to take the Professor Doktor home with them.

Selma and Reba dropped the Professor Doktor at his hotel and then headed for the lounge and afternoon tea. On the way Selma delicately suggested that she might prefer a stiff Scotch. Reba grinned, "Thank God, I need a Martini."

Their long and thoughtful conversation came to two conclusions: first, that it was Izzy's prerogative to decide if and when to introduce Reba to his family, and second, since fate had thrown them together there was no good reason why they couldn't have lunch or at least a drink together on a regular basis. And so began the Selma and Reba bi-weekly-after-work drinks club…Selma treasured her conversations with Reba.

After Izzy's departure the party began to break up. Roz and Morty were next to leave, while Charles and Tina carried out their supplies. Charles said that he would send someone for the equipment the next day.

Selma asked Connor if he'd like to see the rest of the house. She commandeered Jack's flashlight. Con and Ellie went with Syd and Jack to look at photos of Venice. Ellie was really interested in seeing the pictures; Con was pleasantly tired and ready for bed but gracefully succumbed to the developing scheme that intended to deliver him to Venice.

After several rounds of farewell hugs and kisses Selma and Connor were alone.

chapter

NINE

Selma stretched her arms and yawned.

"Are you sure you wanna do this?" Connor said. "If you're tired you can show me around another time, there's no hurry."

Selma shook her head. "I'm wide awake, just a little tired of sitting. Come on, it'll be fun to explain my creation to someone other than my father and brother. They humor me and won't tell me when they think my ideas are dumb. You on the other hand…" She let the thought trail away. "Let's start in the basement that's where I'm building a family room; they were supposed to finish the stairs this week." She opened the basement door and the smell of freshly sawn oak filled the air.

Connor's eye followed the flashlight's beam over the grain of the treads. "What beautiful wood, the smell reminds me of my grandfather's workshop. As far back as we know, every male in the Sullivan family made their living working with wood: carpenters, ship's carpenters and coopers; they're barrel makers."

Selma interrupted. "I know what a cooper does."

"I forgot you're a highly educated product of the Little Flower."

Selma twisted the corner of her mouth downward. "I do cross-word puzzles."

"I'm the first Sullivan who doesn't work with wood, at least not yet. Maybe when I grow up?"

Selma gave him a gentle push down the stairs and closed the door behind. "You sell houses; that's sort of like working with wood."

At the bottom of the stairs Connor reached for the flashlight. "Can I see that?" Connor turned the cowling on the end of the flashlight and the beam widened to illuminate a larger area.

Selma pointed to the left. "On this side is the family room." Connor held the light while Selma paced the perimeter and described the built in cabinets and the wet bar.

Selma pointed to where the TV and furniture would sit; her silhouette danced along the walls in a black and white ballet as Connor followed her movements with the light.

"Papa will use this area the most so I want it to be masculine. I thought pale yellow walls with light oak cabinets, a medium brown carpet and dark leather furniture. Morty told me about this new lighting made specifically for windowless, basement conversions, he says that it simulates sun light and has a switch where you can control the brightness. Does that sound masculine?"

Connor didn't know what to think, he had no experience decorating rooms. "Sure does; sounds like a great place to sit and watch football on Sundays. Maybe I can become one of your father's pals?"

Selma walked back toward the stairs. "If you go bald and belch and fart a lot you might qualify."

She pointed to the space on the other side of the stairs. "On this side are all the practical things: the laundry, furnace, storage cabinets and a powder room with a shower."

Connor shone the light into the far corner. "How about a small wine cellar over there, wouldn't take up much room."

"Humm, that's an interesting idea. Never thought of a wine cellar; don't wine cellars need to be real cold?"

Connor moved closer to the corner area. "Not really cold, not like a fridge. My Dad can tell you what it takes. It's not a big deal, I helped him build his cellar and it only took a weekend to do the whole job."

Selma walked toward the corner. "I'm the only one who drinks wine, Papa…..oooww!" Selma tripped on a bundle of oak stair treads, her shoe stuck under the treads and she started to fall face first to the concrete floor.

Connor turned toward her; as she extended her arms to break the fall she knocked the flashlight from his hand, it fell with a metallic clunk, and the room went dark.

Selma grabbed Connor around the waist, her feet were still stuck in the bundle of treads and she was extended on an angle as if she were in the middle of a dive into a pool. Connor put his hands on her hips and tried to push her to an upright position, much as one would do with a fallen statue. It didn't work, the angle was too steep. He put his left hand on her right shoulder and pushed. When he attempted to place his right hand on her left shoulder it wound up on her left breast instead.

"Sorry, I'm not trying to grope you. I can't see what I'm doing."

She started to laugh, "Okay, okay, just get me upright, then you can grope."

Connor started to laugh as well. He put his arms around her in a bear hug and slowly moved her backward toward the bundle of stair treads. "Don't go too far," she said. "Or we'll fall over the other way."

They reached an upright position with Selma's feet flat on the floor.

"Can you get your shoe free?"

She wiggled her feet. "Don't let go yet. The right one's free but the left one is stuck on something. There's a buckle on the shoe top and I think it's stuck under a wire. Hold on, I'll try and slip the shoe off" Selma twisted and turned her leg and foot to no avail. Her chin was resting on Connor's shoulder; he smelled the floral shampoo scent in her hair, her body was pressed against his, she felt firm yet soft at the same time. Her contorted leg movements pressed her pelvis against his genitals and he was becoming aroused.

61

"This isn't going to work," he said hoarsely. "Here's what we have to do. I'm going to let go of you and get my hands down where I can free your shoe."

"But I'll fall."

"No you won't. Put your hands on my shoulders. When I bend down, lean forward a little and if you feel you're going to fall bend down and put your hands on my back. Got it?"

"Okay, just don't knock me over."

He slid his hands, slower than necessary, down the sides of her body and leg to her ankle.

"Right, there's a wire holding this bundle together and the buckle on the shoe is stuck under the wire. Hold on." He pushed the wire with his thumbs and was able to force it over the buckle. "Okay, you're free. Slide your foot back just a bit. Good, let's get this other shoe back on. Hold onto my head." He placed the shoe under her foot and held it while she wiggled her toes and got it on. "You okay?"

"Yes, I'm fine."

"Good. Just stay put while I try and find the flashlight." He got down on all fours then tentatively felt around on the floor until he found the flashlight. He switched it on, it was still working. He shone the light from Selma's feet to the stairway.

"There's nothing between you and the stairs, walk over there and wait for me." She did as he directed. He joined her, took her hand and led her back up to the kitchen. He was surprised that her hands were so small and delicate. When they opened the door, light flooded down the stairs into the basement. Connor smacked the heel of his hand to his forehead. "If I hadn't shut the door we never would have had a problem; really stupid."

Selma decided not to tell him that she was the one who had shut the door…As they entered the kitchen Selma put her arms around his chest and gave him a big hug. "Thanks for being so calm, I get a little nervous in the dark. I would have panicked if you hadn't been so calm." She looked him in the eyes and grinned impishly. "Okay, now you can grope me."

He returned her grin and kissed her full on the lips. It was a real kiss, their first. He stroked her cheek with his fingers then moved his hands to her waist.

Selma gently rotated her body from his grasp. "On second thought, maybe we'll save the groping for another day."

Connor wiped away the cement dust from his kakis with some paper towels Charles had left behind, while Selma took off the offending shoe. "This one's a goner. The wire put a nice slice through the patent leather. Shame, they're really comfortable."

Connor took her hand and led the way with the flashlight to the Mercedes which, along with Connor's Corvair, had been moved from Jack's driveway.

Connor raised his hand to her face and pushed her long hair so that it fell over her shoulder. "I enjoyed being with you tonight. You're not like any woman I've ever met. Everything about you is different."

She smiled, "Is that a good thing?"

"It's a very special thing."

Selma pushed up on her toes and kissed him lightly on the mouth. "Thanks. It's nice to be special."

She slid into her car, rolled down the window and held up a tan envelope.

"I've got two, free passes for the press preview evening at the Auto Show, Wednesday after next; Mercedes dealer's trying to sell me a new model. You said that you're interested in sports cars. Maybe you'd like to come along?"

"That would be great, I'd love to. Will they have Jaguars there?"

Selma shrugged, "If they have Mercs, I'm sure they'll have Jags." She fished in her purse and pulled out a printed card. "Here, call me tomorrow and we'll work out the details of where to meet. They're doing wine and heavy h'orderves, so don't eat dinner."

"Call me," she said, and shifted into first. As she pulled away from the curb she shouted back, "Hope your hemorrhoids haven't been bothering you too much."

Connor couldn't think of a clever reply so he just waved and looked down at her card.

Jac Simensen

As he drove toward home Connor realized he was still sexually aroused from the physical intimacy with Selma in the basement. He looked at his watch; it was going on eleven-ten. Maybe he'd stop at the 'Sunset Dinner' and see Sylvia. If he remembered right, she got off work at midnight. Sylvia had a crush on Connor and she liked sex; she rarely said no. Sylvia was getting beyond the chubby stage, but she had big boobs and a pleasant face. Connor would drive right past the 'Sunset' on the way home; he still had time to decide.—He thought of Sylvia and bit his lip; he smelled the vestige of Selma's light perfume on his fingers, and grinned.

chapter

TEN

"I really think you should get the 'E-Type.' Not British racing green like the one we saw at the show; candy apple red's the perfect color for an E-Type."

Selma removed the umbrella from her drink. "Connor, why do you keep calling it an 'E Type'? The sign said, 'XK-E' and that's what the salesman called it as well."

"I read in a car magazine that the Brits call it an E-Type not an XK-E. If you want to be aux fait with the sports car set you say E-Type."

Selma shook her head. "I don't want to be aux fait with anyone. I want a stylish two seater that's fun to drive and won't spend half its life in the shop. Jags don't have a great reputation for reliability you know. Morty's father-in-law had a big Jag sedan and it was always crapping out in inconvenient locations. Mostly electrical problems he said. You know the old joke about British sports cars; *Lucas, Prince of Darkness*."

Connor squinted. "I don't get it?"

"You don't get it? You, the aux fait sports car expert. Let me enlighten you. Jags, M.G.'s and most other British sports cars have all of their wiring and electrical parts made by an English company called Lucas which, apparently is known for rather poor quality; hence, *Lucas, Prince of Darkness*. Now you get it?"

Connor sighed. "The E-Type was the most beautiful, sexiest and classiest car in the whole show. It would be a perfect match for a sexy, classy woman like you; perfect."

Selma leaned back into the bar stool. "Tell you what, I'll order the Mercedes in red instead of black like my 190; Red with black leather and a black top. Will that make you happier?"

Connor could see that she was set on the 230 SL. "I've got the best idea. Why don't you buy a red E-type and a red 230 and when the Jag is in the garage you drive the Mercedes. I could help you out and put a few miles on the Jag from time to time, just so the engine wouldn't seize up."

Selma laughed. "Connor what you need is a rich, old woman to buy your toys. You know, like the tan wrinklies in Miami Beach with their diamonds and gold and their young, bronzed boys."

Connor set his glass on the bar. "You cruel, cruel woman, I know that I don't have the highest principals in the world but that doesn't mean I'm ready to become a gigolo." He winked at her, "At least not yet."

Selma changed the subject. "Thanks again for coming with me to my reunion tonight. I'm not good at functions on my own. I know it wasn't the most fun thing for you. You talked to lots of people; I was surprised. If it was your reunion I would have stuck close to your side. What did you tell my friends? After talking with you they treated me like I was a jet setter."

"Oh I just stretched the truth a little and had some fun. I didn't actually lie, but neither did I tell them we both have pretty ordinary lives."

Selma gasped. "Ordinary lives? You call going to the Troc at midnight ordinary; and Dee-Dee Bang-Bang?"

"MISS Bang-Bang to you girl." Connor poked her knee. "I thought that old lady selling tickets was going to choke to death laughing when you asked what time Miss Bang-Bang came on!"

"Alright, enough already. What do you think of this place? I come here with my girl friend usually just for drinks but occasionally we have dinner as well; kind of different, huh?"

Connor swiveled in the stool and looked around. "Is this connected with *The Pub* on the airport circle?"

Selma nodded. "Probably, *Pub Tiki's* a take-off on *Trader Vic's*; tropical drinks and décor and a menu with lots of pineapple."

"I've heard of 'Trader Vic's.' Never been to one; have you?"

Selma shook her head. "There isn't one in Philly; probably have to go to New York."

"If you had asked me before I came in I would have said this looked like a fag place. Hawaiian shirts and leis on guys aren't exactly main stream. But now that we've been here for...." he looked at his watch, "half an hour, it's comfortable in a vacation sort of way. I guess that's the idea; golden beaches, soft music, sexy girls in bikinis...Do you usually wear a bikini when you come here?"

Selma ignored his question." They do a big lunch business and are bursting at the seams with the after work drinks and dinner crowd. It gets quiet by eight or so."

The bartender asked if they wanted another drink.

Connor looked at Selma's drink. "Are you through with your tutti-frutti or will you keep me company for one more?"

She picked up her glass and looked at the half finished drink. "I think I'll trade this in for a Dewar's. Rum punch is pleasant in the afternoon but it's a bit cloying at night."

Selma leaned forward. "Connor, I've had something on my mind all week, something I wanted to ask you; on our way home from the game last Saturday, we saw that fender bender on the expressway and you got all tensed up and didn't say a word for about ten minutes. That's not like you. Are you still having trouble with Maryann's accident?"

Connor took her hand and gently squeezed it. "Thanks for being sensitive; I'm doing okay. I guess there are some things that take a while to work through your system."

Selma looked at his downcast face. Without releasing his hand she stood and kissed him lightly on the cheek. She quietly said, "Connor Sullivan you are a very unique and special person.—Let's go, it's getting stuffy in here." She released his hand, reached into her bag and put a ten on the bar. She gently pulled on Connor's wrist. "Come on, time to go."

The bartender returned and wished them good night.

"You need to come with me to my special place. It's almost eleven now but then neither of us has to get up early in the morning. When do you open the model?"

Connor shrugged, "Ten-thirty, eleven."

She danced ahead, "Come on then, I'll have you back at your car by midnight and you can be home and in bed by one."

"Do I have a choice?"

She was already opening the door on the Mercedes, "Get in."

They turned off of Chestnut and headed west on Market Street. Traffic was light.

They turned right onto the Parkway. The palatial hulk of the Philadelphia Museum of Art loomed ahead of them lit with spotlights like a great ship on the sea. She pulled to the curb just beyond the much smaller Rodin Museum.

Selma locked the car and headed across the wide Parkway toward the Art Museum; she took Connors' hand and pulled him along.

Unlike during the day there were only a few cars parked at the curb and virtually no traffic. There was a steady background noise of cars and trucks moving at speed on the expressway just west of the Museum.

"You come here often?"

She nodded, "I do volunteer work for the Museum, I'm here maybe three or four times a month."

"No, what I meant was do you come here at night?"

She smiled, "Only twice before, and with a friend; I wouldn't feel safe alone at night."

As they approached the Museum it seemed to grow bigger. It was a magnificent Neo-classical structure. They climbed the fifty broad steps to reach the grand plaza and the sounds of the city faded away. Selma ran the last dozen steps and turned back toward the city. Connor finished the climb and stood at her side.

"Isn't the view magnificent?"

Connor had to agree that it was quite a panorama.

The nearly full moon was directly overhead. At the opposite end of the Parkway stood City Hall with William Penn perched on top keeping a perpetual watch over his colony. To the right was the Greek revival home of the Franklin Institute and Penn Station; in the back ground, stood the great, modern, glass and steel PSFS building.

Connor turned in a semi-circle. "I never thought of Philadelphia as an attractive city before; it always seemed a drab, utilitarian place. From up here with the light cutting through the night, the quiet and emptiness, there is a certain grandeur, a feeling of power and permanence, but not beauty."

Selma turned toward him. "My, my, aren't we the poet tonight."

Connor grinned, "It's the wee drop of Irish blood in my veins. On moonlight nights like this I either wax elegant or turn into a leprechaun sized vampire. You lucked out; fang marks on the knee can be rather unattractive."

Selma shook her head and sat on the top stair; Connor joined her.

"I kidnapped you to talk about a couple things."

"Oh?" Connor said, "Serious things?"

"Is it okay if I tell you what I want to tell you? Will you listen to me?"

He saw that she really was serious and nodded.

"My grandmother used to say that only a *piste kayleh* would spit on a grave. That means that only a shallow, empty person would speak ill of the dead. I need to tell you something about Maryann and I'll try hard not to be a piste kayleh.—Maryann worked for my brother Jacob for four years. Her first husband was a pilot and was transferred to Philly just as their marriage was breaking down. After he left her she started coming on to anyone she found attractive; Jacob's construction foreman, workmen and even customers. A few years later Maryann remarried but her behavior didn't change much. Some women are like that. Even some very attractive women need to constantly prove to themselves that men find them desirable. I'd like to balance what I've said by telling you some positive things about Maryann but

I can't; I'm sure that there were lots of good things, but I didn't know her that well.—Then why am I telling you this? Because you're feeling guilty, you think that you were responsible for her death. You think that you were seducing her. You weren't you know; she was seducing you or you were both seducing each other. Connor, if it wasn't you following her home that night it would have been someone else. You weren't responsible for the accident or her death; you were just the one who happened to be there."

Connor lowered his head. "It's more complicated." He paused and focused his gaze down the length of the Parkway. "Seconds before Maryann was killed I was fantasizing about her naked body. I was planning how I would undress her, what I would do with her. Then the pickup slammed into her car and I found her laying there on the seat, staring into space. I stroked her hair and I told her how sorry I was. I told her how ashamed I was that I treated her like a pretty, warm body."

He lifted his head and looked directly at Selma. "You see it's not that I feel guilty; I'm ashamed, ashamed of how I act, who I am, things I've done, girls I've taken advantage of and hurt."

A tear ran down Selma's cheek. She moved closer to Connor and put her arm around his shoulders. He rested his head against hers.

"Connor, you are just too damned honest for your own good. It's good to be outwardly honest with other people, but you can't be so brutally honest with yourself, it isn't healthy. You tell yourself that you're screwing your life up and do you know what happens? After a while yourself believes you and you start to become the person you tell yourself you are."

Connor laughed, "I'm not sure I followed that, could you do it again?"

She stood and moved down several steps so that their heads were at the same level.

"It's simple. You're trying to convince yourself that you are a loser. You like to create little internal dramas with yourself in the starring role. The play you're staging now is called, 'Watch Connor Sullivan Become a Loser.' This play is doomed to be a failure, Connor Sullivan isn't a loser; he's intelligent, perceptive of others, unusually skilled at manipulating people to get what he wants, deeply caring and brutally honest. None of these are the traits of losers. He's also spoiled, somewhat immature and rather lazy. Unfortunately, these traits **are** the traits of losers. Connor Sullivan is young, has an overabundance of male hormones and is quite attractive to women. These are traits of both winners and losers.—Do you see where I'm going? You have all of the things it takes to be a first class human being if you stop telling yourself that you're a loser, and you get some direction and passion into your life."

Selma turned her head away and stared into the distance toward City Hall.

"Connor, I'm so sorry. I apologize. I don't know why I went off on you like that. I have no right…Forgive me?"

He slowly walked down the steps to her level and put his arm around her waist. They silently stared at the city lights for nearly a minute.

"I think that's the best scolding I've ever had. How did you learn so much about me in such a short time? You really care about me don't you?" Selma didn't reply, but turned to face him. They stood looking into each other's eyes until Connor kissed her cheek and released her. She took his arm and they silently descended the stairs.

At street level they stopped to look into the fountain, the pumps were off and no water was flowing, but the underwater lighting made the wind driven ripples on the water's surface iridescent. Connor leaned back against the side of the fountain and looked up at the façade of the Museum. Selma took a deep breath and did the same.

"Connor, do you know what a dowry is?"

"Sure, I actually aced Sociology 101. In the old days a dowry was when an aristocratic woman married a king or prince and her father sent along money and treasure to sweeten the deal. I think that in America we used to have dowry's to help young couples get started. The father of the bride would give the husband a cow or a piece of land, something like that. Did I get it right?"

Selma ignored his question. "My father wants to give me a dowry. In Jewish families it's the father's duty to find a husband for his daughter. An older, unmarried daughter is considered a shame on the family and particularly on the father. My father thinks my being unmarried brings him shame and…"

Connor interrupted. "What do you think?"

"Shame is something that belongs to my father's generation not mine; not to me. I've never had a problem with being single. But my father—well, he's offering a prospective husband quite a lot to take me off his hands: money, a car, a house, even season tickets for the Eagles and Sixers."

"So what does this husband have to do to get the dowry?"

Selma grinned, "Very simple, he has to marry me and if possible, produce a grandchild."

Connor wrinkled his brow. "And what do you think about this arrangement?"

Selma shrugged, "I told Papa that I didn't want anything to do with it and that I wasn't for sale."

She moved directly in front of Connor. "Then tonight, just now, I thought that I might reconsider; but only if you were interested in marrying me."

Her voice broke just a bit and was higher pitched than usual. "I'm not sure if you have the slightest interest, but there could be some real pluses for both of us. You'd get lots of money and some new toys, a nice place to live and a chance to start out fresh; go back to school or anything you wanted. I'd get the opportunity to maybe have a child with a proper father's name on his birth certificate and a home of my own."

Connor put his hand on her arm. "You're really serious, aren't you?"

She looked directly into his eyes. "Yes, I am. It's degrading for me to propose to you and offer you my father's money to marry me; but I like you a lot and I think that we could really help each other have a better life. I think that I could provide you with the support to help you discover the amazing person you really are."

Connor kissed her gently on the forehead and wrapped her in his arms. "My God Selma, you're quite a woman." He whispered in her ear. "Can I have some time to think this through?"

She laughed nervously. "I didn't expect you to sweep me up and carry me away."

He took her hand and started to walk toward the car. "How about we go to some fancy restaurant next Saturday, you choose; if it's expensive, you pay! We'll talk some more. Okay?"

She looked at him and smiled. "That sounds like a good plan."

Selma was enormously relieved. He hadn't laughed or rejected her proposal out of hand. She felt reasonably confident that he wasn't just being kind. Maybe there was a chance?

When Connor turned on the light in his bedroom, he saw that Ellie had left two notes and an envelope on his dresser. Her first note said that his friend Neil Quinn had called: the second, that Dr. Liz Cooper, the Assistant Dean of Students at St. Stephan's, wanted Connor to return her call regarding 'an urgent personal matter.'

The envelope was from the Selective Service System. Connor shook his head; he didn't need to open the envelope, he'd been expecting it. It could wait until tomorrow or maybe Friday.

He turned off the light and slid into the comfort of fresh, clean sheets.

chapter

ELEVEN

Connor woke early. He showered, dressed and went to the kitchen to make breakfast. Ellie wasn't around, but she had left several cups of coffee in the pot. He got out the Sea Toast and butter and cooked three fried eggs in olive oil. He appreciated that Ellie had started buying Sea Toast; she knew it was his breakfast favorite. He remembered childhood breakfasts with Grandpa Jake. He and Grandpa Jake would slather their Sea Toast with so much butter that you could hardly see the big, round cracker, and Granny Marie would scold; "George, don't give that boy so much butter, you'll get him fat." Grandpa Jake would nod in her direction and then slather the butter on the next cracker.

The phone rang. "Connor Sullivan I am here to tempt you with the joys of the flesh. This is Beelzebub your lord and master. You will obey my commands."

"Neil! You yo-yo, when did you get home?"

"I descended with my harem of vegetable virgins to this vile city only last night."

"Ah old queer, have you brought along a tasty vegetable virgin for me as well?"

The conversation was a corny, verbal tennis match; they carried on for a few minutes until Connor lost interest.

"Okay Neil, where are you and what are you doing?"

Neil said that he was staying with his parents in town for the next five days before returning to London to finish his semester abroad. He was going to a birthday party for his ex-girlfriend on Friday night and wanted Connor to join him. They pursued more inane conversation for a few minutes before Connor shook his head and hung up.

Connor cleared his breakfast dishes and poured the remaining coffee into his cup. He took Ellie's note from his shirt pocket and dialed St. Stephan's. He was surprised when Assistant Dean Liz Cooper answered the phone herself.

"Good morning Dean Cooper, this is Connor Sullivan, you left a message with my Mother that I should call?"

"Ah yes Mr. Sullivan. Thank you for returning my call so promptly. Can I please verify with you that you are the Connor Sullivan who recently attended St. Stephan's?"

"Sure, whatever you want." Dean Cooper asked for his former address at school and for his Social Security Number.

"Sorry for the mystery Mr. Sullivan, but I need to speak with you about something quite confidential. Recently we've uncovered a situation in our athletic department and it appears that you may have something to contribute to our investigation. Do you have any idea of what I'm referring to?"

Connor thought for only a moment. "Yes, I know exactly what you're talking about; academic cheating. That's right, isn't it?"

"Yes, Mr. Sullivan, that's the reason for my call. Would you be willing to tell me what you know about this?"

"Sure, it's been over a year, but I remember every detail as if it just happened.—Where would you like me to start?"

"From the beginning, the first time you were aware of the activities in question. With your permission I'd like to record our conversation and then send you a transcript for your review and signature. You're okay with that?"

"Sure, no problem," Connor replied.

"One more thing, Mr. Sullivan; when I start the recorder you'll hear a beep and then again every thirty seconds, to remind you that the recorder is still on; okay? Here's the first beep."

"Fine…Okay…This all started in late November, nineteen-sixty-two. Football season was over; I'd made the team and got to play on the back-up squad all season. I played tight-end and did okay; I got to play in several regular games when we were ahead, even caught a pass for a touchdown. I was feeling good about coming back to play in my sophomore year. When football was over, I tried out for the basketball team, didn't make it; I'm not tall or fast enough. I'm sure you know that basketball's Saint Stephan's main sport and we recruit all over the country. I was a walk on; it was obvious after the first workout day that the other guys were a whole lot better than me, but I was having fun and decided to stick it out 'til the coach made the first cut. I was leaving the locker room a couple days before the cut was announced when Coach Collins approached me; he's an assistant coach on the football team, I think he coaches baseball as well."

"You're referring to Assistant Coach Charles Collins, is that correct?" A beep sounded as she spoke.

"Right, that Coach Collins,—We talked a little about the past football season. He was a lot friendlier than he'd ever been before, I mean, we'd never really had a personal conversation. He asked how things were going with basketball; I laughed and told him that I didn't have a chance in hell of making the squad, but that I was enjoying working out with the guys and maybe could get a slot on the practice team. That's when the tone of the conversation started to change. He said that he could have a word with Coach Rizzo; Rizzo's the head basketball coach. He said that he'd tell Rizzo that I was a real team player and an asset to the football program and that Rizzo should take that into consideration when he made up his cut list. He also said that I was going to get a lot more playing time at tight-end as a sophomore, he felt sure of it.—Then he dropped the other shoe. He asked me if I knew Daryl Summers. I told him that of course I knew Daryl, Daryl's our starting left tackle, a freshman and definitely the best athlete on the team. Probably make it to the NFL someday."

Jac Simensen

Dean Cooper laughed. "I'm a big Saint Stephan's football fan, never miss a game; I know Summers and I'm sure you're right, he's definitely pro material."

Another beep sounded and Connor continued. "Anyway, Coach Collins said that he needed some help from me, help with Daryl Summers. He said that Daryl was about to flunk freshman-comp and as a result he'd be academically ineligible to play football the next year. He said that Daryl was talking about going to an easier school where they wouldn't care if he could write, just play football. I didn't know Daryl well, but always thought that he was a pretty nice guy, as well as a great football player. I said sure, I'd be willing to tutor Daryl…Coach Collins explained that it was too late for tutoring, what Daryl needed was someone to write his compositions."

"So Collins asked you to cheat, to write Daryl Summers papers for him and, in return, he'd put in a recommendation for you with the basketball coach and see that you got more football playing time in future?—Is that correct Mr. Sullivan? I'm not putting words in your mouth?"

Another beep…"No you're not, that's exactly correct. Coach Collins asked me to cheat, to write Daryl Summers compositions for him. In fact, he told me to make sure that the papers weren't too perfect; to put in a few misspellings and grammar errors. The offer to help with the basketball coach and to give me more playing time at tight-end was more subtle, but not the request to cheat, to write the papers, that was crystal clear."

"And what did you tell Coach Collins?"

"I told him that I couldn't help him, that I wasn't prepared to cheat to get a slot on the basketball team that I didn't deserve, or more playing time in my sophomore year. He swore at me, told me I was friggin' stupid and that there were lots more second stringers that would jump at the chance to get his help. That was it, he stomped off."

"What about the basketball team?"

Connor laughed. "I played on the practice squad and had a great time; got free tickets to the games as well, seats right behind the team bench."

"You never reported this incident, never discussed it with anyone?"

"Only with this girl I was seeing at the time. She was kind of a hippie and said that it was good for me to get slapped in the face with the corruption that's everywhere in sports and business. And no, I never reported it; it would have been Collin's word against mine."

"Mr. Sullivan, I'll have this conversation transcribed and a copy sent to you for your signature. We've turned this investigation over to the NCAA. It's possible that someone from that organization may wish to speak with you further."

"I'd have no problem talking with the NCAA; however I've told you everything I know."

"Thank you Mr. Sullivan you've been very helpful."

"Can I ask you one question?"

"Yes Mr. Sullivan?"

"Did this involve more than the football team?"

"Let me shut this machine off," She replied. "Because of the legal implications of the ongoing investigation I can't give you an official answer, but, off the record, quite a few students and coaches were involved and not only on the football team. Mr. Sullivan now that we're off the record can I ask you something that doesn't pertain to the investigation?"

"Okay, shoot, but please call me Connor, I feel like a witness on the stand when you call me Mr. Sullivan."

Her tone and demeanor changed markedly; "Okay, Connor."

"As part of my investigation, I had to review your record at Saint Stephan's. I have your file in front of me now and I find it quite puzzling. You came in here with outstanding recommendations, and SAT's way above our median. Your academic record during your freshman year was excellent. Clearly you were able to handle the kind of work we dish out. Then in your sophomore year your grades started going down-hill and you wound up on academic probation. It looks like during the first semester of your junior year you didn't even attend classes. Connor, you're obviously a bright guy; what happened? Did the cheating incident have anything to do with this?"

Connor was silent for a long moment. "I'm flattered that you took the time to read my file. The cheating did have an impact on my burn out. It was one of several things that made me negative toward school, towards life. But I'm responsible for what I did. Nobody forced me to fail."

"Connor, would you be interested in coming back to Saint Stephan's next term? I think that after what happened and the ethical way you handled yourself, we owe you another shot. What do you think?"

"I have some work to get my life together before I'd consider going back to school."

"I understand, but if you find you're interested in Saint Stephan's please call me directly. I think that I could assist in getting you back in as a junior. You'd have to take a few extra courses to pump up your sophomore GPA, but I'm sure we could work something out. I think we owe it to you."

"Thanks Dean Cooper. I'm grateful for your consideration. If I decide to be a student again I'll certainly give you a call. I don't think that that's where I'm going right now. I think I'm headed somewhere else, but I don't know where just yet."

"Connor it's been a pleasure talking with you. Good luck with your life."

"Thanks Dean Cooper. Goodbye."

chapter

TWELVE

"I don't know a whole lot about Neil other than he's cute, rich and a senior at Florida. Remember that Delta Phi party I told you about? That's where I met him. He's got these piercing blue eyes that look right through you. And, he's really funny; non-stop cornball wise-cracks, that's what I remember. Anyway, coming home from Tampa we were on the same plane. He recognized me, got someone to switch seats with him, and we sat together and talked all the way. That's when he invited me to his former girl friend's birthday party. When he called yesterday, he asked if I had a friend I could bring along. I told him that you were staying with me."

Daphne pulled off the black dress she was trying on and dropped it on the bed. "Cute, rich and funny is a good combination. Did you sleep with him?"

Chloe scowled, "I said that I only met him the one time at a frat party. My date got blotto and I spent most of the evening with Neil and then he drove me home. We fooled around a little, but NO, I didn't sleep with him."

Jac Simensen

Daphne put her hands on her hips and turned on her thickest Mississippi accent. "Now don't you get all huffy with me Miss Chloe, I know you're a proper young lady with a reputation to protect, but I've seen how you stick those big titties of yours in a boy's face when you get all excited."

They both laughed. Chloe was trying on a bikini. She removed the top and cupped her thirty eight 'D's in her hands. "Amazing isn't it how these useless things get them all worked up; probably just because they don't have any of their own," they laughed again.

"Daph, we need to get a move on. Neil and his friend will be here in two hours and we haven't done anything with our hair or makeup yet."

Daphne feigned a sulk. "Who's this friend and what's he look like?"

Chloe clipped the tags from the bikini top and put it back on. She turned from side to side in front of the full length mirror. "I think this one's the best. I'll take the other two back before I leave. Oh, sorry Daph; I don't know anything about the friend except that Neil says he's cute. Let's hope he's better than those creepy blind dates we had at Vanderbilt last year."

Daphne screwed up her face. "Yuck! Don't remind me, Tweedle-Dumb and Tweedle-Dumber."

Daphne pulled the black dress on again; it was a knit and accented her slim waist and perfect rear. "This seems to be the best I can find from the things I packed. Think its okay?"

Chloe grinned impishly. "Any shorter and the string from your Tampax would show! No, just joking, you look great, no kidding."

Daphne stepped back from the mirror. "Should we wear our bikinis under our dresses or what? You said that this is a pool party, right?"

"Yeah, Neil said that it's at this grand estate with a separate pool house and heated indoor pool. There's going to be a band and a bar and dinner at pool side; pretty classy, huh? I'm sure that there'll be a place for us to change. I've got this little beach bag we can put our suits, brushes and makeup in and anything else you need to take. Okay?"

82

Daphne nodded. "I like pool parties. Maybe this friend will have the equipment to fill out his bathing suit?"

———

Neil Lionel Quinn's parent's apartment was bigger than most houses. It included the entire eighteenth floor and roof terrace of one of the newest and most fashionable high rise buildings on the outskirts of Philadelphia. Neil Lionel still had his own bedroom which with each successive year away at college, he used less frequently.

"Mother is going to be so sad that she missed you. She always said that you were the least objectionable of all of my friends." Neil Lionel and Connor were standing on the terrace looking back toward the lights of the city. Connor smiled, he and Selma had shared almost the same view two nights before; although the view from the Museum had been far more intimate.

Connor set his glass on a stone table. "I'm not sure if you know, but our parents still see each other pretty regularly. Your parents always come to our house for my parent's anniversary dinner and my parents always come here for your parents' New Years' Eve party."

"Actually I did know. Nanny told me. Since I've been away at school it seems that Nanny's main job is to assure the family remains connected. Mother calls every few days and Father comes to Gainesville for football and basketball games. They insist that I come home for Thanksgiving and Christmas and we still take regular vacations together. When I graduate in May it's going to be a little more difficult for Nanny to keep us together. I'm thinking about staying on in the UK; that's what they call it over there."

Connor turned his head. "That's a real surprise; you were always the warm weather guy, I assumed you'd want to stay in Florida. I've never been to England, but I hear it gets pretty freaking cold."

Neil shook his head. "Not really, winters are actually milder than in Philadelphia; not much snow but it can get damp and uncomfortable."

"This decision of yours doesn't have anything to do with the weather, does it?"

Neil grinned. "Her name's Emma, Emma Dulforth.—You know my major's golf course design? Emma's father was a speaker at one of our seminars. Trevor Dulforth is an expert on greens design and construction; actually he's a world authority. My semester project's on grasses for greens so I spent quite a bit of time with Trevor and we got to be friends. He invited me to his home for lunch one Sunday and that's when I met Emma. Connor, she is fucking gorgeous; intelligent; funny. She's twenty seven, but you would swear she couldn't be any older than nineteen. I'm really starting to fall for this girl, big time."

Connor looked surprised. "Really, and which Neil Lionel Quinn is courting her, the gentleman or the crazy ass?"

Neil shrugged, "I've sort of been out with her a number of times She seems to enjoy my company but I'm not sure if it goes any deeper than that. English people aren't like Americans; they laugh and joke and have fun, but they don't easily reveal their feelings."

"What does *sort of been out with her* mean?"

Neil shrugged again. "I go to the pub with Emma and her friends, two, three times a week. I've walked her home from the school where she teaches. I've played chess with her on Sunday's at her parent's home. I even let her teach me ballroom dancing so that I could get close to her."

Connor retrieved his drink, "Sounds like she hasn't met Neil the crazy ass yet, only Neil the gentleman."

"Gentleman; that's exactly the problem; Emma is actually Lady Dulforth. I gather that people like the Dulforths stick with their fellow aristocrats. Because I'm an American, I sort of get an exemption from the English system, but if I told Emma that I was falling in love with her I think I'd lose the exemption."

"Do they know that you're loaded? Sometimes money has a way of breaking down social barriers."

Neil shook his head. "I'm sure they've figured out that I'm not poor, but no, they don't know that when I come into my share of the grandparents trust next spring I'll be worth mucho millions."

Connor looked at his watch. "You said we were supposed to pick up our dates at six, right?"

Neil nodded. "We better get moving. Did you bring a bathing suit? I did tell you that this was a pool party didn't I?"

Connor made a face.

"No problem. You can wear one of mine. If this party's like Buffy's last debauch we won't have the suits on for long anyway. Buffy's quite a girl. Sometimes I think that I should have stuck with her." Neil reached in his pocket and threw Connor a set of keys. "Mother said that we should take her car so that the girls will be more comfortable. You don't mind driving do you? I already asked Christian to put your car in the garage. You can stay here if we get back late and you don't want to drive home."

"Whatever you say Neil; go get the suits."

"Turn here and then it's the second right turn; she said it's just beyond the red gates, number seventy-two."

Connor guided the big Lincoln between two red brick pillars into a circular drive, "Nice place."

To their surprise the front door opened and the two girls stepped out. Connor grinned, "Looks like we get to skip the meet the parent's routine, that's a relief." Chloe locked the front door and turned toward the car.

Connor did a double take, "Holy shit! Look at the melons on that, unbelievable!"

Neil grinned. "That's Chloe and those are MY melons." The boys exited the car and Connor walked toward Daphne.

Connor's first impression was quite favorable. Daphne was taller than average, probably five seven in her low heels. The clinging knit dress covered a trim but curvaceous body and the deep cut vee revealed ample cleavage. She had a pretty, freckled face with bright blue eyes, pouty lips and shoulder length red hair. "Not bad." He thought.

Daphne quickly checked Connor out; taller than she; neat, preppy casual, but tastefully fashionable; broad shoulders, and a trim body. And, a hypnotic smile that pushed up from the corners of his mouth to create two perfectly symmetric dimples. "Better than alright, and a new car too," she thought.

"Hi, I'm Connor, Connor Sullivan. I'm very pleased to meet you."

Daphne took his outstretched hand and made an almost imperceptible curtsy. "I'm pleased to meet you too Mr. Sullivan. I'm Daphne

Louisa Breckinridge but you can call me Daph if you care too, every-one does."

"You know Miss Breckinridge I've never met a woman named Daphne before and since it's such a melodic name I think I'll just go ahead and call you Daphne, if you don't mind."

"Why I don't mind at all and I'll just go ahead and call you Connor." Connor released her hand and turned toward Neil and Chloe.

"Connor Sullivan this lovely lady is Chloe Patterson from the University of Miami."

Chloe extended her hand. "Nice to meet you Connor; Neil told me that you've been best friends since childhood."

Connor smiled. "That's because I'm the only one who can put up with his craziness.—Nice to meet you Chloe." Connor forced himself to focus on Chloe's face although he yearned to ogle her large breasts.

Connor turned to Daphne. "Neil, I'd like to introduce my dear old friend Miss Daphne Louisa Breckinridge; you can call her Miss Breck-inridge."

Daphne giggled. "No silly, you can call me Daph, everyone does."

"Hi ya Daph, with that accent you must be from New York, huh?" Neil took her hand.

"Why no, I've never even been to New York. I'm from Starkville, Mississippi."

Neil shook his head. "Could have fooled me; sounds like New York."

Chloe pointed to Daphne. "Daph and I are roommates. Daph, Neil is a senior at the University of Florida and is majoring in golf, right Neil?"

"My specialty is golf ball design; it takes a lot of education to learn how to put the little dimples all over the balls."

Daphne laughed. She turned her head toward Connor. "He's just joshing us, right Connor?"

Connor gravely shook his head. "No my dear, Neil Quinn never joshes, but he does lie a lot," they all laughed.

Chloe turned to Connor. "Where do you go to school Connor?"

Before Connor could reply Neil answered for him. "Connor's a junior at St. Stephan's in Delaware. He's a football player, right Connor?" Connor looked at Neil with eyebrows raised.

"Oh, I like football, what position do you play?" Daphne asked.

"I was a split end," Connor replied.

"Don't you play anymore?"

Neil jumped in. "Connor's had some injuries he doesn't like to talk about."

Chloe frowned, "Nothing serious I hope."

"Nope," Connor said, "nothing serious."

Neil motioned to the car. "We should probably get going. Buffy will be upset if we're late."

The drive to Villanova took only twenty minutes. The girls were comfortable and did most of the talking. By the time they arrived the attentive boys had learned quite a bit about Daphne and Chloe. Connor was starting to get aroused by Daphne's long freckled legs which were barely covered by her short knit dress. When she swiveled to talk to Chloe in the back seat her dress rode up above her crotch and Connor saw the pink flash of her panties. He smiled and forced himself to keep his eyes on the road; there would be time to look at her panties later.

Buffy answered the door. She put her hands on her hips and stared intently at Neil. "Neil you slimy toad, I told you never to come here again. What do you think you're doing and who are these people?" Daphne's intake of breath was audible to everyone.

Neil stepped forward and took Buffy into a great bear hug. "Ah, Buffy, Buffy; ever the charmer." He kissed her and drummed his fingers on her ass. "Taking poison potions again, are we?"

Buffy stepped back and slapped him lightly on the cheek. She turned to Connor and the girls and sweetly smiled. "Now that we've got our greetings out of the way won't you please come in?"

Connor pushed Daphne through the doorway, her mouth was still agape.

Neil stepped back and took Chloe's hand. "Don't be afraid," he said in a stage whisper, "she only attacks men."

Buffy held out her hand. "Hi, I'm Buffy Vanderslice. Sorry if I startled you. Neil and I are the actors in this, former lovers who now hate each other drama. He's the bad guy, I'm sure you could tell."

Chloe introduced herself and shook Buffy's hand.

Buffy turned to Connor. "And Connor, you Irish rogue. I haven't seen you in years. Still propping up this worn out old drunk are you?" She put her hands on his cheeks, and on tip toes, kissed him full on the mouth.

She held out her hand to Daphne. "And oh look, you've brought along the Playmate of the Month. Sorry dear, no insult intended; I'm just terribly jealous of all you skinny, long legged beauties."

Daphne tentatively took Buffy's hand. She almost whispered. "It's a pleasure to meet you ma'am, I'm Daph."

Buffy smiled, "Of course you are dear."

Buffy put her arm around Neil's waist. She was petite and quite sexy in a delicate, elfin way. Neil kissed her again, this time with more passion and purpose. "Happy Birthday my Dutch beauty, you look as if you just stepped out of a Vermeer painting."

She smiled and pinched his rear. "You arrived just in time. Derek is all ready to lead the way to the pool house."

Neil took her hand. "You could be Jewish you know, the way you refuse to give up your traditions."

Buffy turned her head toward Connor and the girls. "When I was a child we always used to have a parade down to the pool house on my birthday, we'd all dress up in costumes. Derek would lead and play his trumpet and daddy would beat on a big bass drum. I found that drum up in the attic a few years ago. Sadly, this will probably be my last birthday at the pool house. Mommy's getting to the point where even with a full time nurse it's difficult for her to stay here. Mathew and Todd both say that we'll never sell the estate and I think that they're sincere, but if none of us live here it will surely go to ruin."

A grey haired man in a faded livery costume entered the front hall and blew what was probably 'the call to hounds' on his ancient bugle.

Buffy clapped her hands. "Okay everyone, follow Derek."

She turned to Neil. "Will you please see that Connor and your guests get introduced to the rest of the party? I think you know everyone except the Caldwell's. I'll be right in back of you."

Neil put his mouth to her ear. "No more sad talk tonight, this has to be the best birthday party you've ever had, the one you'll always remember."

She smiled broadly and kissed him on the cheek. "How sweet; when did you say we were going to get married?"

He squeezed her hand, "Just say the word, 'Barkus is willing!'"

Derek opened both of the front doors to reveal eleven golf carts parked in a line. Each cart had been decorated with tinsel rope garlands and each had two multi-color lanterns hanging from the roof. On the rear of the first cart was a red sign that said 'FOLLOW ME.' Derek got into the first cart and the guest couples loaded into the others. Ken Pratz, Buffy's current boyfriend and ersatz fiancé drove the last cart that was decorated to look like a peacock's tail. Buffy was the last to exit the house. She had quickly donned a sequined, multi-color caftan that reflected the changing lights of the lanterns.

"Let the birthday parade begin!" she shouted. Derek blew his bugle and the golf carts trundled down the drive the 200 yards to the pool house with everyone singing 'Happy Birthday.' They circled the pool house three times and then parked the carts at the entrance.

The pool house was an incredible structure. The semi-circular pool had a marked competition lane along the straight axis. The opposite curved side of the pool started at three inches deep and gradually increased to eight feet where it intersected with the marked lane. One of Buffy's cousins explained to Conner that Mr. Vanderslice had designed the pool to provide for the training needs of Buffy's eldest brother Mathew who had been a member of the U.S. Olympic Swim Team, and also to serve as a recreational pool for the family and their guests. A greenhouse structure with sliding glass walls that opened in the summer rose high above the pool. Ceramic tiles that mimicked the texture of a sandy beach covered the adjoining patio. The huge patio area was covered by a sloping roof that joined with the greenhouse at the apex. Entry to the pool house was through two eight foot tall doors carved with images of whimsical South Sea creatures. Palms in containers dotted the patio. A waterfall gurgled at the far end of the pool. A dozen or more chairs, tables and lounges filled the patio without making it appear crowded.

Along the left side of the patio were two spacious changing rooms. Between the changing rooms was a sauna with enough room for a large group of sweaty bodies. On the other side of the patio a large room that had once been the venue for Mr. Vanderslice's high stakes poker games had been divided with moveable partitions into a guest bedroom and living area. A well stocked bar sat in front of the sauna. Two round tables each with ten place settings and huge candelabra stood near poolside. A small piano and a drum set were next to the entry. Arrangements of flowers bloomed all about the patio.

Daphne was beginning to regain her composure. "Look at this place Connor it's like a movie set!"

Connor whistled softly to himself. "There's some serious wealth in these Main Line towns."

Daphne tilted her head to one side, "Main Line?"

Connor took her hand and led her toward the changing rooms. "It refers to the railroad that leads into Philly. You know, the main line as opposed to the secondary lines. Living on the Main Line was pretty important back before cars; now it's a status thing. Let's put Chloe's bag and our suits in the women's locker room, you can fish my suit and Neil's out later when we swim." Connor pushed open the swinging door. "Hello, anyone in here? Naked I hope." No one replied so he entered.

"My, my; just look at this." Daphne turned to a ten foot long mirrored counter full of bottles, jars, containers of perfume, lipsticks, eye shadow, combs, brushes and all the things needed to add or subtract from a woman's appearance. There were four satin covered stools in front of the counter.

Daphne picked up one of the perfume bottles. "This is the real stuff! How exciting. Wait 'til Chloe sees this, it's just like Hollywood!"

Connor opened the first locker; it was labeled 'Marilyn Monroe.' The next locker was 'Judy Garland.' "Daphne, do you feel more like Marilyn or Judy tonight?"

Daphne looked at the lockers and giggled. "Oh I'll take Marilyn of course."

Connor grinned. "We're not going swimming till after dinner but if you like I can help you change into your swimsuit now and then I could give you an expert opinion on how it fits."

Daphne put her finger to his lips. "You are so fresh Mr. Sullivan; you'll just have to wait until I change to get a better view."

He put his hand on her back and gently pushed her toward the door. "Let's get a drink Marilyn. What would you like?"

"Yes sir, what can I get you?" The barman asked.

"Any red wine?"

A tiny smile crossed the bartender's lips. "We're serving a nineteen-forty-seven Chateau Margaux with dinner. Could I pour that for you now? If you'd prefer something else I can send someone up the house; the Vanderslice cellar is well stocked."

Connor shook his head. "Unbelievable, forty-seven Margaux for twenty people, that's unheard of. You really have enough to go around?"

"I've decanted eight bottles but we brought down another four should they be needed. There's another case in the cellar." The barman poured Connor's wine, "And for your lady?"

"She said that she'd like something sweet; any ideas?"

The barman held up a bottle of Bol's Crème de Cacao. "Does she like chocolate sir?"

"She loves chocolate."

"Then I'd suggest a 'Black Russian', Crème de Cacao and vodka; sweet and strong."

"That should do the job," Connor said and then lifted the wine glass to his nose. "Good lord, that's ethereal!"

The bar man smiled. "Yes it is rather, isn't it? I have to taste the bottles when I decant them, make sure they're sound you know."

Connor put two dollars on the bar. "I'm sorry, sir, but we've been instructed not to accept tips."

Connor returned the money to his pocket. "You can tell that I'm not used to classy parties like this one."

"Oh sir? Neither am I."

Connor picked up the glasses. "You could have fooled me."

The barman smiled. "I like to watch old movies."

Connor handed the glass to Daphne. "The barman made this just for you darlin'."

Daphne raised the glass to her lips. "That's perfect! It's like a chocolate milkshake, doesn't even taste like alcohol. What's it called?"

"A Black Russian."

She frowned. "Why's it called that?"

"I think it's a play on words. It's made with Russian vodka. White Russians were the soldiers who were loyal to the Czar during the revolution. I think it's just a switch from White to Black."

Daphne bit her lip. "I thought it was only the British and the Haitians who were against us in the revolution? I don't remember any Russians."

Derek quietly entered the patio from a side door and approached Buffy; he had exchanged the faded livery jacket for a tweed sport coat. "Miss Clarissa, they said that you needed me down here."

She took his hand. "Yes Derek I do." She led him to the tables at poolside and tapped on a wine glass with a spoon. Derek stood to the side looking uncomfortable. She tapped the glass once again and conversation died.

"My friends, tonight is a very special birthday for me. For eighteen of my twenty-five years my very close friend Derek has led the parade from the house to the pool house. Sadly, this will be his last parade. Next month he will be retiring from his long career taking good care of all of the various Vanderslices and returning to live a happy and I hope long life with his sister in his native Cornwall. If I say much more I'll cry and all of my makeup will run down my face. You wouldn't like to see that, not pretty. So I'll just say, 'Thank you Derek'. Thanks for being my father's confidant and friend, for protecting my mother from the mice and bats, for telling me I looked pretty during those pimply pubescent years, for taking the blame when the horses escaped an unlocked paddock to dine on father's vegetables, and for holding my hand when we lowered daddy into the ground. Thank you Derek, I will never forget you."

The barman approached Derek with a glass of red wine on a silver tray. Derek lifted the glass to his nose. "Eeeem, this must be the '47. It was your father's favorite. I thought we finished all of this before he died. He'll be disappointed that he left some on this side of the river."

Everyone laughed, raised their glasses in a toast and sang 'For He's a Jolly Good Fellow." Derek finished his wine; Buffy embraced him and kissed him on the nose. He departed as quietly as he had entered.

Buffy turned to the guests. "I want you to know that I invited Derek to join us for dinner but he said that his favorite TV show was about to start and declined the invitation."

The dinner was good; as good as a catered meal for twenty cooked in the afternoon and served in an outbuilding with no kitchen facilities could be. The trio played through dinner, mostly light jazz and show tunes.

Dinner conversation at both tables was bright and carefree. The meal ended with poached pears and a rare pre-war vintage of Chateau D' Yquem.

Daphne put her mouth next to Connor's ear. "I can't understand why you all make such a big fuss about that nasty, sour wine. These Russian things are so much better. This yellow stuff isn't too bad though. Do you think that someday when I grow up I'll get to like wine?"

Connor stroked the back of her neck. "It doesn't matter sweet Daphne, as long as you're having fun that's all that counts."

She smiled. "Oh I am having fun, I've never done anything like this before and the people are all so nice."

He took her hand. "C'mon let's dance."

Daphne was an excellent dancer. Her steps were graceful and her rhythm faultless. Two other couples joined Connor and Daphne on the floor. Soon Connor noticed that the four older couples had said their good-byes and exited. That brought the number of guests down to twelve. The party was starting to fizzle out fast, Connor thought.

Buffy emerged from the changing room in a French bikini. She talked with the pianist. The tempo and style of music instantly changed from light jazz to pop. Ken joined her in his bathing suit. "Okay," Buffy shouted above the music, "show time."

Connor turned to Daphne. "Why don't you find Judy, Marilyn?" Connor walked with her to the door of the ladies changing room. "Maybe you could toss out my suit and Neil's as well?"

Daphne kissed him on the cheek. "Maybe you could get me another one of those Russian soldiers from the revolution?" Chloe strutted in the door behind Daphne and patted Connor on the rear as she passed.

Neil came up behind Connor. "I think these sweet ladies are feeling their booze and starting to get wet panties. You agree?"

Before Connor could reply Chloe emerged through the swinging door with their bathing suits in hand. "Okay now, who has the cute little Hawaiian Surfers?" Connor pointed to Neil and Neil pointed to Connor. Chloe hung the suit on Neil's outstretched finger. "I think that Mr. Quinn must be the undiscovered surfer boy." She tossed the black European style suit to Connor. "This says you all over it."

The boys ambled to the men's changing room. Connor had finished undressing and was pulling on the skimpy suit. "Christ Neil, have you tried this on recently? It hardly covers my balls!"

Neil stepped back and viewed the effect. "It's fantastic; you can see the outline of all the goodies inside, the girls will love it.—So, what do you think of Daph?"

Connor endeavored to tuck his pubic hair up into the leg openings of the suit. "She's very sexy in a little girl sort of way. Makes me want to take her home and lick her lollypop. I don't think I have to ask you what you think about Chloe. Have you seen her face yet?"

"No what's it like?"

"Aside from the warts and crossed eyes it's not too horrific. You better have a look though the drooling may put you off."

Neil laughed loudly. "Chloe told me that her parents won't be back until Monday, she said it in a way that implied an invitation. I think that we should plan on taking them back to her house. What do you think?"

Connor was satisfied that he had packed everything under the suit as well as was possible. "Why don't we just see what happens?

I get the feeling that this party will die soon, half of the guests have already left."

Neil smirked. "Don't bet on it."

Connor stopped at the bar to re-supply the Russians.

He was standing outside the women's changing room with glass in hand as Daphne exited in a white bikini. "Okay, what do you think? Do I pass?"

Connor was taken back; Daphne really was the Playmate of the Month. She was very, very close to the 36-29-34 formula of perfection.

"My God Daph," he stammered. "You pass with flying colors."

Daphne beamed. Chloe followed in Daphne's wake. Her bikini was black with silver accents across the top of the bra and cleavage. It seemed that both of her breasts were barely contained within the bra and would burst out at any moment. Neil moved beside her and put a gin and tonic in her hand while he placed his other hand on her hip.

The underwater pool lights had been turned up and the room lights down. There were tall stacks of pink and white bath towels on a table near the pool edge. The dinner tables had been removed and the trio was playing a melodic but driving tune. Buffy walked to the end of the diving board and bounced up and down. She reached behind her back removed her bikini top and dropped it carelessly into the water. Her medium sized breasts were firm with large brown nipples. She bounced up and down again; every male eye fixed on her breasts. She turned with her back to the patio and wiggled out of her bottoms. She did a little pirouette to face the patio and the guests; her pubic hair had been shaved in the shape of a heart. The guests laughed and then clapped as Buffy did a creditable back flip into the pool. She swam leisurely to the edge where she emerged and dried herself with a pink towel as the guests clapped again. Buffy smiled, dropped the towel into an adjacent wicker hamper and walked up to a woman who Connor remembered being introduced to; Margie something-or-other. She was a bit pudgy and had changed into a red, one piece suit. She had a Mediterranean complexion with dark hair that fell below her waist. Buffy whispered in Margie's ear and then turned to the bar as Margie slowly strutted to the diving board. Buffy said something to the band and the percussion increased. Margie walked to the end of the board. The sexual tension in the room was becoming palpable.

Daphne clutched Connors hand. She looked directly into his face. "Connor, I can't do this! I just can't."

He saw that she wasn't teasing. There was real fear in her eyes. He put his arm around her slim waist and drew her close. "It's okay Daph; nobody's going to force you to strip. Really, it's not a big deal. We can leave now if you're uncomfortable."

She put her arm around his waist and gave him a toothy smile. "No silly, it's not about showing off my little boobies; I can't swim. I'll panic if I have to go on that board!"

Connor laughed and patted her ass. "No need to go on the board."

Connor looked around. Soft lights were coming from the guest bedroom suite and the door was open. Buffy, Ken and another couple had disappeared. Margie was on the diving board with her bathing suit around her ankles, her ample rear pulsing to the tempo of the music. Lorna, the blond Connor was seated next to during dinner, had decided not to wait her turn and along with her boyfriend had already stripped. Connor took note that she really was a blond.

Connor turned to Daphne. "I think it's likely to get a little kinky around here."

Neil and Chloe came up in time to hear Connor's comment. "If it's anything like last year it'll get more than a little kinky," Neil said. "Margie in particular has a taste for the bizarre and she and Buffy can put on quite a show. Ever hear of a double dong?"

Connor ignored Neil and looked at Daphne. "It's only ten thirty; maybe we should all change and go back to Chloe's house?"

Daphne looked at Chloe. "Can we do that Chloe?" Chloe grinned. "My parents won't be back until Monday, we have the house to ourselves for the weekend."

chapter

THIRTEEN

Connor managed to get five hours sleep and felt bright and rested. He usually opened the model at ten thirty on Saturday but he arrived early and unlocked the door at ten. More people came through the model on Sundays but in his short experience Saturdays produced more sales. Connor had sold six of the remaining nineteen houses and had a hold on two others including the model home.

Jack was delighted with Connor's performance and told Con that Connor was a natural salesman. "He doesn't push anything, just helps customers talk themselves into the sale."

The sales office at Sunny Slope Farms was on schedule to open in three-and-a-half months. Jack planned to sponsor Connor for his real estate license before the opening so that Connor could take on greater responsibilities for sales agreements and contracts.

To Connor's surprise he discovered that he got a bonus when a house sale closed. His first sale closed on Thursday and he found an envelope next to the coffee pot with one hundred dollars in crisp new bills. Connor whistled when he saw the money. Perhaps he would surprise Selma and pay for dinner; then again, maybe he would put the cash into his apartment fund. One hundred on top of the one fifty he had already saved would give him plenty to cover the security deposit and first month's rent on a nice place.

"No," he thought. "I'll pay for dinner. There's another closing next week and that bonus will go in the apartment fund." Getting his own apartment had ratcheted down in his priority list since Maryann's accident; he didn't understand why.

He made coffee and had just sat down with the paper when the phone rang. He smiled when he heard Selma's husky voice.

"Hi, do you have anyone with you?"

"Uh huh, there's a brunette laying on my right side and a blond on my left."

"Alright smart ass, I meant customers."

"Under the current circumstances, it looks like I'm the customer."

"How can you give me so much crap this early in the morning?"

"Alright, there's no one here but me, I just sat down with the paper and a cup of coffee but I'm fantasizing that the brunette and blond will show up any minute."

She decided to ignore him. "The reason I'm calling is that we're going to have to change our dinner arrangements for tonight. I just found out that my father and his lady friend will be going to Torrello's at seven thirty; our reservation is for eight and I don't want to intrude on their privacy so we'll have to book somewhere else, okay?"

"Fine with me, where would you like to go?"

"Last week you mentioned The Pub on Airport Circle. I've never been there and thought that it might be fun to go someplace different. What about it?"

"Sure, The Pub's good. It might be a bit down market for your refined tastes."

"Hmmm?"

"For starters, they don't take reservations and on Saturday there will probably be a half hour or more wait for a table."

"They have a bar don't they?"

"Yeah, there's a bar and a nice lounge area. Great grilled steaks. They have these open charcoal grills around the perimeter of the restaurant where chefs in white uniforms and big hats do the cooking. You can smell the steaks a mile before you get there. It's pretty casual; you'll see everything from open-necked shirts to cocktail dresses and suits."

"Sounds like fun, I really love grilled steaks."

"In that case, you'll like The Pub. What time should I meet you?"

"I'm babysitting Jacob and Syd's kids starting early tomorrow morning, after the regular babysitter goes home. So, I'll be driving back to Jack's house tonight after dinner. Any time works for me."

"Hey, I've got a better idea. Pick me up at the model at six thirty; we'll drop my car at Jack's and then I can drive your car to The Pub and bring you back after. You can relax and I can have fun driving your car."

"Your Corvair's automatic, can you handle a manual?"

"No problem, I learned to drive on a stick. My first car was a fifty-two Ford with the gearshift on the column."

"Okay, so I'll meet you at the model at six-thirty, don't be upset if I'm a bit late, traffic going in and out of town can be difficult on Saturday nights."

"Great. See you then.—Oh Selma, hold on. It would really make me happy if you wore something that shows off your beautiful figure instead of those loose fitting things you usually wear. Don't get mad now, you always look terrific. It's just that it would be fun to look at your curves once in a while."

Selma laughed, "You mean my rear, don't you?"

Connor acted hurt. "Now why would you say that? Did I even mention your derriere?"

"Don't apologize I'm not offended; I'll see what I can do to satisfy your lurid fantasies. See you at six-thirty."

"Bye; and I wasn't apologizing."

"Goodbye Connor."

Selma put down the phone and immediately dialed another number. "Hi Reba, it's me again. I just talked to Connor and I need your advice about where I can get something that shows off my rear but isn't sluttish." Selma laughed. "Yes, it seems that he's infatuated with my ass. Could be worse, he could be hooked on my nose." Selma laughed so hard that she nearly dropped the phone. "Thanks, I really appreciate your help. I'll be there in forty-five minutes. Maybe we can have lunch as well? Okay, I'll just brush my hair and I'm on my way."

Connor dumped the cool coffee in the sink and poured a fresh cup. He sat down with the paper and started to read the Real Estate section. The phone rang again. Connor expected Selma with another plan change, but it was Neil.

"Hey Buddy, you get home alright last night, you okay?"

"No problem except for the claw marks on my back."

"I'd love to get the details but I can't screw around talking now. I broke a crown this morning and have to get it fixed before I leave. Our family dentist agreed to come in today just to take care of me so I don't dare be late."

"Is it painful?"

"Nope, it just cracked in half and fell off. The tooth feels strange but doesn't hurt. Look, I just got off the line with Chloe; the girls want to know if we can come over tonight. Chloe said that she'd get some beer and pizza and then we could just hang out and play Monopoly or Old Maids. They're headed back to Florida Tuesday so this is our only chance for a repeat performance."

"I can't make it; I have a date tonight."

"Com'on. Can't you be coming down with leprosy or something? I mean these girls are gorgeous and available."

"Neil, I'm not sure I could handle Daphne again. Anyway, this is a special date, there's no way I can break it."

"You've been holding out on me, huh? Who is she?"

"It's kind of complicated. It would take a lot more time than you have to explain."

"It's your loss. I'll tell Daph that she just wore you out. Maybe I can interest them in a three-some?"

Connor chuckled. "Good luck. Sweet, innocent Daphne may turn into a wild woman in the sack but I'm pretty sure a two-some is her limit. She's an old-fashioned girl at heart."

"Look, I gotta go. I'm flying out on Tuesday; I'll ring you before I leave and tell you the lurid details of your lost opportunity...Cheerio old pip."

"Bye Neil, safe trip."

'Just for Two: Intimate Apparel' was tucked away in a small shop off Locust Street. The left side of the shop window featured sexy lingerie, garter belts, bustier and crotch-less panties. The right side of the window displayed gowns and cocktail dresses. Selma seemed transfixed by the display. "Reba, are you sure about this? We're going to a restaurant not a bordello."

Reba grinned. "Don't be put off by the window. Julie has some of the most beautiful, Italian and French designer clothes in Philadelphia. Julie was a costume designer before she opened this shop. I've been buying things from her for over ten years. Come on, you asked me to find something fabulous. Julie is our ace in the hole."

The compact shop was bursting with racks of clothing seemingly in all colors, sizes, shapes and styles. The asbestos tile floor was chipped and faded and the walls probably hadn't been painted since the 1940's. An old, plastic Philco radio was pouring out the live Saturday matinee performance from the Metropolitan Opera. Julie was in the rear holding up tutus for two emaciated teens to inspect. She smiled and waved to Reba. "Be with you in a minute dearie." The teens took the tutus into the dressing room.

Julie waddled up to Reba and embraced her. "I do the costumes for the girls in the Pennsylvania Ballet. Not very interesting, but it pays the rent."

Julie looked to be four foot ten; she was stocky with long false eyelashes and crimson lipstick. Her clothing was unique; it looked as if she had put on parts of several different outfits, one part over another.

She turned to Selma and embraced her as if they were long standing friends. "So this is the pretty little girl who needs some help with her butt; in my day we just said ass but now we all have to be polite and say butt."

Selma quickly decided that she liked Julie. "I don't mind if you say ass, I've always thought that butt was an unfeminine word for such an important piece of our anatomy."

Julie patted Selma on the cheek. "I'm going to like this one."

The teens emerged from the dressing room in tutus and stood on a platform in front of the three panel mirror.

Julie turned back to Reba. "Let me get these two pinned up so I can give you my full attention. You know your way around. The latest designer things are on the far wall."

Julie turned and bent and generally fussed over the first girl. She put in pins and made chalk marks. "Now stand over there Justine, and don't move."

She repeated the performance for the second girl but skipped the pinning and chalk. "Margaret, it's amazing how this size is always a perfect fit for you. You can just put it back on the hanger; make sure it's the one with your name tag."

She turned to the first dancer. "Alright Justine let's see if we can slide this off without puncturing you. There's only us girls, we can do it right here." Julie carefully unhooked and unzipped the tutu.

Selma was taken aback with Justine's protruding rib cage and childlike breasts.

The girls changed into their street clothes and left; Julie waved after them. "They're such sweet kids; it's criminal how they force them to starve. Would you believe that Justine is nearly twenty and weighs less than a hundred pounds?"

Julie took Selma into the changing room and had her strip to her bra and panties. She measured poked and prodded all around Selma's body. "You have such a wonderful figure my dear this is going to be an adventure."

For the next forty minutes Julie and Reba presented Selma with outfit after outfit until they found one that pleased them all.

Selma looked smashing in a pale apricot, silk blouse and charcoal grey trousers. The blouse had a loosely fitted bodice with a narrow plunging neck that was generous in its display of cleavage, and loose puffy, long sleeves. The trousers fit snugly over her hips and rear and then gradually relaxed to end at the ankle in an understated flare. Selma looked in the three mirrors and was pleased with what she saw.

"Absolutely perfect," Reba cooed.

Julie nodded. "If your boyfriend doesn't fall in love with your ass in these trousers then you need to dump him and find a real man."

Selma turned sideways. "There is just one thing. The crotch is a bit on the snug side. I think that if I sat in these trousers for more than an hour they could get uncomfortable. You wouldn't happen to have the next size up?"

Julie shook her head. "With these designer clothes it's rare that I have more than one piece. Not a problem, I can let the crotch out a touch in less than ten minutes. I need to fish out a lift and separate bra for you as well; it'll give the effect that you're not wearing anything under the blouse. You're a thirty-six B?"

Selma shrugged, "Depends on the bra whether I'm a B or C."

"Probably a B in a lift; I'll get both out so we can see. You can wait while I sew or walk up to Mario's for coffee and Italian pastries, your choice."

Reba put her hand on her stomach. "I'm starved, let's do coffee and pastries."

Selma nodded. "Great! Can we bring back something for you Julie?"

Julie beamed. "Thanks; just tell Mario that it's for me. He knows what I like."

Selma changed her clothes and Reba and Selma started for the door; Julie called after them. "Wait Selma, I need to check your crotch." Selma grinned and then the three of them dissolved in laughter.

chapter

FOURTEEN

Maryann had been right. Crawford Borden was the only banker willing to go out of his way to put together a mortgage solution for the Jankowskis. Pete and Arlene Jankowski were in their mid-twenties and both teachers in the Cherry Hill school system.

Arlene had fallen in love with a *Hampton,* a mid-priced, four bedroom, raised ranch. Even with the income from their summer jobs, together Pete and Arlene earned only twenty-three thousand a year. Since their wedding day they had lived modestly and managed to save enough for a down payment. The difficulty was that the house was on a premium lot that commanded an extra sixteen hundred dollars. None of the banks would finance the mortgage with the extra cost nor could the Jankowskis come up with that much more in addition to their down payment. Connor called around the banks and S. & L.'s but no one he spoke with could accommodate the Jankowskis needs except Crawford.

At eleven o'clock Crawford called Connor and gave him the good news. The loan committee had decided that as established teachers, the Jankowskis were 'assets to the community and low risk borrowers' and were making an exception to bank lending policy.

"Crawford that's the best news I've had this week. Pete and Arlene strike me as quality people and I'm sure that your bank won't regret its decision."

"I agree Connor, I'm always happy when we can help our local teachers; we pay them peanuts and dump our problem children in their laps, the least we can do is to try and help them find a decent place in town to live."

"How did they react when you told them?"

"That's why I'm calling. I want you to tell them. I know that you put a lot of effort in on their behalf and I thought that it would be appropriate for you to be the hero."

"I'll call right away. What should I say?"

"Just tell them that their mortgage application has been approved and that they need to call me on Monday to make an appointment to go over what we'll need for closing."

"Right, Crawford. Thanks for your personal involvement in this; you can be sure that I'll put your business card on the top of the stack when it comes to future referrals."

"My wife and I have four kids in the Cherry Hill schools and one in college I'm pleased to help the Jankowskis stay in town. Thanks Connor, goodbye."

"Thanks again, see you Crawford."

Connor put down the phone and smacked himself on the forehead. "What a great guy; and I thought that he was an incompetent old fart and maybe a fag!"

Connor heard a 'thunk' as Arlene Jankowski dropped the phone.

Pete picked up the phone. "Who is this? What's wrong?"

Connor repeated Crawford's message.

In a slow, quiet voice Pete said. "Oh my God; this is no joke is it Connor?"

"No joke Pete, you got your house."

"Hold on Connor." Connor heard Pete gently put the phone down; he could hear Arlene and Pete deliriously shouting. He smiled and hung up. This was a time for them to be alone.

Ten minutes later Pete and Arlene called back. They were each on separate phones and Connor found it somewhat difficult to hear through their excitement. They thanked him effusively; he made sure to give Crawford Borden most of the credit.

"Connor, what do you drink?"

"Pete, that's not necessary, I get paid to help people buy our houses."

"Come on Connor, what do you drink?"

"Mostly wine, but please, I'm happy that Crawford and I could help you and Arlene."

"We'll always be grateful to you Connor." Arlene said. "If you excuse us now we have a few calls to make to family and then we're going out to celebrate. Talk to you soon."

Connor put down the phone. He felt good. He felt good that Pete and Arlene were going to get their new house; he felt good that Crawford Borden was a nice guy; he felt good that he would see Selma in a few hours and that they would spend the evening together; he felt good that he was proving to be less of a screw up than he had aspired to be.

———

Selma was early; the traffic in center city had been lighter than she anticipated and she arrived at the model at six instead of six-thirty. She knew from the Plymouth station wagon in the drive that Connor would have a prospective customer with him. She thought about waiting in the car, but didn't want to get her new outfit any more wrinkled before Connor got the full effect so she entered the house through the side door into the garage/office. She crossed to the mirror on the far wall and primped her hair. She listened for voices from the rooms above but heard nothing except the background music being piped through the house. Her heels clicked on the tile floor as she moved up the stairs to the kitchen. There was a fancy gift bag on the table along with two wine glasses with blue bows tied to the stems, but no Connor.

She wandered into the living room; draped over the arm of the couch was a woman's jacket, a waist length, dressy jacket, the sort that might be worn over a cocktail dress. She picked up the jacket; it was a petite size and not particularly well made. Her imagination started to race. Who was in the house with Connor and where were they? She dropped the jacket back on the sofa and turned toward the bedrooms just as the front door opened.

"Oh hi...I'm Arlene." A small athletic appearing woman approached Selma with her hand outstretched. She was flushed, excited and out of breath. She pointed at the jacket which was an obvious match with her scarlet pants.

"In all the excitement I left without my jacket. Connor is so wonderful; you buying from him too?"

Selma was struggling to imagine what sort of drama she had walked in on.

"Pete, my husband and I are going out to celebrate. Connor got our mortgage approved. I don't know how he did it but he did. We were two blocks away when I missed my jacket. Is that your car? It really is beautiful."

Selma took Arlene's hand only to have it quickly withdrawn.

"I gotta run; we have reservations at 'The Woodbine Inn.' Normally we only go there on our anniversary, but tonight's special, we're celebrating."

She gave Selma the once over. "Don't you look fantastic; I wish I could wear sexy things like those."

Selma handed Arlene the jacket as Arlene turned and hurried out the door. "Bye honey."

The door closed and she was gone as quickly as she had arrived. Selma looked out the front window and saw the Plymouth backing down the drive. She let her breath out slowly.

Selma turned back toward the master bedroom; she heard the sound of water running. The thick carpets muffled her steps and Connor didn't see or hear her enter the bedroom. He was in the process of shaving, standing at the sink in the en suite bathroom. He had obviously just showered and had a bath towel wrapped around his waist. He was quietly humming an aria Selma recognized, she thought it was from *Carmen*. She stood and watched him for over a minute; he really was a well built young man. She searched for something clever to say but came up with nothing, so she loudly cleared her throat.

Connor quickly turned to face her, his razor still in hand and the left side of his face covered in soapy foam. "Good God, Miss Katz, you scared the B'Jesus out of me!" The towel fell away from his waist; he made no effort to catch it. As she stared at his masculinity he dropped the razor onto the floor and walked from the bathroom toward her.

"Oh no you don't!" She laughed. "I don't want that foamy stuff all over me!" She dashed out of the door and retreated to the kitchen; to her relief, Connor didn't follow.

Connor shouted. "I'll be out in five, help yourself to a glass of wine it's in the fridge, the corkscrew's on the counter. That was you Selma in those sexy pants wasn't it? I never got above the waist."

"That was you Connor without the pants wasn't it?" She called back. She was going to echo that she never got above the waist but thought better of it. He continued his song, now louder with lots of 'la, la's' mixed in with a smattering of random words…Selma didn't bother with the wine.

Connor let out a wolf whistle as he entered the kitchen.

"Who is this incredible lady? No it isn't. Could it be? Yes it is!" He took her hands, held them above her head and then turned her from side to side. What great curves, long slim legs, a peak-a-boob blouse and sexy pants. Where did you get the outfit, it's terrific?"

"Oh, it's just something I had in my closet; haven't worn it since college."

He bumped his hip against hers. "Okay kid, let's party!"

Selma dropped her keys into his hand. "You're the chauffer."

———

Connor loved driving Selma's 190 SL. As he shifted he fantasized that it was a Jaguar E-Type. The traffic toward Philadelphia had ebbed and they moved along with little interruption. While they drove Connor told Selma the details of the Jankowski's mortgage adventure.

"How old is this Crawford Borden guy?"

Connor shrugged. "I'm not good at ages once people get past thirty. He's probably around forty-five. Why do you want to know?"

"Well it's probably a silly idea but I'm going to need to find someone to help me with the business soon. Once Jacob gets started with his new development, what's it called?"

"I think that he's decided to keep Sunny Slope Farm."

"Sunny Slope: anyway, once he gets going on Sunny Slope I'm going to be really, really busy; there's no way I can successfully look after the trust as well. Think that you could introduce me to Crawford sometime soon?"

Connor downshifted to second and the exhaust tone rose and burbled.

"Sure, I owe him one. I thought he was an old fart and queer as a three dollar bill."

"He isn't?"

"You'd be safe. He's got a dozen kids."

They were approaching Airport Circle; the municipal airport the circle was named for had ceased to operate in the fifties. Connor pointed to a boarded up café restaurant on the right. "That used to be The Place when I was in high school, 'Clifford's.' On any weekend night there would be dozens of hot cars in the parking lot, gunning their engines and laying rubber; Corvettes, Super Sports, GTOs, custom rods, you name it. My parents put it off limits to me but I managed to sneak over once in a while with one of my friends. Some pretty rough characters hung out there, lots of dope and stolen car parts changed hands. The police finally closed it down and then they bulldozed the old runways so that the kids couldn't use them as race tracks anymore…pretty exciting stuff for a seventeen year old."

Connor turned into The Pub parking lot, pulled up to the Concierge Parking sign at the restaurant entrance and handed the attendant two dollars. "Put this right up front where you can keep an eye on it, okay?"

The attendant handed him the car check. "Yes sir, I'll put it right next to the Lincoln." He pointed to a new Lincoln Continental parked directly across from the entrance.

As Selma slid from the 190's low seat she was aware that the second attendant was surreptitiously looking down her blouse while he was opening the door. He would be the first of a number of men that night that showed their appreciation for Selma's well proportioned body. She blushed; Julie certainly knew how to make a girl get noticed.

The Pub was crowded but not overly so. Connor and Selma managed to get seats at the bar while they waited to be called for dinner. Selma sipped a Dewars and soda while Connor twirled a glass of red wine.

"Why are you playing with your glass like that?"

Connor grinned. "So that I can appear cultured and sophisticated instead of the bozo I really am." She raised the left corner of her mouth. "You think that's sophisticated? More like a child playing with his chocolate milk if you ask me."

Connor gave her an exasperated look and put the glass on the bar. "A true oenophile, that's wine lover for you cretins, swirls his glass to get the wine to mix with the air and produce a bouquet that one can appreciate with one's nose." As he spoke Connor gestured toward the wine glass and nearly knocked it over.

Selma laughed. "Wouldn't it be more efficient to use a straw and just blow bubbles?" She turned to the bartender. "Could my friend have a straw for his wine please?"

The bartender looked quizzically at Connor, Connor shook his head. "Sorry, she's a highly educated product of The Little Flower Convent and isn't used to being allowed out at night unless there's a full moon."

The bartender frowned and moved to the opposite end of the bar. Connor stared at Selma. "Now look what you've done, we'll never be able to get another drink."

The piped in muzak paused and a nasal female voice came over the speakers. "Mr. Bond, party of two, Mr. J. Bond."

Connor stepped down from the stool. "Come on double-0-eight that's us."

Selma shook her head. "Do you think you'll ever grow up?"

Connor grinned. "I hope not, adults are so boring."

From the time that Selma and Connor began to follow the hostess until they were seated, a number of men paused to examine Selma as she passed.

"Connor, people are staring at me. Do I look that out of place?"

Connor reached across the table and took her hand. "Selma, I give you my solemn word as a secret agent that you look absolutely smashing. You're just not used to getting so much male attention. You have a fantastic figure but you don't often dress to show it off so you're not used to men ogling you."

Selma shook her head. "I don't know; this may take some time."

The waitress came for their orders. Connor released Selma's hand. "Would you like another Dewars or would you enjoy some red wine with your steak?"

"Wine would be good."

They both ordered onion soup, Delmonico steaks medium-rare, baked potatoes and asparagus. The waitress told them to help themselves to the salad bar but they declined.

"You know Selma I've had a really strange week. The good news is that with the Jankowskis I've sold a total of seven houses and that means that I can actually afford to pay for dinner. The bad news is that I'm screwing up less than planned."

"You seem happier; crazy as ever, but happier. Are you?"

Connor shrugged. "I feel different; not sure why, but I'm pretty relaxed about things. I mean, I'm still a self centered, spoiled brat, but I'm a more relaxed brat."

Selma tilted her head. "Big deal, I grew up with an adoring, Wealthy father, a doting grandmother, and two protective older brothers; we could have a competition about who's the most spoiled, it wouldn't be close."

Connor shifted in his seat. "We said that we'd talk about…uh, the conversation we had at the Art Museum. I've done a lot of thinking and have some things I need to ask you. I'm nervous; I'm not sure that this is the right place to talk?"

Selma pushed back in her chair. "If you're going to tell me that you're not interested you can do that here and now. I won't cry, I promise."

Connor smiled. "That's not it at all Selma. You know I like you a lot. It's just that we have some heavy stuff to discuss."

Selma finished off her scotch, "So….talk."

"Okay," he said, counting on his fingers. "There's love, my draft status, sex, some details on the dowry and, to be brutally honest, I've wondered why you've never had a nose job. Those are the things I need for us to discuss."

Selma laughed: "Love, war, sex, money and a nose job; great title for a movie. Seriously, the nose job is probably the only topic we should do somewhere else; there's a good chance I might cry. But, everything else…well." Selma glanced up as their waitress approached the table. The brass colored pin on her blouse announced her as 'Beatrice.'

She held out the bottle of red wine in front of Connor for his inspection. "That's fine," he said. Beatrice took a waiters corkscrew from her pocket and fumbled with the capsule that covered the top of the bottle. "I'm sorry," she said. "I've never had to open a wine bottle before. Where I used to work they only had wine by the glass and the bartenders opened the bottles."

Connor smiled at her. "No problem, opening wine bottles and beer kegs is one of the few things I truly excel at; let me do it for you."

Beatrice whispered. "I can't, if my supervisor catches me letting you open the bottle I'll get an earful."

"Okay, Beatrice. Let me walk you through this. First use the pointy end of the screw to peel away the top of the capsule; the right way to do it is to use that little knife blade in the handle to cut the top off, but I find that seldom works." Beatrice followed his instructions.

"Okay, that's good. Now stand the bottle on the table and gently push the end of the screw into the middle of the cork…Right; now twist the screw around until it's in about an inch from the top of the cork. Good, you got it. Okay, this is the most difficult part. See that little arm on the side with the two notches?" Beatrice nodded. "Now put the top notch on the edge of the bottle…Great, you got it. Keep your left hand around the neck of the bottle and push in with your thumb where the notch is sitting on the bottle rim; gently pull up on the main lever. Perfect. Now put the longer, second notch on the edge of the bottle and pull up again, hold the neck of the bottle just like before. Okay, you almost got the cork out. This is the tricky bit; you don't want to spill any of the wine. Hold the neck of the bottle with your left hand; wrap your right hand around the corkscrew so that the screw part comes out between your fingers and pull up gently."

The cork popped and Beatrice beamed. "Well, look at that!"

Connor gestured toward the corkscrew. "We're not done yet. Unscrew the cork…Right, now put it close to your nose."

Beatrice frowned, "You're joking?"

"No this is important. Does the cork stink and smell rotten?"

Beatrice shook her head.

"Once in a long while a cork will decay and rot and make the wine disgusting and undrinkable. It'll probably never happen to you but if it does, then tell the customer that the cork's gone bad and take the bottle back to the bar; the bartender won't know what you're talking about until he tastes the wine, then he'll know."

Beatrice set the bottle in front of Connor. "Now Beatrice, you pour just a little wine in my glass, about a half inch. Wait for me to taste…Okay, that's fine, now pour about a half glass for Selma first and then the same for me…That's it! You're a sommelier, an expert."

Beatrice laughed, "I can't wait for someone else to order a bottle; I'm ready!"

"Connor, that was brilliant, you should be a teacher."

"Only when it comes to tapping beer kegs or opening wine bottles, not much demand for those courses."

Beatrice returned with a loaf of hot, garlic bread on a wooden board and two bowls of cheese encrusted onion soup.

"So," Selma said. "Where were we?"

Connor pulled his chair closer to the table. "Let's start with the draft, that's the most straightforward. Now that I've lost my college deferment, I got a notice from the draft board to report for a physical next Thursday. If I pass, as I'm sure I will, I'll be classified 1-A and eligible to be drafted until I turn twenty six. I'm told that there's about a one in three chance that I'll be drafted within three months of being classified 1-A."

Selma interrupted."And if you were married would that change anything?"

Connor shrugged. "Maybe…currently there's no difference between 1-A married or single. However, I talked to a counselor at Saint

Stephan's yesterday. He says that the President is very likely to sign an Executive Order later this year that will change the system so that men who are 1-A and single will be drafted first and the 1-A married guys only if there aren't enough singles to fill the draft board quotas."

"What does the counselor think the chances are that the President will make the change?"

"He said the chances are high, there's political support for it and Kennedy personally likes the idea. He also said don't plan your life around it passing."

"So if you were married there's a possibility you'd be able to avoid the draft?"

"Maybe, but the point that I'm making is that if we got married soon there's a chance that I'd be drafted and you'd be on your own for a while."

Selma thoughtfully bobbed her head up and down, "Okay."

Connor lifted his glass. "I guess I'm a little frazzled, I forgot to toast. Why don't you make the toast, I'm doing all the talking."

Selma shook her head. "I'm not clever like you, you do it."

"You don't have to be clever, just say what comes to mind, what you feel."

Selma thought for an instant and then lifted her glass. She looked him straight in the eyes. "I wish you a happy life with someone who will appreciate and love you."

Connor laughed, "Aw shit Selma, I didn't mean for you to be that direct, you're trying to bias this conversation."

"You said for me to say what I felt didn't you?"

"Yes, I did, but I didn't really mean it. You were just supposed to say cheers or *mazel tov,* not something meaningful. That's not fair."

She grinned, "Whoever said that I play fair? It's the prerogative of the weaker sex not to play by the rules."

Connor looked at the floor and shook his head. "Alright, so much for the draft, now we turn to love."

Beatrice returned with their dinners. The steaks were thick and seared with cross hatched grill marks. The asparagus had been finished on the grill as well and looked delicious. She suggested that they cut the steaks to see if they had been cooked to their satisfaction.

Selma tried hers first. "Perfect, warm in the middle just the way I like it."

Connor pushed his chair back. He stood, put his hand on Beatrice' back and guided her a few steps from the table.

"Beatrice, I'm about to propose to this beautiful woman. I would really appreciate it if no one interrupted us until we finish eating. You'll be able to tell when we're done. If I'm crying, that means she accepted; got it?"

Beatrice smiled. "Yes sir! I'll make sure that you're not bothered by anyone."

Connor sat.

"What was that about?" Selma asked.

"Oh nothing, I just told Beatrice that I was about to propose to you and asked her to leave us alone."

Selma smirked, "Yeah, right."

Connor grinned. An advantage of having a reputation as a non-serious person was that you could say serious things and expect for them not to be taken seriously.

"Selma, I'm going to ask you a few questions, mainly so that I can get some time to attack this fantastic steak while you talk."

"Mmm, fantastic is right. I haven't had a steak this good in a while, perfectly cooked. Okay, shoot." Selma was hungry, she hadn't had anything to eat since the Italian pastries at noon.

"First question: are you in love with me?"

Selma dabbed at her lips with the white napkin. "Excuse me for talking with my mouth full; being the youngest in a verbal Jewish family, I developed a talent for talking and eating simultaneously. That one's easy; no, I'm not in love with you, but I like you a lot. As you are well aware you are physically attractive. You're fun. You make me laugh. You're bright, articulate, witty and honest. Most importantly, you make me feel good about myself. You treat me like I'm a beautiful, intelligent, sexually attractive woman. When I'm with you I feel like a beautiful, intelligent, sexually attractive woman, even though I know that's stretching the truth.—Your turn; do you love me?"

"Let me just finish chewing this bite. Asparagus is great, have you tried it?"

"Mmmm," she repeated, "put some butter on it, it's even better."

Connor set down his fork. "Okay, I'll try and give an equally direct answer. I like you a lot. You're intelligent, witty, funny, strong and classy and you have a great body. You fix your hair, choose your clothes, select your jewelry and put on your makeup in such a way that all of those things become part of you, of your personality. You are entirely feminine, one hundred percent woman. The thing that pleases me the most about you is that you are at peace with who you are; you don't pretend to be a little girl, you don't put on the helpless routine, or sexually tease, you're just you."

Connor paused, reached across the table and took her hand. "I guess the most important thing is I've discovered that I like myself the best when I'm with you; you kinda fill in the things I'm short on."

Connor released Selma's hand and took a sip of wine. "Sounds like the spoiled brat definition of love, huh?"

Selma had stopped eating while he spoke. She looked down at her lap. "Connor that's beautiful. That's exactly how I feel as well. When I'm with you I feel glad that I'm me, big nose and all. Please, that's enough. If you say anything more, I'm gonna cry and then I'll blow my cover and reveal that I'm not the strong, composed woman you think I am."

"Try the sour cream and chives on the steak; it's even better than on the potato."

Selma looked up at Connor and impishly grinned. "Suddenly I'm feeling quite full. Could we move on to the sex please?"

Connor held up his finger to signal that he needed some time to chew. He drank more wine and daubed his lips on a napkin…"This one's straight forward. Sex is extremely important to me. You said yourself that I have an over abundance of male hormones; that's true. I couldn't conceive of being in a relationship with a woman unless we both felt sexually satisfied. Does that make sense to you?"

Selma nodded. "Women need sex and the physical expression of love even more than most men. I'm a very sexual woman, I need to make love and have love made to me frequently. Does that answer your question?"

Connor smiled. "Sure does."

Selma played with the sour cream and chives with her fork. "What did you have in mind?"

"A honeymoon."

She laughed, "Honeymoon?"

"Before we go any further with this relationship I think we need to make sure that we are sexually right for each other. If we were the average couple we would have had some steamy sex by now, but we're not the average couple, and this is not the standard American love story. I propose that we have the honeymoon first; not in some motel but in a fancy suite at a class hotel. Atlantic City would be nice. What about it?"

"Connor, you sure know how to smooth talk a girl out of her panties…You're on, when?"

"How about the Monday after next? We could drive to the shore in the morning spend the day and night and then drive back on Tuesday. I'm sure Bernice, Jack's assistant, will cover for me on Tuesday until we get back."

Selma put her fork down and leaned back. "Do you want me to make the arrangements? I have a connection at the Chalfont-Haddon Hall, since it's off season I might be able to get the bridal suite?"

Connor drummed his fingers on the table. "Yes, please; the bridal suite!"

Connor noticed that Beatrice was staring at him while she took the order from a couple a few tables away. He gave her the thumbs up. She smiled and flashed 'OK'.

Connor turned back to Selma. "Enough serious talk, let's do the dowry bit on the ride back."

Selma smiled, "Let see, we've covered war, love and lust; yes I think money can wait its turn."

Two bus-boys came and cleared their plates away. As the boys and leftovers departed, Beatrice and another waitress appeared. Beatrice was carrying a small white frosted cake topped with two flaming candles. The second waitress carried two glasses of champagne.

Beatrice set the cake in front of Selma, "Congratulations to both of you, we all hope that you'll be very happy."

Connor thanked them and lifted the champagne. Selma looked at the cake wide-eyed and opened-mouthed. The diners at nearby tables smiled.

"Connor, what's going on, what prompted this?"

"You didn't listen to me. I told you that I told Beatrice I was going to propose to you; obviously she assumed that you accepted."

Selma laughed and raised her glass. "I guess I did, didn't I?"

chapter

FIFTEEN

Connor paid the bill and left a generous tip for Beatrice. The Pub was full; the couples waiting in the bar were two deep. As they exited Selma got even more male stares then when they had entered. She smiled; maybe she could learn to like this.

"Connor, that was so nice. Best steak I can remember and the grilled asparagus was a treat. You should have tried the cake, the butter cream icing was perfect. I hope you left her a big tip."

"Tip? I left her a bill for the corkscrew lesson. You don't think I give away that kind of valuable information?"

Connor looked in the rear view mirror. A police car was closing fast. "Uh oh, New Jersey's finest are on our tail." He checked his speed. "Fifty in a forty five zone; not likely they'll pull me over for that." He dropped his speed to forty five. The car pulled closer, it was the State Police. They continued following for forty tense seconds and then pulled to the left lane and quickly accelerated away.

Selma waved to them as they went by…"What was that all about?"

Jac Simensen

"Beats me; maybe they thought we looked like criminals…Bonnie and Clyde? This triple-black Merc could give the impression of mafia."

"Alright Clyde, you wanna do the dowry part now or wait till we get back?"

"Let's do it now."

Selma swiveled in her seat toward him. "Remember what I said at the Art Museum. Papa thinks that since I'm thirty, unmarried and not a great beauty that the only way I'll ever find a decent husband is if he provides a prospective husband with some incentives."

"And you told him to stuff it…Right?"

"Uh huh; but as I said before, maybe the dowry isn't as crazy as it sounds. You and I just agreed we like each other a lot. We enjoy being together…Mmm?"

"That's what we both just said."

"So if we agree to marry you get the dowry and the carefree, independent life you've said you lust after. You get twenty-five-thousand cash every year. A new XK-E every three years and season tickets for the Eagles and the Sixers. There's a catch with the tickets though; the seat's next to Papa and his friend Herman so you'd have to put up with a lot of farting and belching."

Connor laughed, "I knew there had to be a catch."

"Also, the Cape would be Papa's wedding present and be in both our names."

"Tell me again; what's in this for you?"

Selma put her hand on his knee. She was aware that the scotch and wine were making her bolder. "Beside your sexy masculine body, I get to have a home of my own, and the chance to have a child, maybe two."

Connor shook his head. "Selma, you do realize that this is totally insane don't you?"

She squeezed his knee. "Life's insane."

Connor changed the subject. "This twenty-five-thousand; is that just for me or would I have to pay for groceries and stuff?"

"It's all yours. I'd pay for all of the family expenses."

"You make enough to do that?"

"Uh huh, Jacob pays me well and I have some money of my own."

Connor downshifted and entered a traffic circle. "Tell me about Jewish weddings."

"You'd want a Jewish wedding?" she asked.

He shrugged. "I'm an apostate protestant and you're a convent raised Catholic. Sort of makes sense."

"Let me tell you about my friend Cleo's wedding. It was last July."

Selma had just finished describing Cleo's wedding as they pulled up to the model. Connor turned off the ignition. "Tell me again why they step on the glasses?"

"So that no one else can ever drink from them again, it's like vowing your fidelity to each other."

"I guess that rules out beach weddings?"

Connor unlocked the door stepped inside and turned off the burglar alarm. He looked at his watch it was ten-twenty. "Turn on some lights; I have to call the security company. Don't want the patrol barging in with guns drawn…Be with you in a minute."

He dialed the phone. "Hi this is Connor, seven-seven-three. I need a variance for tonight…no, just for tonight. The password's TROJAN. No TROJAN. T-R-O-J-A-N…Okay thanks."

Selma was seated on the arm of the couch and laughing. "T-R-O-J-A-N; surely that doesn't refer to a Greek soldier?"

"That was Maryann's little joke, I have no doubt that it refers to the condom. I found a large box with just three left hidden in the bottom drawer of a file cabinet. I have a feeling that this house has quite a lurid history…Come on in the kitchen and we'll open some wine."

Selma kicked off her shoes and followed.

"I have no idea if this is any good. It's a gift from Pete and Arlene, a Pinot Grigio from Italy." He opened the bottle with a pop and looked at a shoeless Selma.

"My God girl, you've shrunk. You didn't take that potion with the note that said 'drink me'? Or was it the 'eat me' apple that made Alice shrink?"

Selma nodded. "It was the potion, the apple made her grow tall again."

"Are you sure about that, it's most important you know."

Selma wrinkled her lower lip. "I'm positive that it was the potion that made her shrink but I'm not as sure that it was an apple that made her get big, maybe it was a cookie?"

Connor poured some wine for Selma. "You taste first, if it's awful you can spit it out."

In a mocking manner Selma twirled the wine in her glass then tasted. "Ummm, it's dreadful you wouldn't like it, more a woman's wine."

Connor tasted. "Not bad, dry with a little fizz at the end." He picked up the bottle. "Shall we go into the living room?"

Selma shook her head. "I'd rather stay here if you don't mind. In my experience kitchens are the best places for serious conversation. Probably has some connection with our ancestors sitting in front of their hearths during the dead of winter…Are there any tissues in here?"

Connor looked around. "Only paper towels, there are tissues in the bathroom, I'll get them."

"Don't bother paper towels are fine."

Connor set the towel holder with a nearly full roll of towels on the table. "Think that'll be enough?"

She nodded. Connor filled their glasses and pulled his chair up to the table. Selma sat with her hands folded in front of her.

"I told you that my mother died when I was two?"

Conner nodded. "Yes you did."

"What I didn't tell you was how she died…She was asphyxiated, choked to death. Her name was Hannah. I need to trust you with dark family secrets."…She held out her little finger, "Pinky promise that you'll never tell a soul?"

Connor looked at her quizzically, "Pinky promise?"

"It's like wishing you would die if you ever told the secret. We put our little fingers together like so, and that's all there is to it, you've just promised that you'll never tell."

Connor looked at his little finger. "Powerful little thing. Okay, what're the lurid secrets?"

"Most of what I know about my mother I learned from my Aunt Sally and from Jacob. Jacob was twelve when she died so he remembers her well. After my mother's death, Papa destroyed all photographs of her but Aunt Sally had a few snapshots with my mother and baby Morty and my mother holding me as an infant. She gave me those pictures so I have a fair idea of what my mother looked like. Mama was a lot like me; she was shorter and slimmer but we share the same nose. I guess if I'm honest, mine might be a bit more prominent."

Connor interrupted. "Why did your father throw away the photos?"

"Be patient for a minute, I'll get to that."

"Everything I'm telling you now is what Aunt Sally told me when I was about sixteen. She said that my parents weren't exactly thrilled when they found out that my mother was pregnant with me, they weren't planning on any more children after the two boys.

Sally said that Papa started doing strange things; he would stay out late and pick up women in bars; then just before I was born he started keeping a mistress. She said that it was as if someone had taken over his mind, he was a different man. Shortly after I was born Mama confronted him and told him that either the mistress went or she would divorce him. Papa told her that he was unhappy living with an unattractive woman and that he wanted her to have a nose job. She refused but he kept at her and at her. In the end she agreed to go ahead with the nose job if he dumped the mistress."

Connor pushed back in his chair. "Selma, I'm sorry to keep interrupting, but I didn't know they did nose jobs back in the thirties."

"Actually, rhinoplasty became fairly common after the First World War when surgeons learned how to repair facial injuries soldiers got from shrapnel or bullet wounds."

"Sorry, I won't interrupt again."

Selma sighed. "It's okay, this is a complex story."

"One thing I forgot to tell you; Aunt Sally is an M.D. She's semi-retired now, but in the thirties she worked at Jefferson Hospital. Anyway, Sally recommended a young surgeon to Mama, someone who worked at Jefferson. Papa and Mama met with the surgeon and for whatever reasons, Papa didn't like him. Through his cronies he found another surgeon who practiced at Philadelphia General. No one ever told me this, but I think that one of the reasons Papa opted for Philadelphia General was that it was considerably less expensive. Papa can have this miserly side to his personality."

Connor poured more wine in their glasses.

"Do you know anything about rhinoplasty?"

He shook his head "Only that when a girl in my high school history class had a nose job she had black eyes for weeks."

"Let me tell you the little I know. When the surgeon does a nose job he works mainly on the inside of the nose. He cuts and pulls away the skin and tissue that's attached to the bone and cartilage; after he cuts the bone and cartilage to the shape of the new nose, he replaces the skin and tissue removing any excess in the process. Aunt Sally says that it's a complex operation and that surgeons have to assist in dozens of procedures before they're able to do rhinoplasty on their own. In my mother's case everything went wrong." She paused and tore off a paper towel.

"First, the surgeon screwed up the operation; he failed to cauterize the blood vessels correctly. Next the surgical recovery room staff failed to recognize that she had received more anesthesia than was indicated and neglected her long enough for sufficient blood to drain into her lungs and asphyxiate her; she drowned in her own blood."

Connor put his hands on his head. "Good God Selma, that's horrible!"

Selma dabbed at her eyes with the paper towel. "In those days doctors were Gods; people didn't sue doctors or hospitals. Philadelphia General gave my father a fabricated version of my mother's death with enough medical complexity so that he was unable to question their story. The story broke down however when Aunt Sally got involved. It took a while, but in the end Philadelphia General admitted their errors and the surgeon was barred from conducting further operations at that hospital and by implication, any other Philadelphia hospital. It wasn't much, but at least my father knew the truth."

Selma blew her nose. "Connor, I'm so sorry, but could you get the tissues, these towels are rough on the skin."

"Be right back."

Selma paced around the kitchen table. Connor returned and replaced the roll of towels with the tissues. He put his arms around her and held her close. "I'm sure that it was incredibly painful for you to live with that memory all through your childhood."

Selma nearly whispered. "The worst part is that I never knew the details of my mother's death until I was sixteen."

She struggled to regain her composure. "Connor I'd like to sit down please." She sat quietly with her hands over her eyes.

Connor gently stroked her hair. After a few minutes she wiped her eyes with a tissue. She laughed a small childlike laugh. "I'm sorry, my mascara's run; I must look a mess."

Connor smiled. "Would you like to finish this another time? I can drive you to Jack's if you're ready."

She took a few more tissues from the box. "No, I'll finish, I don't want you to have to see me like this again." She paused and then resumed in what was nearly her normal voice.

"Of course Papa was desolate, haunted with guilt. That's when he destroyed all of Mama's pictures; I don't know why he did that. Sally said that for the next few months he didn't eat much and spent the evenings listening to violin music in the dark and crying. Grandma moved in right away and became our mother for the next eight years. As far as I was aware, she was my mother, the only mother I ever knew. We were very close. When grandma died, Jacob was in Massachusetts at college and Morty was in New Jersey in military school. I was going on eleven and pretty mature. Papa had hired Violet Weiss as our housekeeper; she cleaned and organized but I always cooked dinner for Papa and me. We probably lived what most people would consider a strange life but for me that was just the way life was; I didn't know anything different. I went to school, came home, listened to the radio soaps with Violet, made dinner, did my homework and went to bed. On the weekends Papa and I would do fun things; go to the movies or the zoo or a football game or a museum or shop for clothes and toys for me. Jacob and Morty both married but things at home went on pretty much the same for Papa and me. Are you staying with me?"

Connor reached across the table and took her hand. "I'm with you."

"When I was sixteen there was a girl in my class named Libby."

"This was at the Little Flower?"

"Good Connor, you finally got it right…Except for her crooked nose, Libby was an exceptionally pretty girl; clear skin, long black hair and a nicely, developing body. When Libby came back after spring break she had bruised, dark eyes and a small, delicate nose.

She told us all about her nose job. Mostly she focused on the pain and discomfort, but clearly she was pleased with her new nose…I was jealous, really jealous.

The next weekend when I was making breakfast for Papa and me I announced that I wanted to get a nose job. I was standing with a platter of toast in my hand. Papa's mouth tightened to a red slash, his body shook, I mean really shook and then he hit me. He slapped me on the cheek so hard that I fell to the floor and smashed the platter. He grabbed me by my blouse and hauled me to my feet. I was fearful that he would hit me again and started to cry. Papa had never hit me before, not a spanking not even a gentle slap.

He screamed. 'Don't you ever say that again! No nose job! Not while I'm alive!'

I struggled from his grasp and ran to my room. My cheek was throbbing and I was bleeding from the corner of my mouth. My whole world had changed in an instant. Papa, my loving father, had turned into a monster; he hit me, he assaulted me. I locked my door and prayed that he wouldn't come after me. I dove into the bed and covered myself with the blankets. What had I done? Why was Papa furious with me?"

"After a while I stopped shaking and tried to decide what I should do. Papa hadn't followed me to my room. I picked up the phone and called Jacob; he wasn't home. I called Aunt Sally and got her answering service. I left what I'm sure the operator thought was a hysterical message.

I was about to call the police when Aunt Sally called back. She was there in less than a half hour and took me to her apartment. Papa wasn't in the house when I came out.

Aunt Sally listened to me, bathed me, gave me some cocoa laced with brandy and then tucked me into bed for a nap. The brandy did its job and I slept for several hours."

While I was sleeping Sally called Papa. He was frantic. He had run from the house after he hit me and when he returned I was gone. Sally told him in no uncertain terms to stay away until she called. When I awoke, Sally gave me some sandwiches and cakes with warm milk.

It took a long while for Sally to tell me the story of my mother's life and death; she didn't pull any punches and Papa didn't come out of it looking too good. But I understood; I knew why the mention of a nose job had pushed him over the edge."

"Later Sally called Papa and he joined us for a light dinner. Neither Papa nor I ate much; I don't think either of us was able to swallow. Papa drove us home.

When we went in the house he cried; he got down on his knees and cried. 'Selma, please forgive me. I swear I'll never hit you again.' I kissed him and went to bed…I knew that a nose job wasn't a possibility."

Connor moved behind her chair. He gently massaged her shoulders, they were tense.

"Umm, could you do that for an hour, it's so nice."

He raised her hair and massaged her neck. "Come on Cinderella, I need to get you home it's almost twelve."

She stood and faced him. "What's the matter, you don't like pumpkins?"

Connor embraced her; without shoes the top of her head just reached his chin. He kissed her mascara blotched eyes, he kissed her nose, and he kissed her lips a long lingering kiss. Selma opened her mouth and ran the tip of her tongue across his lips. Connor reached down took her rear in his hands and drew her close to him.

Selma stepped back. "I think we agreed to cover sex next week didn't we?"

Connor laughed. "Wouldn't hurt to get a head start would it?"

Selma shook her head. "War, love, money and a nose job are about all I can handle tonight. Lust will have to wait 'till next week."

chapter

SIXTEEN

Ellie had only a few unchanging habits; her most sacred was sleeping late on Sunday, making a special breakfast and then spending several hours with the Sunday papers. On this particular Sunday for some reason she awoke at seven-thirty feeling bright and rested and decided to modify her routine and make breakfast for herself and Connor. On Sundays she knew that Connor left for work between nine thirty and ten so she had lots of time to make his favorite, Eggs Benedict. She knew that Con would prefer scrambled eggs with sliced ham; she would fix that for him when he decided to get up.

She fluffed her side of the duvet to maintain the warmth and tucked it around the sleeping Con, it was the first really cold autumn morning of the year. In the bathroom she turned the shower on full to allow it to warm up. The separate shower room that Con had designed when they built the house was a luxury she reveled in, it had a ceiling shower head with another head on the wall, the two could be operated independently or together. She wasn't going to wash her hair this morning so she only turned on the wall mounted head.

Ellie stepped back to look at her naked body in the full length mirror. She tussled her still red hair and patted her reasonably flat tummy. "Not bad for forty-seven." She said aloud. She stepped on the scale, 'one twenty one.' 'Great,' she thought. 'No concern about what I eat today.' Ellie weighed herself every morning and when once or twice a year she got close to one twenty five she would go on an immediate, brief diet to get herself back to one twenty. Ellie knew that at its core the love that she and Con shared was based on passion and physical attraction and she was determined to continue to be as physically attractive for Con as she could.

She let the warm jets of water slide down her neck, shoulders and back for several minutes without moving and then soaped up and finished washing. She smiled; life was good. Having Connor home was an unexpected pleasure. Connor had changed; his needs were now very different than when he had been in high school or even recently during college summer breaks. He seldom asked her for advice or opinion and she had learned not to volunteer. Most of all, she was elated by the growing warm relationship between her husband and her son. Ellie had no idea what had changed between them but there had certainly been a major shift in the way they interacted with each other. Con seemed to be learning to respond to Connor as an adult and Connor seemed to be genuinely enjoying the time he spent with his father. Whatever had sparked the change she earnestly hoped it would continue.

Ellie toweled off, slid on a pair of sweatpants and pulled a comfortable, worn cashmere sweater over her head. She exited the house through the garage, shivering in the cold and collected the two Sunday papers. She looked at the headlines in the *Philadelphia Inquirer* as she went into the kitchen; nothing too exciting, seemed like this Vietnam conflict was getting more front page space each week. She dropped the papers on the kitchen table anticipating a long, leisurely read after Connor left for work. She filled a frying pan with water, a slug of vinegar and a pinch of salt and placed it on the stove to warm for poaching eggs. She thinly sliced the ham left over from dinner and began to concoct her version of Hollandaise sauce.

"Hey Mom, what are you doing in the kitchen this early? It is Sunday isn't it?"

Ellie laid the whisk in the mixing bowl, gently pinched Connor's cheeks and kissed him lightly on the lips. "I didn't get to see too much of you this week so I thought that I'd make your favorite breakfast before you run off."

Connor looked at the sliced ham and the Hollandaise in the making. "Okay, Eggs Benedict! Haven't had your special recipe in ages, you do it so much better than the diners."

Ellie grinned. "I think it's the ham instead of Canadian bacon that makes it special, more flavorful. Canadian bacon can be so tough. Put some coffee on while I toast the English muffins, okay? Coffee beans are in the fridge. I read that coffee stays fresher longer if you keep it in the cold. Speaking of cold, dress warm it must be near freezing today. What time do you have to leave for work?"

"Not for about an hour, I try to be there a little early on Sundays. We don't officially open until ten thirty but on Sunday people start coming by around ten. In my short experience selling houses I've found that the early ones are the recreational lookers, the serious buyers don't show up until afternoon, but you never know."

Ellie poached the eggs and assembled their breakfast while Connor ground the coffee beans, filled the coffee maker and looked over the front pages of the papers.

"Wow, things are getting bad in Vietnam now that they killed this Diem guy, seems like the whole place is coming unglued. It says here that over fourteen thousand American troops are there as advisors. I think that Kennedy is trying to soft pedal our involvement by calling the soldiers advisors. Looks like they're fighting and dying more than advising." He shook his head and picked up the Sports section.

Ellie put the plates of Eggs Benedict on the table and Connor poured the coffee.

"I ran into Mrs. Meakins, Frankie's mother, at the grocery store yesterday. She told me that Frankie is going in for the draft board physical on Thursday like you. She asked me if you could give him a ride into Camden, his car was in an accident and will be in the shop for a while."

Connor grinned, "Haven't seen Little Frankie since high school; it was a miracle he graduated, he was really dim. I'm not even sure that he could read or write very well. He's a good kid though and was a great offensive tackle. I think the teachers took pity on him; he was polite and always tried to do the work, probably the only kid to ever graduate with straight Ds'. Sure, no problem, I'd enjoy talking with Frankie. I hope he can fit in my Corvair, he was about two seventy at graduation."

Ellie laughed, "I saw Frankie about six months ago. He came to the shelter with his girlfriend. She wanted to adopt a cat. We found a pretty little black and white kitten for her. Frankie looked great, he's lost a lot of weight, couldn't be much over two-hundred. His girlfriend was attractive, around six-foot almost as tall as Frankie. They make a nice looking couple."

Connor cut through the ham and English muffin to create mouth sized pieces. "You can tell Mrs. Meakins that I'll pick him up at six thirty, okay?"

"Sure, I'll call this afternoon."

"Mom, this is the best you ever made. Someday you have to teach me how to make this sauce, it's so good."

Ellie smiled at the compliment. "Anytime you want, it's not difficult to make."

They ate in silence for the next few minutes while Connor cut and devoured his second stack of egg, ham and muffin.

Ellie got up and refilled their coffee mugs. "How are you feeling about this draft board thing? Are you worried?"

Connor finished chewing and wiped his lips with a napkin. "I figure that it's like when you're a little kid and you have to go to school. Everyone has to go, so you just go. You don't think about whether or not you want to go or if you're going to be an outstanding student or a dunce, you just go. Then day by day things happen, you make choices. It's the same thing with the draft. I take the physical, get classified, wait to see if I get drafted and if I do I try to figure out the best way to work with the system, just like school. The draft board quotas are still pretty low so I have a better than fifty-fifty chance of making it to twenty-six when I'm no longer eligible, on the other hand this conflict could become a full scale war and I could be in basic training in a few months and in Vietnam or some other nasty place a year from now. I'm not happy with the prospect of being drafted but I'm not going to move to Canada. Whatever happens, I'll work with it when it happens, not in advance, not now."

Ellie stood and put her empty plate on the counter. "Your father's right Connor Sullivan, you really have become quite a man." She moved in back of his chair put her hands on his shoulders and kissed him gently on the head. "You need to know that we're both very proud of you; both of us."

Connor stood and embraced her. "Thanks Mom, I know you are and I love both of you. Thanks for the great breakfast."

Connor went to brush his teeth. Ellie cleared the table and stacked the dishes in the dishwasher. He returned a few minutes later in a leather jacket with a pair of gloves in hand. "Not sure when I'll be home, I'll call you this afternoon when I know what I'm doing. I may just stop by the diner for a sandwich later."

"I think that your father wants to drive up to see his mother. If we don't answer the phone it means that we've decided to take her out to dinner. There are lots of things in the fridge; there's half a meatloaf if you want to fix yourself a sandwich and there's some leftover spaghetti and meat balls in the bowl with the foil."

"No problem Mom, I can fend for myself." He turned toward the door, "Oh, one other thing; I may be starting to get slightly serious about this girl I've been dating for the past couple months. I'll let you know if anything's on the horizon, anything serious I mean."

Ellie threw the dish towel at his head, he ducked. "You scamp! You think you can just drop a bomb shell like that, run out and leave me to think about it all day?!"

Connor was already half way out the door. "Bye Mom, talk to you later, love ya."

Sometime in the early morning Jackie had crawled into bed with Selma. She awoke to find him asleep, snuggled in under the covers against her side. Jackie had just turned five. Although she would never tell anyone, Jackie was her favorite of her nieces and nephews. He had

Syd's delicately crafted facial features and her blue-gray eyes with Jacob's dark hair. He was a gentle, beautiful child.

Selma glanced at the bed side clock radio; it read 9:10. She had slept late. She heard the TV coming from the rec-room on the lower level, cartoons. The twins were up.

She thought, "Lord only knows what they're eating." Hannah and Sally were nine and shared a formidable sweet tooth that seemed to emerge whenever Selma took care of them. She would always remember when they were four and she walked into the kitchen in the early morning to find the two of them sitting on the floor, each with a stick of butter in hand and a sugar bowl between them. Selma had watched as they politely took turns dipping their butter sticks into the sugar and then to their tiny mouths.

She carefully rolled away from Jackie and slid out of the bed. Jackie stirred a bit but continued sleeping. Selma put on her dressing gown and pushed her hair from her face. She quietly made her way down the stairs and peeked around the door to the rec-room. The twins were watching cartoons, sitting on their bed pillows and sharing a box of Frosted Flakes; they were eating from the box with their hands.

It was eleven when Reba called. Selma had gotten herself and the children fed, washed and dressed. The four of them were sitting on the rec-room floor playing gin rummy. Selma was exasperated, all three of the children, even five-year-old Jackie, could play the game better than she. She was losing for the second time and was pleased to be interrupted by the phone call.

"I'm sorry Selma, I couldn't contain myself any longer, I had to call. Your father just went out to the car for cigarettes and I had to find out how things went last night. Can you talk?"

Selma smiled. "Much better than okay, we had a wonderful time, he loved my outfit. The Pub is great; the people treated us so nice."

"Enough about the restaurant, did he accept your proposal?"

"He sort of did. I think that he's at least part of the way there. We're going away for our honeymoon next Monday and if all goes well I think he'll agree."

"Your what? Your honeymoon?"

"It's kind of hard to explain, we both agreed that it's important we're sexually compatible so we're going to do the honeymoon first to make sure."

"Well, that's a new approach to getting into a girl's pants!"

Selma laughed loudly. "That's exactly what I told Connor!"

"Where are you going for this honeymoon?"

"Connor suggested Atlantic City and I thought that with your contact at Chalfont-Haddon Hall that maybe you could help us get the bridal suite for one night? If not the bridal suite, then a nice room?"

"No problem, I'll call Norbert tonight. Next Monday you said?"

"We'll arrive early Monday afternoon and leave mid-morning on Tuesday, okay?"

"So how are you feeling about Connor, do you still like him as much as you did?"

"Reba, I'm in love, hopelessly and completely. I think that Connor and I were created for each other. He's perfect for me: funny, serious, intelligent, loving, helpless and, well, just Connor."

"My, this is serious! In that case we need to get you in to see Julie to get your honeymoon outfits together. What day's good for you? Woops, can't talk anymore…I'm in here on the phone talking to Barbara…I'll call you tomorrow and we can set a time. I'm so happy that things are going well for you Barbara and I'll check my availability for next Monday and get back to you. Bye for now."

Selma laughed. "Goodbye Mrs. Katz."

chapter

SEVENTEEN

Little Frankie Meakins had lost a lot of weight. At six foot two and carrying a muscular two hundred pounds, he looked trim. He came around to the driver's side and Connor rolled down the window.

"Hey Connor, thanks for the ride, how ya doin', haven't seen ya since graduation."

"Hey Frankie, good to see you."

They shook hands through the window. Frankie came around and slid into the passenger seat. He looked around at the inside of the Corvair.

"Nice car, yours?"

Connor nodded. "My parents bought it for me when I went away to college. It's about three years old now." Connor backed out of the drive.

"I got a fifty-eight Buick that used to be my Grandfather's. Grandma gave it to me when he died. Only has twenty-eight thousand on it. Milk truck backed into it last Tuesday so it's in the body shop now, supposed to get it back tomorrow. Angie was driving but nobody got hurt. Angie's my girlfriend. We're getting' married in April."

Connor smiled, "Hey that's great Frankie, congratulations. My Mom said that she met Angie when you guys came into the shelter to get a kitten. She told me that Angie is really pretty and that the two of you make a good looking couple."

"Angie loves that cat, really spoils it and spoils me too."

"You're looking great; lost a lot of weight. Did you go on some kind of diet?"

"No, no diet. I work at DeMeidio lumber and do a lot of lifting and hauling; building materials, heavy stuff. Tough to stay fat when you work that hard. That's where I met Angie, she works in the office; her father owns the place. I was thinking about looking for another job before I met Angie but now I guess I'm there for good. Job security ya know, marrying the owner's daughter. But that's not why I'm marrying her. She's real pretty and smart and big like me. She cooks for me, buys my clothes and helps me figure out what to do with my money. We're savin' to buy a house."

"Angie sounds special. Maybe I'll get to meet her sometime."

"You could come to the wedding if you want. It's at Saint Joe's on Westfield Avenue. Angie's Catholic, I have to turn Catholic for her. My Dad don't like the idea too much but I don't care. I'm not anything now so after I turn Catholic I'll be something. We're taking these classes together with the priest. It's pretty complicated, but Angie understands and explains it to me afterward; she's smart. You're not Catholic are you Snake?"

Connor laughed, he hadn't been called Snake since high school. "No Frankie, I'm like you, I'm not much of anything."

In Camden, Connor parked in a dollar-a-day lot. He and Frankie walked to the Federal building where the local draft board had its offices. They checked in with the gruff, elderly receptionist and entered the stark holding area where they were surprised to find three of their high school classmates. There was a coffee urn and a box of tired looking pastries. Frankie was one of the few to chance the pastries. Altogether there were twenty young men in the room: nine black, ten white and one Hispanic.

A balding, middle aged man in a cheap suit with a clipboard in hand entered and called the role, two names went unanswered.

"Listen up," he squeaked in a small, nasal voice. "Out this door and to the right are the men's rooms. I suggest that you visit them now as there will only be one rest stop between here and Perth Amboy. In exactly ten minutes I will lead you down to the bus. Following your induction exam you will return by bus which will arrive here at about 3:00P.M., when you will be free to leave. You will be given a cold drink and box lunch in Perth Amboy prior to re-boarding the bus. I'm told that selections are limited, trade amongst yourselves if you don't get what you want. Any questions?"

The lone Hispanic raised his hand. "Will they tell us if we pass or fail?"

The balding man cleared his throat. "You will be told if you have passed or failed the exam, but nothing else. Any other questions?"

Silence…"Ten minutes back here."

The bus rumbled along the New Jersey Turnpike. Several of the men smoked and played cards most of the others stared dully at the passing traffic. Connor sat alone and read the morning paper passing on sections to others as he finished and then turned to a dog eared copy of Jack Kerouac's *On the Road*. Frankie sat next to 'Grouch' Bauer a former lineman who told dirty jokes non-stop; some of them were actually funny.

In Perth Amboy they joined another bus load of recruits, were divided alphabetically into two groups and told to strip to their tee shirts and undershorts. After placing their clothing and personal belongings in lockers, Connor's group of ten were led into a room with rows of school desks. During the next hour and a half they were given two written tests. One appeared to be a general intelligence test and the other an aptitude test. Connor found the tests exceptionally basic and completed both in less than half of the time allowed. Most of the other men completed the tests early as well. One man was led away when he told the examiner that he couldn't read.

The young men in Connor's group were each given a manila folder and then one by one processed through a series of stations where Medical Corpsmen checked their sight, hearing, blood pressure, feet, rectum and anything else that could be checked. The results of the tests were noted on the forms in the manila folders as the men moved along.

Midway through the process Connor was called into a room where there was a civilian doctor in a white coat. The doctor was a small man with tight black curls. He smiled and pointed to Connor's tee shirt; "St. Stephan's Football."

"Yeah," Connor responded, "I used to play there."

The doctor extended his hand, "I know, don't you remember me?"

Connor shook the doctor's hand, looked carefully at his face and broke into a huge grin. "Doctor McCord! Of course I remember you. You're the team doctor, you set my fractured thumb. What a small world!"

"Sullivan, right, Connor Sullivan?"

"You got it! How did you ever remember me; that was almost three years ago?"

"Tell the truth Sullivan, your name came up just a week ago. I was part of the NCAA academic investigation at St. Stephan's. The assistant dean, I forget her name…"

"Cooper," Conner interrupted. "Liz Cooper."

"That's right, Dean Cooper, good looking woman."

Connor shook his head. "I only talked with her on the phone."

"Dean Cooper read your statement to the investigating committee; seems that you were the only student who refused to cooperate with the cheating. Good man Sullivan. I can't tell you the details but a lot of folks have been disgraced. The cheating was happening throughout the whole athletic department."

"I thought so."

"So what are you doing here Sullivan? Didn't volunteer, did you?"

Connor laughed. "I may not be the smartest guy on wheels but neither am I crazy. Somehow, my patriotism isn't in high gear for this war they're getting ready to fight. I'm having a tough time understanding how these Vietnamese guys are a threat to me and America."

Dr. McCord shrugged, "At the rate they're pumping kids through here the politicians are surely up to something. Okay Sullivan, drop your shorts and we'll see if that hernia of yours' is getting any worse."

Connor screwed up his face in a quizzical expression, "Hernia, what hernia?"

Dr. McCord placed his hand firmly on Connor's groin. "Cough…. Now again." He moved his hand to the other side. "Repeat….Cough again." The doctor took a form from Connor's folder and started to write. "Sullivan, that hernia isn't any better or any worse than when I examined you a few years ago."

Connor was mystified. "Hernia? Are you sure that it was me you remember with a hernia?"

Dr. McCord shook his head and stared into Connor's eyes. "Yes, I'm quite sure it was you. You do remember don't you?"

Connor got the message. "Yes, Doctor McCord, I remember like it was yesterday."

The doctor smiled. "Before you finish you'll be checked by an Army physician. He'll ask who told you that you have a hernia and you'll tell him, 'my doctor.' Now of course that's perfectly true since I was your doctor three years ago."

Connor fought back a grin, "right, got it."

The doctor removed his latex gloves and held out his hand. "It was a pleasure to see you again. Good luck with your life and remember; what goes around comes around." Connor shook his hand.

———————

The Army physician was either a Lieutenant or a Captain; Connor knew that both ranks wore one or two bars and that some of the bars were gold, others silver but he wasn't sure which went with what rank. The Army doctor flipped through Connor's folder and then scowled as he looked Connor up and down. "Drop your shorts and turn around." Connor did as he was told and they repeated the groin pressing and coughing exercise several times. "Who told you that you had a hernia?"

Connor hadn't had much practice lying so he decided to make his answers as short as possible. "My doctor."

"When did he tell you?"

"About three years ago."

"Three years?"

"Yes."

"Have you seen your doctor since then?"

"Yes."

"When?"

"Recently."

"What did he say then about your supposed hernia?"

"He said it hadn't gotten any worse or any better."

"That's all?"

"Yes."

The Army doctor looked at Connor with a look of disgust and shook his head. He took a form from Connor's folder quickly wrote in a large scrawling hand and then placed the form back into the folder. "Give this to the guard at the desk down the hall…Next."

The security guard was seated at a desk doing a crossword and didn't look up when Connor handed him the manila folder. He pointed to the left. "Down the hall and into the locker room; get dressed and then wait in the lounge until your name is called. Leave the key in the locker."

Connor washed his hands and arms up to his elbows with lots of soap and warm water. He took the key on the elastic band he had worn through the exam and opened his locker. After hurriedly dressing he exited into the lounge where there were about thirty young men of various colors, sizes and shapes sitting at cafeteria style tables eating lunch. At the end of the room was a counter, behind which, a large, black woman was handing out boxed lunches. Connor waited in the short line. When it was his turn the woman gave him a big smile. "And what would you like, honey? I got turkey on a roll or baloney and cheese on white bread."

Connor returned her smile. "Can I have the turkey please?"

"You sure can, and what would you like to drink? There's Coke, Seven-Up or orange drink and coffee over there in that urn; I just made it a few minutes ago."

"I'll have some of your fresh coffee, thanks."

She handed him a box. "Here's the turkey honey; now you enjoy, I made this up fresh this morning."

Connor gave her his best smile. "Thank you ma'am, I'm sure I will."

Connor didn't recognize any of the men in the room so he sat at an empty table. The box contained a turkey sandwich with tomato and lettuce on a Kaiser roll, a small bag of potato chips, a Hershey bar and an apple. Connor hadn't eaten since five-thirty and was quite hungry. He quickly polished off the contents of the box and drank two cups of coffee.

By the time Connor finished eating, Frankie and five of the men who had been on the bus from Camden arrived and sat at the table. Conversation was subdued. It was clear that everyone was relieved to have finished the process.

A matronly woman entered the lounge and began to call names. "Preston, Maurice, P."

The man who had said that he couldn't read got up and approached the woman. She pointed to a door to her right. Preston, Maurice, P. gestured toward his lunch companions, took a bow and then strutted toward the door. Most everyone nervously laughed.

Connor took the remains of his lunch to the trash bin and poured a third cup of coffee. "Sullivan, Connor J." She called. Connor winked at Frankie and crossed the room to the woman. She pointed to the door. Connor asked. "Can I take this coffee with me?"

She nodded.

Connor walked through the open door; to his left was a large mirrored window and to the right a counter, behind the counter stood two older men in white shirts and ties.

The first man looked up. "Sullivan, Connor, J.?"

Connor nodded. "I'm Connor Sullivan."

The second man put a form and a pen on the counter in front of Connor. "Sign here. This says that all of your clothing and personal property was returned to you."

Connor signed. The first man made a check mark on the list that lay on the counter and then looked up at Connor. "Mr. Sullivan, you have been found unacceptable for military service. Your local board will provide you with further details of your classification by mail within two weeks. Please wait in the holding room at the end of the hall where you will be called for your bus."

Connor thought that he must have misheard, "Unacceptable for service? That means I failed?" The first man looked up at Connor. "Yes Mr. Sullivan, unacceptable means you failed. Please, down to the end of the hall."

Connor shook his head. "My, my, my," he muttered.

On the way back to Merchantville, Connor stopped at 'Cappy's' package store and bought a bottle of champagne to celebrate with his parents. Before he got to the cashier he went back to the cold case and picked up a bottle of sweet Asti Spumante.

He waved to Cappy who was putting a new tape in the cash register in the adjoining bar and grill. "Hey, Connor, come on in, buy you a beer."

Connor shook Cappy's outstretched hand. "Hey Cappy…Good to see you. Have to take you up on your offer another time, got someone in the car waiting for me."

"How's the new job, ready to come back yet?"

"Cappy, I'm making so much money that I think I just might buy you out next year, always wanted to own a gold mine."

Cappy laughed. "Wonderful! I'll make you a great deal and then go play in the sun with some teeny-bopper."

Connor waved. "See ya, Cappy."

Connor put the champagne on the back seat and handed the Asti to Frankie. "Hey, thanks Snake. What's this?"

Connor slid into the driver's seat. "It's champagne Frankie. It's a type of fizzy wine that people drink to celebrate something important."

Frankie took the wine out of the paper bag. "Oh yeh, I seen this stuff, it's what the baseball players shake up and squirt all over each other when they win the World Series. What are we celebratin' Snake?"

"Frankie, we're celebrating that you and I aren't gonna get shot up in Vietnam."

"That's good, huh Snake?"

"That's good Frankie."

chapter

EIGHTEEN

Connor had a hangover. The Sullivan's had done a great job of celebrating his 'hernia.' Between the champagne and the bottles of red Burgundy Con liberated from his wine cellar, Connor had quite a bit to drink. The aspirin had tamped down the headache but he was still feeling thick-tongued and slightly disoriented. Fortunately business was slow. At eleven there had been an older couple who had a quick walk through the model, and then in the early afternoon, a man who was relocating from California stopped to ask when the first Sunny Slope Farm houses would go on the market. Connor was surprised, the new development hadn't even been announced and already someone was interested in buying. The Cherry Hill real estate market was hot.

Selma and Reba had enjoyed themselves immensely. With Julie's help they had assembled Selma's honeymoon trousseau. Selma had a comfortable outfit for the car trip to Atlantic City, a glamorous dress for dinner, a sexy negligee for the bedroom and another comfortable outfit for the trip home. She was pleased with her choices and was feeling increasingly at ease wearing figure flattering clothes. Except for the French negligee the rest were from Italy. They had lunch at Torello's on Chestnut Street before Selma returned home with her prizes.

———

Sometime about four, Connor finished the last of the club soda and bagel he brought from home. He was feeling almost normal. The phone rang; it was Selma. He had tried to call her the night before and again this morning to tell her the news of his glorious failure but she hadn't answered.

Selma was agitated, her first words were. "Connor, turn on the TV right now."

"The TV, which channel?"

"Any channel," she said. "They all have the same story, the President's been shot, he's dead."

Without putting down the phone Connor turned on the TV on the kitchen counter. "Where did it happen?"

"Dallas, he was in a motorcade with his wife and the Texas Governor. I think the Governor got shot too."

"Do they know who did it?"

"I don't know anything more; I just got home from shopping and switched on the TV."

"Did they say when it happened?"

"I haven't heard, but it must have been within the last few hours."

"They said that he's dead?"

"I'm pretty sure that they did, I only watched for a few minutes before I called. He was hit in the head"

"Good God, that's terrible."

Selma's voice cracked. "His poor wife, she was sitting next to him and was covered with his blood."

Connor shivered at the image of the always impeccably dressed Jackie soaked with her husband's blood.

"I guess that's the last time you'll ever see an American president ride in an open car. The world is getting really nasty."

148

Selma and Connor stayed on the phone and watched the developing news together. The reporters confirmed that the President was indeed dead and that his body was being taken to Air Force One for return to Washington. Vice President Lyndon Johnson, who had been a few cars behind the President's limo, took the oath of office and became the thirty-sixth President of the United States of America.

"Selma, I have to go, someone just came in the front door. I'll call you back as soon as I can. You're okay, aren't you?"

"Yes, I'm okay…I'm scared Connor, please call me back."

"I'll call as soon as I can. Why don't you fix yourself a stiff Scotch?"

"Okay, I will. Please call as soon as you can."

"I will, I promise."

Arlene Jankowski was standing in the middle of the living room. She had tears running down her cheeks and was dabbing at her eyes with a wad of tissues. Connor had forgotten that Arlene was coming to pick up a set of documents that Jack's secretary had left that morning.

"Connor, the President's been shot I just heard it on the car radio."

Connor nodded. "I've been watching TV. Kennedy's dead and Johnson's been sworn in."

Arlene started to sob, "It's terrible, terrible!"

Connor took Arlene's arm and guided her to the couch where she continued to sob. Within a few minutes she regained her composure. "I'm sorry Connor. It's such a shock; I don't usually fall to pieces like this."

Connor put his hand on her arm. "Don't apologize; the whole country is in shock. I'm sure that lots of tears are falling everywhere."

Arlene vigorously shook her head side to side. "It's not like I thought that he was a great President or anything, I mean, I didn't vote for him. But that doesn't matter, he was the President and now he's dead. It's so sad, so sad. His poor wife; how do you tell little children that their father's been shot and killed?"

Connor went to the kitchen and returned with a box of tissues and a manila envelope. He put the tissues on the coffee table and the envelope on the couch next to Arlene. She pulled a few tissues from the box and blew her nose. "Thanks for listening to me Connor." She took a few more tissues and picked up the envelope. "I'd better get home and see what's happening on TV. I'll need to know as much as the kids tomorrow or they won't give me any peace.—Do they know who killed him?"

Connor shrugged. "Not that I've heard, not yet."

Arlene walked to the waste basket in the corner and dropped in the used tissues. "Better take a few more of these with me. I'll talk with you soon."

Connor watched Arlene open the door; a gust of cool autumn air blew into his face as it closed behind her. He felt a shiver start in his lower back and move upward to his shoulders and neck.

He sat on the couch and stared at the opposite wall for a long while…"So that's how a great life ends," he thought. "Kennedy's family and friends will mourn him. His supporters will shed tears and be saddened. Ordinary people will be shocked at the brutality of his murder and be swept up in the details. His political cronies will show their sad faces and perhaps their tears to the cameras while they position for their place in the new order."

Connor smiled a tight lipped smile. He remembered something Grandpa Sullivan told him shortly before he died; it puzzled Connor at the time.

Grandpa Sullivan was no philosopher, hardly an intellectual; neither was he outwardly warm and loving. He was a gruff man with a deep voice and thick accent that tended to keep his grandchildren's affections at arm's length.

Connor had been telling Grandpa about his plans for college when Grandpa looked him straight in the eye and placed his hands on Connor's shoulders. "Connor whatever happens to you never forget that the great life is the small life. The small life is the only life that's really yours."

For the first time Connor understood Grandpa's message.

Connor dialed the phone, Selma answered on the first ring. Selma was calm but Connor sensed that she wasn't herself. "Did you have that Scotch?"

"No, I didn't feel up to whiskey, I made some coffee instead. They said that they caught someone who might be connected to the shooting. They have a man in custody now. They said he shot a Dallas cop and then ran into a movie theater where the police caught him. Someone saw this same man come out of the building where they think the shots came from. Air Force-One is on the way back to Washington where they're going to do the autopsy. That's what's happened since you've been gone."

Connor told Selma about the conversation with Arlene; Selma didn't seem at all interested. "Selma, are you okay?"

"I'm fine…No actually I'm not. I'm feeling a little strange. I've lived in this big, old house and this neighborhood for my entire life and always felt safe and secure. Tonight it doesn't feel safe, it feels threatening. No reason: no sounds or suspicions, it just feels different."

"When do you expect your father home?"

"Papa's not coming home tonight he's staying in town with his friend."

"Selma, I think you need to get out of there. I don't think you should be alone tonight."

"I'll be alright it's just all this talk of killing and bloodshed has got me spooked."

"Why don't you call Jack and stay there tonight? I'd feel a lot better if I knew you weren't alone."

"Jacob and Syd and the kids are in Miami for the week; they won't be back until Tuesday."

"How about Morty?"

"Morty and Roz really don't have the extra room, besides I'd rather not be around Morty at a time like this, he's been really down on the President."

"Look, how about I come over there and stay with you. I could pick up some take-out on the way."

Selma laughed, "No way! This is a very old fashioned neighborhood; at least what's left of it. Within ten minutes everyone on the block would have heard that Selma Katz is alone in the house with a strange man. A half hour later Mrs. Lieberman from across the street would be at the front door to see if everything was all right; not a good idea."

"Fine, then you come over here. The bed in the master bedroom is the only one that's real, the other two have cardboard mattresses, but that's no problem, I can sleep on the couch, certainly wouldn't be the first time. I'll go out and get some Chinese food and a bottle of wine and we can watch the horror show on TV together. Come on, go pack. All you need is a tooth brush and nightgown. There's shampoo, towels, even a hair dryer."

To Connor's surprise Selma didn't argue, "Okay, you talked me into it, but forget the Chinese. I'll stop at the store and pick up some things to make us a real meal, one without MSG."

"MSG, what's MSG?"

"Never mind, you don't need to know. You could go up the road and get us some wine; I don't know what I'm cooking so better get both red and white."

Connor picked up on her brightening spirit. "Okay and if you still can't decide what you're cooking we'll mix them together and have rose."

Selma was pleased that she wouldn't have to spend the night alone. She was even more pleased that she would be with Connor. She retrieved her overnight bag from the hall closet put in a pair of corduroys and a light weight sweater, some shoes, undergarments, makeup bag and tooth brush. She took a comfortable flannel night shirt from her dresser and placed it on the top. Selma paused, broke into an impish grin, opened one of the boxes from Julie's and fished out the French negligee. She clipped off the tags and held it up to her body. 'Not bad,' she thought. 'Not bad at all.' She tucked the negligee under the night shirt and closed the bag.

Selma came in through the front door. "Connor, I'm here." There was no response. She carried the brown shopping bag into the kitchen, "Connor?"

He hollered. "I'm in the bathroom, be right with you." She took off her coat, hung it on the coat tree and was unloading the groceries, when he came through to the kitchen.

"How many people did you bring with you? That's enough food to feed a large family." She turned to find him in the doorway and moved to embrace him. They held each other without speaking.

"Thanks for inviting me. I don't understand why, but I was frightened to be alone tonight."

Connor kissed her gently.

She smiled, "That's nice, I feel much better now. Could you just hold me a little longer?"

He held her tight and then kissed her again, this time with considerably more passion. Selma stroked his cheek with her finger tips. "Okay, I can go home now, I feel much stronger."

Connor smacked her on the rear. "You're not going anywhere until you make us this spectacular dinner, I'm famished."

She took his arm and led him to the kitchen counter. "Let me show you what I brought: linguini with white clam sauce, some crispy Italian bread that I'll turn into garlic bread and the makings for a Caesar salad. You do like your Caesar with anchovies don't you?"

Connor nodded. "I'm part Norwegian, remember. I ate mashed anchovies as baby food."

She twisted up the corners of her mouth. "Ugh! You're okay with white clam sauce?"

He clasped his hands together "An all time favorite."

"I got some vanilla ice cream and some chocolate sauce if you have room for dessert. Here's some cheese and some crackers for us to eat while I cook. If you get a knife you can slice up the cheese for me and open some wine please, I'm getting the DT's, haven't had a drink since lunch."

"Okay Miss Bossy but first we need to have a brief conversation about a very important subject." He took her by the waist, sat her at the kitchen table and retrieved a bottle of wine from the fridge, "White okay?"

She nodded. He opened the bottle set two glasses on the table and poured…He sat, rested his head on his arms and grinned. Selma grinned back.

"Okay buster, what's the mystery?"

He lifted his wine and they clinked their glasses in salute, "To hernias!"

"*Hernias*?" She repeated.

"Especially to my phantom hernia. I failed the draft board physical; I'm unacceptable for military service!"

Selma let out a shriek. "Oh my God, Connor! You're serious?"

Connor nodded, "Deadly serious."

"But you have a hernia?"

"I don't have a hernia, nothing's wrong with me."

She set her glass on the table. "I don't understand…."

Connor laughed and replayed his adventures in Perth Amboy for her.

"So your friend Frankie failed too. Did he have a hernia?"

"Frankie's a good kid, not a mean bone in his body, but neither is there much of a brain in his head. I think his hernia was the IQ test and the fact that he can't read or write too well. They don't tell you why you fail but in my case I'm sure it was the hernia that Doctor McCord diagnosed."

"You really believe that because you didn't get involved in the sports cheating that the doctor made sure you failed?"

Connor shrugged, "Like he said, 'what goes around comes around.' That's 'war' crossed off our list."

Selma clinked his glass, "No war for you, no war for us."

Connor stood, "Okay boss lead me to the cheese I need food."

Selma was pleasantly surprised that Connor knew how to cook. While she fixed the garlic bread and cooked the linguini, he tore up the lettuce, added a raw egg, sprinkled in the cheese and olive oil and soaked the canned anchovies in milk.

Selma looked at him oddly, "Why the milk?"

He winked. "It takes out the excess salt and leaves the little fishies succulent."

"Where did you learn that trick?"

"Everything that I know about cooking I learned from my Mom; I've cooked with her from the time I was three or four. My Dad hated it; he always said that cooking was woman's work. He used to have pretty rigid concepts of male and female roles. He's mellowed over time but still won't cook. Coffee is the only thing he'll make for himself."

Selma wrinkled her brow. "So you're close with your mother?"

Connor nodded. "Really close; like I told you once before, I didn't meet my dad until I was almost three; when he came home from the war. My mom and I lived with my grandparents during that time and everyone thoroughly spoiled me. My mom was very young, just out of high school. She and I sort of grew up together; in many ways she's more like my big sister than my Mom.

Early in their relationship she and my Dad had troubles that were the direct result of my Dad being very, very tied to his mother. My Mom decided that she didn't want the same thing to happen to me, especially since she couldn't have any more babies and I was destined to be an only child. She raised me more like a buddy than a son. It's difficult to explain."

"You're doing great, keep going."

"My Mom and I used to do things together, go places together, take walks, and sometimes go to the movies if my Dad didn't want to go. What happened is that I had a close relationship with my Mom and a more 'regular dad type relationship' with my Dad…Mom was my big sister. I think I told you before that I called my Mom by her first name until I was about twelve. You can see how that would cause some stress between my Dad and me."

"A touch of Oedipus complex?"

Connor grinned, "Showing off our Little Flower wisdom again are we Miss Katz? In any case I didn't gain these deep psychological insights until I got old and wise; last month I think it was."

Selma squeezed his hand. "You really can talk intelligently when you try."

Connor pushed his chair back from the table. "That was a truly magnificent meal from start to finish; especially the Caesar, don't you think?"

She ignored his question. "You were right about the milk and the anchovies, it makes a big difference. I'll do it that way from now on when I make a Caesar. Do you want some ice cream with hot chocolate sauce?"

"No thanks, I don't have much of a sweet tooth after I eat dinner. Can I fix some for you?"

"I think I'll pass, maybe I'll have some for breakfast. Ice cream for breakfast is one of my secret sins."

Connor smiled, "How about cheesecake, cherry cheesecake?"

"Mmm yes, or blueberry," She licked her lips. "Any more wine?"

"There's some red; Beaujolais. It's a light, fruity red."

"Oh, I like Beaujolais; yes, I'll have some please."

Connor opened the bottle poured two glasses and started to clear the table.

Selma raised her glass, "To a good cook and bus boy."

"I don't wash them; I just put the dishes and pans in the trash, saves time."

Selma shrugged. "They're not my dishes; I could care what you do with them. Seriously, this kitchen is well equipped for a model home isn't it?"

"It's just old junk Maryann accumulated. I don't think I'll take this stuff to Sunny Side."

Selma tilted her head back quizzically, "So you've decided to go to Sunny Side?"

"Actually, I never thought about going or not going. Between you and the draft board I've had bigger things on my mind; but yes, I'm going to Sunny Side."

"Between me and the draft board huh? Am I supposed to take that as a compliment?"

Connor shrugged, "Com'on, let's go in the living room and turn on the big TV, see if they discovered anything new. Now that the draft board's gonzo I only have you to worry about."

There was little new news. An amateur photographer had captured the entire assassination on 8MM film and was negotiating with the media to sell the pictures. The probable assassin had a name; Lee Harvey Oswald. He was being interrogated by the FBI, Secret Service and the Dallas Police. The reporters were strongly implying Oswald's guilt. Kennedy's body was being autopsied at Walter Reed. Johnson was being briefed on the urgent affairs of state. Funeral arrangements for the former President were being put in place. The police had retrieved the murder weapon from the warehouse; it was a high powered Italian made rifle. Texas Governor Connelly was out of surgery and would recover. The reporters were less frantic then they had been earlier in the day and their reporting was starting to get back to normal.—As the British say, 'The King is dead. Long live the King!'

Selma and Connor were sitting on the couch, the bottle of wine and their glasses on the cocktail table. She had her head on his shoulder; he had his arm around her neck and was gently stroking her hair. "Had enough news for now?" He said.

"Why don't you just turn the sound down in case something important happens?"

Connor adjusted the TV audio so that the sound level was barely noticeable. He went to the Motorola console stereo and started up a record that was already on the turntable. Soft guitar music filled the room.

"Oh, I like that. Who's singing?"

Connor sat next to her. "I just got this; it's this new stuff, Bossa Nova, from Brazil. The singer is Jobim, Antonio Carlos Jobim. He plays the guitar and writes the songs as well. I've only played this a few times but I'm getting ta like it; very sensuous and sophisticated."

Selma grinned, "Umm, just like me." She folded her legs onto the couch and laid her head in Connor's lap.

"Yes, Little Flower, just like you."

Connor moved his hand to her left breast and gently ran his index finger in a circle around the nipple. She placed her hand over Connor's finger and stroked the back of his hand.

He lowered his head and kissed her, she opened her mouth and their tongues played together. He slid his hand beneath her short skirt and under her panties; she was wet. He stroked her clitoris and she spread her legs wider.

Selma pulled away and sat up on her knees, "Why are we groping on the couch like a couple of teenagers when we have a king size playground in the next room?"

"You're okay that we don't wait for the bridal suite?"

She nodded, "I'm okay, you?"

"I'm okay. I was starting to think that the whole bridal suite thing was kinda contrived; this is a lot more natural."

Selma stood up, "Give me five minutes and then you can come in the bedroom."

She walked toward the door and Connor started to count aloud, "One, one thousand, four, one thousand, ten, one thousand."

"Five minutes." She called back.

Connor flipped the Jobim LP and turned up the volume then took the glasses and bottle to the kitchen. He went to the guest bathroom, striped to his tee shirt soaked a wash cloth in warm water pulled back the foreskin of his enlarging penis and carefully washed the head and shaft. He walked to the bedroom door and called. "I'm looking for a young maiden to ravish, have you got any of those?"

Selma replied, "Okay, you can come in."

Selma had turned down the bed and adjusted the lighting low. She stood in the arched doorway that led to the en-suite bath, the doorway framing her as if she was the subject of a sensual portrait. Her pale blue negligee plunged to the waist in front and had no back. A delicate strap formed of tiny, pink rosebuds, ran around her neck. It continued downward to outline the front panels that were making a half hearted attempt at covering her breasts. The gown stopped just above her knees. Selma had pulled her long, brown hair back over her shoulders. She extended her arms to the sides. "You like?"

Connor struggled for words to express his delight. He walked up to her took her hands and turned her from side to side. "Beautiful, beautiful," was all he could think to say.

"If you like the wrapper let's see what you think of the candy." She reached behind her neck and released the rosebud strap. With a silken rustle the negligee fell to her feet. Connor was visually overwhelmed. Her full breasts were capped with delicate pink, upturned nipples, her fine, brown pubic hair had been trimmed to a small patch, her belly had a slight, sexy curve, her legs were perfectly proportioned all the way from her ankles to the pouting lips of her vagina, and her skin was flawless.

Connor stepped back and words came to him without searching. "This must be how King David felt when he first saw Bathsheba bathing on the roof top. You're gorgeous, perfect."

Selma bent to remove the gown from her ankles. She looked at his penis and started to laugh. She pointed, "Oh how clever!" Connor's erection had lifted up the front of his tee shirt forming a drape around his penis, with only the head protruding. "Oh look, he has a little hat."

Selma reached down and slid the foreskin back. "What a big healthy fellow!"

Connor pulled off the tee shirt and dropped it on the floor. He reached around Selma's body and cupped her ass in his hands. He pulled her close and kissed her. She held his penis and began to rub it against her. Their embrace became more energetic and their kiss more desperate.

Selma began to guide Connor inside her but he pulled back.

"Some things are better horizontal, at least the first time. Come with me my little Jewish Princess." He took her hand and led her to the big bed.

chapter

NINETEEN

"That's enough. All everyone wants to talk about is Kennedy…I wanna hear about last night. I take it you decided to cancel the trip to Atlantic City?"

Selma put her fork on the plate. "Umm, it was Connor's suggestion. Strange, he said exactly what I'd been thinking."

Reba took a small sip from her Gibson, "And that was?"

"It was too contrived. Driving down there knowing that the purpose was to have sex would have made the whole experience less special."

"Can I assume from the wall-to-wall grin on your face that last evening was successful?"

The bartender interrupted, "Are you finished Reba?"

"Thanks Dean, you were right, the tarragon in the chicken salad adds a nice zing."

"Selma?"

Jac Simensen

She wiped her mouth with the starched napkin. "I think I better finish this salmon, I need the energy." The women laughed while Dean turned away with Reba's plate.

"Seriously Selma, it was really that good?"

Selma shifted closer. "I lost count of the orgasms and how he accomplished them. We were exhausted and sound asleep before midnight. Then he woke me up about four a.m. drawing designs on my belly with his tongue. When the sun came up I returned the favor and woke him up with my tongue. If it wasn't for the fact that we had to straighten up before Connor opened the model, I think that we'd still be in bed!"

Reba shook her head. "Selma Katz, you're making this up."

Selma crossed her heart.

The bartender returned. "Is it a two drink lunch today ladies?"

Selma winked, "At least. You can take my plate I'm too busy talking to eat. Thanks Deano."

"Let me tell you what he said when he first saw me naked… 'Now I know how King David felt when he first saw Bathsheba!'" They laughed so loud that a few of the customers looked their way. "Honest Reba, I don't know if he plans what he says in advance or it just pops into his head."

Reba patted Selma's hand. "Does it matter? No one ever quoted the Torah to me when I was naked. You sure he's not an Irish Jew?"

Reba fished the onion out from the bottom of her glass while the bartender set down a fresh drink.

"Thanks Dean…So now what? Have you made any decisions?"

"Uh huh…He said that we should get married."

"That's it? He just said you should get married?"

Selma put her arm on the bar and smiled. "No, it was a bit more prosaic. It was during our sunrise session, I was on top. I think he watched my face and timed it a few seconds from the explosion when he said, 'Selma, we're perfect for each other, I think we should get married.' I wanted to shout YES but all I could do was pant! Romantic, huh?"

Reba shook her head. "I'll say this; it's a moment you'll never forget."

162

"Selma, for just one minute let me play the pseudo step mother, I know it's a role I'm not entitled to, but I'd never forgive myself if I didn't."

Selma squeezed Reba's hand. "Reba, you're my dearest friend. Ask me anything you want."

Reba looked at the floor for a few seconds and then raised her gaze to Selma's eyes. "I've never met Connor but from your stories I feel that I know him well. He's good looking, he's charming. But is he honest? Sincere and…"

Selma interrupted, "Connor's honest to a fault."

"Okay, he's honest. He's fun to be with, he treats you well. You're both witty and sophisticated, you more than him. You love him, he says that he likes you a lot but he's never said that he loves you…"

Selma interrupted again. "He doesn't love me yet. I don't think he knows how to love, but he can learn, I think I can teach him."

Reba sipped her second Gibson. "Okay, here's the tough part. Do you honestly think that Connor would suggest that you two get married if you hadn't offered him the money, the car, the house and everything else? Do you think he would want to marry you if you weren't wealthy?"

Selma patted Reba's hand. "Connor doesn't know I have money, he thinks that I live on a salary that Papa and Jacob pay me for taking care of their books."

"Selma, I don't like to be confrontational, but isn't that dishonest?"

Selma smiled, "I said that Connor was honest to a fault not me… It's complicated; when I told Connor about the dowry I never told him that if he accepted, the money would come from me not Papa. Papa can give us the house as a wedding present, and, we need to talk about that later, but I don't intend telling Papa anything about a dowry and I'll make sure that Connor doesn't bring it up with him either."

"You didn't answer my question; would Connor agree to marry you if you hadn't offered him the dowry?"

Selma took a deep breath. "The simple answer is no, he wouldn't. When this all started, I thought the dowry would help persuade him that we could have a good life together. He'd get the toys and the no pressure life he said was important to him; I'd get a husband. I'm sure he likes me; he likes to be with me. And now that we know the sex is especially good, I think that the money may be less important to him. I don't know that for sure. What I do know is that I love him and want him for my husband and lover."

Selma paused to collect her thoughts. "Connor Sullivan is the man I've always wanted but could never have. He's the cute boy who I wished had asked me to my senior prom. He's the good looking, well-dressed guy I wanted to be seen holding hands with around the campus at Temple. He's the handsome man I dreamed loved me and asked me to marry him. He's the loving husband and father to my beautiful children."

Selma paused and looked at the floor. "For the last seven years I've tried to build a life that didn't include that man. I had my work to keep me busy, my charities and organizations to fill time, Martin for sex and companionship and Papa and my family for love and support. I wasn't exactly thrilled with my life, but I was content…Then Connor came along. Through a chance meeting and a constellation of seemingly destined events I started to believe that there was a possibility for me to have a real life; a chance for the ugly duckling to…"

Reba stood and gently kissed Selma on the cheek. "Enough already, Snow White; do it. Go after your Prince Charming."

Selma smiled, "There's no doubt about it."

Reba hoisted herself back on the bar stool. "Now what's this about the house you said we needed to discuss?"

Selma was pleased to change the subject. "This morning before he opened the model, Connor and I went to the diner for breakfast. As you might imagine, we talked about lots of things. We didn't really disagree on anything, but the only decision we made is that we want to move into the Cape at Quail Run. Connor likes the house and he said that he thinks the way I redesigned it would work well for both of us. So, the obvious question: what to do with Papa? There's no way he can stay in the old house alone."

Reba grinned and shook her head from side to side. "You're right Selma, there's a bit of destiny at work here. Your Father and I are going away to the Bahamas for the Hanukah-Christmas holiday. It's my intention to give the old man an ultimatum; either he moves in with me full time or else!"

Selma curled her lip, "Or else what?"

Reba frowned. "I hadn't thought about that, I assumed he would just say yes."

"Not Izzy Katz, he likes to bargain, he needs to know all the options."

Reba thought for a moment. "You're right, I need to figure out an 'or else.' How about I say I've been offered a new job in New York and I'm going to move there and live with my sister?"

"Do you have a sister in New York?"

"No, I don't."

"Does Papa know that you don't have a sister in New York?"

"No, we've never talked about my sister."

"Where does your sister live?"

"I don't have sister."

"Reba, this is getting dumber and dumber. He'll smell a red herring if you say you're going to take a new job. He knows how much you like what you do."

Reba sighed and sat back into the stool. "I guess you're right, forget the New York idea."

"Can I make a suggestion?"

Reba nodded.

"I've lived with Papa for thirty years, I know him real well. He likes to put on that he's a cantankerous, tough guy; he can be pretty formidable in business negotiation. But when it comes to the people he loves, he's Mr. Softie, he can't say no. I know he loves you so he won't be able to say no to moving in with you. Besides, after I tell him he's gonna give the Cape to me and Connor he'll have to find somewhere to live. He never wanted to move to Cherry Hill, the timing's perfect."

Reba finished the last of her drink. "Don't let me have another one of these, I'm feeling wild and crazy enough as it is. Okay, now that we've shot down the ultimatum, what do I say?"

"Tell him that you love him and that you don't want to be alone any more. Tell him that you feel sad and empty when he isn't with you. Shed a few tears; tears always break down his resistance. He'll need to talk around the idea for a while; let him talk. When it looks like he's done, give him a kiss or sit in his lap or take his hand or whatever comes naturally and wait for him to say yes."

Reba squinted her left eye. "Are you sure that we're talking about the same Izzy Katz?"

Selma grinned, "Trust me; I've used this approach ever since I could talk and I can't remember a time when it failed. He loves you. Mr. Softie can't abide the thought of a woman he loves being sad, unhappy, lonely. There's nothing he can do but say yes."

The bartender approached, "Another round?"

"Dean, if you promise to walk me home and put me to bed, I'll have another."

The bartender grinned. "That's the most appealing offer I've had in a long time. Unfortunately my shift doesn't end until four, but if you can wait that long you're on…Selma?"

"Can you just pour a slug on top of what's in here?"

"Oh what the hell," Reba said. "If I have to hang around until four I might as well have one too, put a little ice in it please, Dean."

"Okay Selma, I'll try it your way. Your father's and my relationship has always been based more on mock battles and arguments than any outward show of affection. Maybe if I appeal to his protective, male nature he'll be taken off guard."

Selma patted her hand. "It'll work, you'll see…I'm curious, you didn't mention marriage. Do you want him to marry you or just move in?"

Reba nearly choked on the cocktail onion she had in her mouth. "Good God, no! Three marriages are enough for one life time."

"If he's going to live with you full time I think that he's going to have to acknowledge that you're his partner, at least to Jacob and Morty and come to think of it, me too."

The bartender returned with their drinks. He winked at Reba. "It's two ten now, I'll let you know when it's four."

After he moved away Reba whispered. "You don't think Dean's serious do you?"

"If we hang around until four you'll find out."

166

Reba bobbed her head from side to side. "Maybe I should tell him I have a pacemaker?"

Selma laughed, "You don't have a pacemaker."

"I know I don't, but if Dean thought I did, he'd be gentle with me."

They both laughed.

"Seriously Selma, it's up to your father to tell people about us or not; I don't mind either way. Might be fun to be part of the family and get involved in family functions. On the other hand I enjoy my privacy and not having outside demands on my time…When are you going to tell Izzy that you're getting married?"

Selma frowned. "I'm not sure, Connor wants us to take his parents to dinner tomorrow night and tell them then. Do you and Papa have dinner plans for tomorrow?"

"We'll probably go to Torello's it's your Father's favorite place on Saturday night."

Selma grinned, "Wouldn't it be a gas if we showed up at Torello's with Connor's parents?"

Reba shook her head. "No, no, no, no! Too many surprises at one time can lead to heart attacks."

"I guess you're right, it's just that the sooner I tell Papa I'm getting married, the sooner you can tell him that he's going to move in with you."

Reba frowned, "I don't see the connection."

"It's simple, when I tell him that I'm getting married and that he's giving us the house for a wedding present he'll have to start thinking about where he's going to live. I mean he'll realize that he can't stay in the neighborhood; he doesn't know how to cook. Violet Weiss cleans but she doesn't cook and Papa loves to eat. Maybe you should cook tomorrow night?"

Reba drummed her fingers on the bar. "Hum, good idea. He loves my pot roast…some roasted potatoes, maybe a nice Caesar salad."

Selma took Reba's hand. "Let me tell you about soaking the anchovies in milk."

"Milk?"

"Yes, milk."

chapter

TWENTY

The man in the dark suit and grey hat stepped out from the tight knot of reporters and fired his hand gun into Lee Harvey Oswald's abdomen. The police who were transferring Oswald from the Dallas police station to the county jail swarmed over the man.

Ellie sucked in her breath, "Oh my God!" She set the iron down and moved closer to the small black and white TV.

"Con, come here right away!" Con was in the garage and didn't hear her. The scene on the TV was confused, bodies swarmed around the center of the picture. She called out again, "Con!" He had just opened the door to the kitchen and heard her call.

"What's wrong?" He said as he moved quickly to the utility room.

"Someone shot the guy who killed Kennedy; it might have been one of the reporters."

An hour later Oswald's shooter had been identified; Jack Ruby, a local Dallas night club owner. Ellie and Con had moved to the larger TV in the living room.

Con sipped his coffee. "Sure looks like someone was trying to shut Oswald's mouth. I don't think that this Oswald is just a crazy man, taking a shot at the President; maybe the Russians were behind this?"

"Good Lord, I hope not. This could be the start of another war." Ellie shook her head from side to side. "I know this sounds unpatriotic but I'm sure glad that Connor got classified 1-Y. She stood up, "I can't take anymore of this I'm going to finish ironing."

Con put his arm around her shoulders. "Right, I'll turn it off, we can hear the details later when they know more. I don't think it's healthy to listen to all this supposition and rumor." Con moved to the TV.

Ellie took their empty cups and started for the kitchen. "Remember, Connor and his girlfriend will be here at six-thirty. We'll have time for a glass of wine here before we leave for dinner."

"Have you figured out who this girl is yet?"

Ellie smiled and put the coffee cups back on the table. "Sit down," she said. "I don't have any direct evidence, but I think it's someone we know."

Con sat back on the couch. "Someone we know, both of us?"

"Uh-huh. In fact you know her better than I do."

"That's crazy; I don't know any of the girls Connor's been out with. That Cindy Prescott he took to his high-school prom was the last of Connor's girls I met. She was a pretty, little blond. Not her?"

"Nope, Cindy got married last summer."

Con frowned. "There's that chubby waitress down at the diner with the huge boobs. I think he's been bonking her for quite some time. Couldn't be her, not his type; unless of course she's pregnant?"

Ellie grinned, "No, not the waitress."

"Come on, he never brought anyone home while he was at college and he's only been home for a few months."

Ellie sat on the edge of the cushion. "Who's the last woman that you've seen with Connor?"

Con put his hand to his chin. "The last girl I saw with Connor was at Izzy and Selma's party….. No, it couldn't be Selma, not Selma, not Connor!"

Ellie patted his knee. "Think back. Connor and Selma danced together; they sat next to each other and talked throughout the meal.

They stayed behind so Selma could show Connor the house, remember?"

Con nodded. "Yeah, we went to Jack's to see the Venice pictures. Funny, now that you mention it, I remember Syd saying that when she and Jack took Connor's and Selma's cars over to the Cape the lights were on but they didn't notice anyone moving about in the house. I didn't think anything of it at the time."

"I'm not a real nosy mother, well not so much anymore, but there are things you can't help noticing. The morning after that party I was doing Connor's wash. First thing I saw was that the chinos he wore that evening were full of dust, sort of like he was rolling around on the floor. Then, his jockey shorts had what could have been semen stains on the front."

Con pushed back into the cushions. "It couldn't be Selma. She's not Connor's type. He likes the petite, pretty girls who laugh and giggle a lot. That's not Selma…Selma's not unattractive but you'd hardly call her pretty, and she's serious, not giggly. I think you got this wrong, it couldn't be Selma."

Ellie grinned, "Wanna bet?"

Con shook his head. "No, it couldn't be Selma…Okay, you're on."

"Usual stakes?"

Con shook his head. "I don't know if I'm up to your kinky sex anymore. Alright but I don't think you have a prayer of winning this time."

"Rest up old man!"

Ellie took the coffee cups and started for the kitchen. Con smacked his palm against his head. "The dowry, Izzy's dowry! I forgot about the dowry!"

Ellie put the cups on the table for the second time. "Good Lord, you're right, I forgot all about it too."

"Now it makes sense. Connor gets money, a car, a house and he retires at age twenty three. Sound like our son?"

Ellie plopped onto the couch. "This is terrible! I don't want him to marry Selma for Izzy's money, it's not right. Don't get me wrong, Selma might actually be a good match for Connor. He could use a little seriousness in his life; but not for money."

Con started to pace. After two trips back and forth to the TV he turned to Ellie. "Seems like there are two ways to go, we could confront Connor and tell him that marrying for money doesn't make sense; tell him to wait for someone he'll love and who will love him."

Ellie twisted in her seat. "Don't think so. If he's gotten to the point where he's ready to announce their engagement he's not likely to reconsider just to make us happy."

Con continued pacing. "You're right, especially if they're sleeping together."

Ellie interrupted. "There's no doubt about that. Not only the chinos and the jockey shorts, but he said that he needed to stay with 'his friend' overnight on Thursday after Kennedy got shot. They probably didn't play chess."

Con grinned, "No they probably didn't," he paused. "The other way to play this is to ignore the dowry and see where Connor's going with his plans."

"What do you mean ignore the dowry?"

Con sat next to her. "I mean let on that Izzy never told me and I never told you. You didn't mention the dowry to Connor did you?"

Ellie shook her head. "I'm sure I didn't, there wouldn't be any reason."

"I'm sure I never said anything either. Maybe that's the right approach."

Ellie wrinkled her forehead. "What approach?"

"Don't say anything about the dowry. Let Connor and Selma, if it is Selma, do the talking and we can see how much the dowry is a factor in their relationship."

Ellie stood and started to pace. "We're moving too fast with this. What Connor actually said was that he was 'getting sort of semi-serious' with a girl and that he wanted us to meet her. Maybe they're nowhere near marriage yet. Maybe I'm wrong and it's not Selma. I'm pretty sure that he's been sleeping with someone named Daphne. I overheard a phone conversation on Tuesday morning he was having with Neil Lionel."

Con gave her the eye.

"Don't look at me like that, I wasn't spying. I just happened to be passing through the kitchen while he was on the phone. I knew it was Neil Lionel because I'm the one who answered."

Con motioned her to sit beside him; he put his arm around her shoulders. "You're right, we're moving way too fast. First, let's see who shows up with him. Then we'll all have a nice relaxed dinner and let the two of them do all the talking. Tomorrow you and I can decide if there's anything for us to discuss…I'll tell you one thing, since Connor's been home from college he's been a different boy, man. He seems genuinely happy and he's matured almost overnight into someone whose company I enjoy. If it is Selma he brings home and if she's responsible for the metamorphosis then I'm all for the match, dowry or not."

Ellie squeezed his hand and kissed him on the cheek. "Damn, you're so perceptive! The bet's still on though, if it's Selma I win."

Con put his hand on her breast. "No, I think I win."

It took a while, but the coffee cups finally made it to the kitchen.

chapter

TWENTY-ONE

Izzy Katz was elated! Selma getting married and to Con and Ellie Sullivan's son! His life's work was soon to be completed, he could die in peace.

As soon as Selma's car had left the driveway Izzy called Con and Ellie. Ellie answered.

"I hope you two are at least half as happy as I am!"

Ellie thought the voice sounded familiar but she couldn't fathom the message. "What? Who is...Izzy!"

"Yes, it's me Izzy, the father of the bride. Are you happy? I hope you're happy."

Ellie laughed. "Izzy, we're thrilled, we're really happy. Hold on a second. Con pick up the phone, it's the father of the bride."

"Izzy, congratulations!" Con nearly shouted.

"Hey Con. You're happy? I hope you're happy about Selma?"

Ellie responded, "Selma's a wonderful girl. The two of them are so relaxed together, and they're so much alike."

"They are?" Izzy choked.

"They told us last night at dinner." Ellie said. "But they made us promise not to call you they wanted to tell you themselves."

"Yeah, they just left. Connor asked me for her hand. What, I told him, you crazy? You can have hands, arms and legs and all the rest as well. He thought that was funny. He thought I was joking!"

Con and Ellie laughed; Izzy coughed. "Did they say when they were going to get married? Real soon I hope before Connor can change his mind."

"Izzy don't be like that. They're two kids and they're in love."

"I'm sorry Ellie; it's just that I thought that I would never see this day."

"January Izzy, they said January."

"You're not Catholics are you?"

"No Izzy we're not really much of anything."

"My housekeeper, Mrs. Weiss, she's a Jew not a Catholic. Her neighbor introduced her to this Saint at the Catholic Church, Saint Juda. Mrs. Weiss says that whenever she wants something real bad she goes down to the Catholic Church and gets the Father to light some candles to Saint Juda. She says that it always works and she gets what she asks for. The deal is that after Saint Juda gives you what you want you have to go back and light more candles in thanks. Well two months ago, Mrs. Weiss told me that she was going to stop at the church on the way home and have the Father light some candles for her sister's gall stone operation. I figured, what the hell, so I gave her five bucks and asked her to light some candles for me that my Selma would get married!…That's something. Isn't that something?"

Con laughed, "Izzy that's amazing."

"Con, I'm going down to the church right now with fifty bucks for thank you candles. I want to keep this guy on my side."

Ellie interrupted, "Izzy, I think it's Saint Jude with an 'E' not Saint Juda."

"Too late, Juda's the one I asked so he's the one I gotta thank. I like the way the Catholics do business. While I'm at the church I may just look into what it takes to become a Catholic. I wonder if you can be a Jew and a Catholic at the same time?"

"No problem with that Izzy," Con said. "Jesus was a Jew and he was the first Christian as well."

"Hey, I gotta go call my friend. She'll be as happy as I am about Selma. Con, see you next Friday if not before. Ellie, you might think about lighting some candles for Saint Juda so we can have a grandson real soon, Selma's getting kind of old for kids you know."

———————

For a change, Selma was driving. "I'm glad that you didn't say anything to Papa about the dowry. I think that it would embarrass him to talk about it openly."

"Why would I want to discuss it with him? What's to discuss?"

Selma down shifted around a curve. "Nothing really, you're right. No big deal, but I think it would be best if we kept the dowry between you and me. You haven't told anyone have you?"

"Not a soul, not even my parents."

"Good, neither have I."

She patted Connor's knee. "You still okay with an informal wedding, no chicken dance?"

Connor put his hand over hers. "I'm happy with whatever makes you happy, it's your show. Were you planning on a big, white, poufy gown and veil or maybe bowling shirts?"

Selma laughed, "Could we get them with 'Sullivan Lanes' on the back and our names on the front? Actually, I was going to go to Julie tomorrow and see if she could put together something sophisticated but casual, maybe in cream or pale pastel. What do you think?"

"How about something like the blue negligee? You know, backless and almost frontless."

She ignored him. "You'll need a new suit; a dark, blue worsted with a regimental stripe tie and black shoes would be nice."

"Fine," he said. "What about the underwear? Jockey, boxer, white, striped?"

Selma frowned, "Forget it I was only trying to be helpful."

Connor stroked her hair. "I could use your help. I'm okay when I need to dress like a Pat Boone look alike, but I don't have a clue about suits."

"Where do you buy your suits?"

He laughed, "I don't. The only one I have is about five years old. I think Mom bought it for high school graduation; it think it was from Robert Hall."

"There's something serious I need to discuss with you. Think you could do a few minutes of serious?"

Connor frowned, "Serious good or serious bad?"

Selma shrugged, "Depends on the point of view, I'd say serious good."

"Okay, for serious good, I'll be serious."

Selma pulled to a stop at a red light and shifted in her seat to face Connor. "It's about children. I'm going to be thirty-one in April. The older a woman gets the more difficult it is for her to conceive and the greater the odds become that she could have problems with the pregnancy. We already agreed that we want a child, children, right?"

Connor nodded, "We agreed."

"So what I'm trying to say is that we shouldn't wait, understand?"

Connor chuckled. "Didn't your grandmother teach you it takes nine months to have a baby?"

The light changed; Selma engaged the clutch and burned rubber as she moved away at speed. "Connor, you promised to be serious."

"I'm sorry. Yes, I agree, we shouldn't wait. So what are you proposing?"

She settled into forth gear. "Well, I thought that since we've discovered that we're sexually excellent together it's probably unlikely we're going to restrain ourselves and wait for our honeymoon?"

Connor grinned, "I like this serious conversation."

She looked across at him. "So, I was thinking about discontinuing my birth control pills. I mean it could take four, five, six months for me to get pregnant. I could be thirty-two before our baby is born. We're getting married in less than two months, so if it happened sooner rather than later, no big deal."

Connor massaged the back of her neck with his hand. "Okay, I don't have any problem with you stopping the pills. I'm getting to like the idea of having a little kid to play with, my little kid. Once you decide to get married then having children stops being an abstract concept; you can actually imagine holding a squirmy little thing and changing smelly diapers. Okay, you should stop the pills now and we'll see what happens."

"Connor, that was too easy. I thought that maybe you'd say that we should get to know each other better first, that we should wait a year before we get into the stress of raising a child. Are you sure?"

"Everything you said makes perfect sense to me, why wait? Can I stop being serious now? I'm getting a headache."

Selma laughed and rubbed his leg. "Okay, here's my plan for tomorrow. You go into town and order your Jaguar. You don't need my help for that?"

He shook his head. "No ma'am, I could probably fill out the order form for the salesman in Braille."

"I'll go see Julie and get started with the dress. Then we both drive to the Cherry Hill Inn and have a look at the facilities. I'll call them first thing in the morning. After we'll have lunch and then go over to Jacob Reed's in the Mall and order you a suit and all the trimmings. If you're up for it, pardon the unintentional pun, we could stop off at the model and practice for our honeymoon."

Connor grinned from ear to ear. "Is this what it's going to be like being married to a Jewish nymphomaniac? Shop all day, screw all night."

Selma frowned, "Don't be silly Connor; you know I don't like shopping."

In only a few hours Izzy had gone from a state of elation to total confusion; things were not going at all like he expected; Reba wasn't the least bit interested in marriage.

"Let me explain another way," He said. "Now that Selma's getting married I won't have the responsibilities of maintaining a family home for her any more. I'm going to be a free man; I can remarry. You and I have been together for six, seven years. I mean, we're just like a married couple except that we don't live together all the time. So why not get a bigger, newer apartment, get married and live together. It's just like we're doing now but we'll be together all of the time instead of most of the time."

Reba shook her head. "It would be nice to get a newer place, maybe down by the river where they're doing all of the redevelopment; that's a good idea. It would make me very happy if we could live together, all of the time; that's a good idea. Getting married; now that's a bad idea."

Izzy was waving his hands in the air in frustration. "I don't understand, we live together all the time and get married or we live together all the time and don't get married. It's the same thing."

Reba laughed. "Exactly! You said it, it's the same thing married or not married. I agree, I chose not married. Understand?"

Izzy smacked his hands on top of his head. "This is crazy! Women always want to be married."

Reba grinned. "I don't. I've been married three times and what do I have to show for it? Two divorce judgments and a corpse."

Izzy shook his head. "But what about security, what if I die tomorrow?"

Reba put her hand on his arm. "You take care of me very well. I don't need much taking care of, but you do it well. If we move in together tomorrow and you die I can take care of myself like I've always done."

"But that's not right; I want to make sure you're taken care of after I'm gone."

Reba stroked his nearly bald head. "That's very kind of you, but we don't have to be married for you to do that, you just need to talk with your lawyers."

Izzy started to pace. "Since my wife passed on you are the only woman I've ever loved. I always wanted us to marry and live like normal people; but there was Selma. It's been my duty to keep a family home for her. But now Connor's going to do that I don't have to take care of her any more. I want us to be married. I want you to be part of my family. I want you to meet Selma and Jacob and Morty and to sit with me at Selma's wedding and at family parties and dinners. I want you to be my wife. That's what I want."

Reba stood from the arm of the chair where she had been sitting and embraced Izzy. "You really are Mr. Softie aren't you, and I didn't even have to shed a tear." She kissed him on the nose.

"What are you talking about?"

She pulled on his arm. "Sit. I have a few things to tell you."

When she finished she took his hand. "Are you angry that I deceived you all this time? It wasn't willful you understand, it really was a chance meeting. Selma and I decided that it was up to you to decide if or when you would introduce me to your children, your family. I love Selma like a dear friend, maybe even a little like a daughter. I went through the whole Connor love affair with her and I think I even deserve some small part of the credit for how things turned out."

Izzy grinned from ear to ear. "The day after you did the translating at the Museum I found a program on the floor in the back seat of my car. Your name was on the program and I knew that Selma was organizing the event. I put two and two together and bingo, a couple of conniving rascals emerged."

Reba stood up and put her hands on her hips. "All this time you've known and you never said anything!"

Izzy patted the cushion next to him but Reba didn't sit. "I haven't known anything, I just suspected. The calls from 'Barbara' that ended very quickly when I came in the room, the occasional credit card receipt you left laying around from the Pub Tiki when Selma was telling me she often went there for lunch with a girlfriend. But most of all, I noticed the change in Selma. Since she met you she's been much happier, more talkative and open with her feelings. You've been good for her and no, I'm not the least bit unhappy with what the two of you did, in fact I love you for it."

Reba sat next to Izzy. She curled her feet up under her and put her head on his shoulder. "So, when were you thinking about telling your children that we're going to be living together?"

chapter

TWENTY-TWO

Con, Izzy and Jack were standing at the large, main bar inside the great hall where the wedding and reception would take place. The bartenders hadn't arrived so Jack was doing the mixing and pouring. Izzy had his customary Manhattan in front of him and Jack was pouring some red wine for Con.

"So this is the good stuff, eh Connie?"

Con nodded. "Depends on what you like, I think it's excellent. Try some, you might be surprised."

Jack took another wine glass from behind the bar. He poured a small amount. "I don't know Connie; I never developed much of a taste for wine, red or white; too bitter, makes my tongue curl up." Jack attempted to swirl the wine in the glass as Con had done. He lifted the glass and drank the contents in one swallow…You're right, I could get used to that stuff. Not bitter at all. What is it?"

Con set his glass back on the bar. "It's French. It's called Pomerol, that's the place it comes from; made with a grape called Merlot."

Jack tilted his head. "How do you spell that?"

"M-e-r-l-o-t; you drop off the 't' when you say it in French."

Jack poured himself a full glass. "That's the trouble with wine, it's too complicated. If I tell a bartender I want a CC and Seven any bartender anywhere knows exactly what I mean." Jack took another large sip. "I like this a lot, write down the name for me Connie so I can order Pomerol next time I'm in a class place. They have this whole book of wines at the Latin Casino." Jack produced a pen and Con wrote the name on a cocktail napkin.

Izzy was looking at the sky through the far windows. "Starting to get dark. This so called Rabbi, Gellman's his name, he let the two of them write the whole wedding service; it's nothing like a real wedding. He let them do anything they wanted except start the wedding before sundown. No veiling and no ketubbah. The only reason they're having yarmulkes is because I threatened to wear a baseball cap if they didn't. Young people have no respect for tradition."

Jack frowned, "Papa, don't be such an old grouch. Connor's not Jewish and Selma isn't much of a Jew either. Neither are you or I for that matter, we haven't sat Seder since Grandma died. Morty and Roz are the only ones in the family that act like Jews and even they have a Christmas tree."

Izzy energetically shook his head. "I think it's sad when the young turn their backs on their traditions."

"Papa, what's this I hear about you lighting candles at the Catholic Church for Saint Jude?"

"Juda," Izzy said. "It's Saint Juda. He's in the Torah, he's a Hebrew Prophet, I asked the priest. You can check it out yourself."

Jack put his hand on Izzy's arm. "Smile Papa; your only daughter is getting married today. Not too long ago you would have been thrilled for her to marry a Hindu in a mosque, or where ever Hindu's get married."

"At least they have a huppah," Izzy sulked.

Connor entered through a side door. "Hey you guys are in the wrong place. They just opened the bars outside in the foyer and they're putting the hors d'oeuvers out. You gotta' see it, it's amazing. A caviar bar, you know black fish eggs, huge, colossal shrimp, lobster and pink wine pouring out of an ice sculpture of Cupid!"

Jack laughed, "Where's the wine coming out from?"

Connor posed with his arm out, "Sorry Jack, it's pouring from his outstretched hand."

Izzy set his glass down on the bar. "What about Morty's Roz' father? Nothing kosher, he'll starve. Lobster! Might as well have ham sandwiches!"

Connor put his arm around Izzy's shoulders. "Papa, Selma's got a whole separate section of kosher food. I'm not sure what it all is, smoked fish and some strange looking stuff, but she says it's good. There's even kosher wine, but no ice sculpture. I guess they don't make kosher Cupids."

Izzy was about to complain when Connor pre-empted him. "Gentlemen, you are wanted upstairs, suite three-six-one. Reba sent me to get you, they're going to put on your flowers and make sure you look presentable. I already had the once over, your turn. Papa, Selma said to tell you that this is going to be an unusual wedding and that she wants to see you smiling all of the time. That's her message."

Izzy stepped back from the bar. "You talked to Selma?"

"Of course."

He pointed at Connor, "When?"

"Just before I came to get you."

"She had her dress on?"

"No Papa, she was naked. Of course she had her dress on."

Jack whispered in Con's ear. "I think this boy's not going to have any trouble handling the old man."

Izzy shook his finger at Connor. "It's very bad luck for the groom to see the bride in her gown before the wedding, bad luck."

"Papa you'd better get yourself upstairs before Selma comes down to get you then everyone will see her dress. Today belongs to Selma. Whatever she says we have to do, you and me both, Papa." Connor put his arm around Izzy's back and guided him toward the door; Izzy continued to gesture and complain. Con and Jack followed behind.

Connor hadn't exaggerated. The selection and quantity of food was overwhelming. The two bars had been going full tilt for an hour and the wedding guests were relaxed and in good spirits. Most of the men wore the ivory, satin yarmulkes that had been distributed at the entrance; they had been embroidered, 'Connor and Selma, January 28, 1964.'

At exactly seven o'clock a drummer and two trumpeters dressed in matching red shirts and black vests appeared on the long curving stairs that led down to the foyer. A drum roll quieted the crowd and the trumpeters and drummer proceeded with a fanfare for several minutes, while a uniformed, hotel staff member opened the huge doors that led to the grand hall. Two young bell boys unrolled a red carpet from the curving end of the stairs to a multi-level platform that had been set up in the great hall.

The platform was crowned with an awning made from garlands of flowers: a huppah. On the upper level of the platform, under the huppah were two large gilded chairs with scarlet, velvet cushions. On the next level were six smaller, similar chairs and another four at floor level. On the floor in front of the platform was a pile of large, white cushions. To the right side of the platform a harpist was seated behind a golden harp.

There was another drum roll and a brief fanfare and then the harpist began to play a bright, melodic tune that gave the rhythmic feeling of skipping or prancing.

Selma and Connor were the first to descend the staircase, they were holding hands. Selma's hair was piled atop her head. She wore an ivory gown that at first glance appeared to be a lovely, conventional wedding dress. On closer inspection it became clear that her gown consisted of two parts. A strapless, floor length, gown with a beaded, fitted bodice and a large, delicate lace shawl that covered her head, fell to her shoulders, crossed to cover her breasts and extended backward to form a train that fell behind for six yards. Hannah and Miriam, Jack and Syd's twins carried the train and their brother Jackie followed with a gold ring pinned to a cushion. Connor was wearing the dark blue worsted suit and regimental tie that Selma had selected. Connor and Selma laughed and waved to their guests. Next came Con and Ellie and Izzy and Reba, they walked abreast holding hands; then,

Aunt Sally, Jack and Syd and Roz and Morty. All of the remaining family members and guests followed.

Rabbi Gellman stood at the top of the platform and welcomed the wedding party. Selma stood to the Rabbi's left, Connor to his right. Izzy, Reba, Con and Ellie stood in front of the chairs on the next level. The two end chairs remained empty. One was covered with a frayed, woolen, prayer shawl that Grandmother Miriam had worn when she came to America from her village in Treshias. Izzy sat next to the other empty chair where a pair of suede gloves that had belonged to Hannah Katz, Selma's mother, were folded neatly on the seat. Jack, Syd, Roz and Morty stood in front of the chairs at floor level and the children, including Roz and Morty's two teenage boys sat on the cushions.

Selma and Connor waved, blew kisses and pointed to friends and family as they all passed in front of the platform. When all of the guests were seated the harpist stopped playing and Connor motioned for the wedding party to sit. He spread his arms and the room fell silent.

"Selma and I and our parents would like to welcome you and thank you for being a part of our wedding celebration. Rabbi Gellman who over the past few weeks has become our friend as well as our advisor has kindly agreed to lead the marriage ceremony."

Rabbi Gellman raised his hands and led a brief, non-sectarian, nearly non-religious prayer. The Rabbi spent the next five minutes talking about the joys and responsibilities of marriage in an engaging, humorous manner, with specific references to Connor and Selma and their families.

When he finished he motioned for Connor and Selma to stand and take each other's hands. He approached Connor.

"Connor Jakes Sullivan you have stated your desire and intention to be married to this woman, Selma Amanda Katz, Is that true?"

Connor looked at Selma and nodded. "Yes, that's true."

The Rabbi turned to Selma. "And you, Selma Amanda Katz, do you wish to be married to this man, Connor Jakes Sullivan?"

Selma's face lit up and she smiled at Connor. "Yes, I do."

Rabbi Gellman stepped back from the couple. "Connor and Selma, these are difficult times; times of war, of rampant divorce, of materialism, of greed, violence, disease and selfishness. Have you considered the impact of these challenges to your future in making your decision to marry?" The intake of breath from the assembly was audible and the group discomfort palpable.

Connor raised their intertwined hands to chest level and smiled broadly. "Together we will each be twice as strong as either of us alone. Together we will comfort each other. Together we will nourish what is best and noblest in each of us."

The Rabbi turned his gaze to Selma. "And you Selma?" She looked around the room and then turned her gaze to Connor.

"I forgot what I'm supposed to say," she whispered loudly.

After a second's pause Selma spoke up. "I agree with Connor and I love him."

The room erupted in laughter and Connor and Selma embraced.

The Rabbi walked down to the floor and helped Jackie unpin the ring from the cushion on his lap. He returned and handed the ring to Connor. Selma extended her right hand. Connor held the ring above his head, lowered his hand and placed the ring on Selma's finger.

"Selma Amanda Katz, I declare to all assembled here and to the Gods that you are my wife. I promise to care for you for the rest of my life." They embraced and kissed.

Rabbi Gellman turned to the guests. "This assembled company has witnessed that Connor and Selma have willingly expressed their desire to join in marriage and that Connor has declared Selma to be his wife and placed a ring on her finger in testimony of that declaration. According to the laws of God and the State of New Jersey I declare that Connor and Selma are husband and wife. So be it."

The guests clapped and cheered.

Izzy turned to Reba. "Selma didn't say anything. She didn't even say that she took him as her husband. I don't get it?"

Reba grinned, "I thought that you were the traditionalist. In the old days that's how they always married. The bride said that she agreed to the marriage and then the groom said that she was his wife and gave her a ring. The part about the bride taking vows is all modern. Selma wanted to do it the old fashioned way."

Izzy tilted his head and frowned, "Are you sure? I never knew that."

"So? There's lots you don't know. Now I don't want to hear another complaint from you about this wedding, ever. We're going over to the other room to eat, drink, dance and have fun. You're gonna do everything you can to make this the best day in Selma's life. Got that?"

Izzy kissed her on the cheek. "So be it."

The harpist resumed playing and the moveable partition forming the left wall of the room slid away revealing the bars, tables and chairs that had been set for the reception in the adjoining room. Selma and Connor hugged and kissed their parents and family members. With the children dancing around her, Selma arranged the family in a receiving line at the base of the wedding platform.

After the last guest had been shuttled to the reception area and the photographer's last flash bulb ignited, Connor and Selma followed the spirit of Jewish custom and went unaccompanied, to a small room near the grand hall.

Connor helped Selma remove the delicate lace shawl that comprised the traditional half of her wedding dress. They toasted together with vintage Champagne in delicate crystal flutes and ate a few cocktail sandwiches. She shifted the wedding ring from her right hand to her left.

Connor stepped back and framed her with his hands. "Selma that dress is nothing short of sensational. You look like a film star getting ready to make her appearance at the academy awards."

Selma beamed, "Make sure to tell Julie how much you liked it, she put an immense effort into getting it just right."

"I met so many people that I can't remember which one was Julie."

Selma laughed. "Julie's hard to forget. Flaming red hair with a dress that looks like it was patched together from six or seven other dresses, that's her signature."

Connor nodded. "Short, kinda chubby?"

"That's Julie."

Connor nodded. "I'm happy you finally got to meet Neil and his parents. Neil's mother, Billy, is a famous surgeon; I've known them all my life. Neil's English girlfriend seems nice, I love the accent."

"Connor you missed something."

"I did?"

"Neil's girlfriend is actually his fiancée; didn't you notice the huge diamond on her left hand?"

"The little devil; he never told me."

The nine piece band was excellent. The violinist and reed players did a creditable version of klezmer music to accompany the Hora, the traditional circle dance. Their vocal rendition of 'Daddy's Little Girl' even sounded like the Mills Brothers. The food was exceptional, the wines excellent and in abundance.

Selma was elated; Connor, exhausted but happy. Con and Rabbi Gellman stood at the bar and talked about wine for an hour and then traded phone numbers to arrange future visits to each other's cellars.

At one o'clock, Izzy Katz, the founder of the feast, rolled into bed with a smile on his face, Reba joined him an hour later. Ellie and Con and Jack and Syd closed the bar at two thirty. Family and friends went home with a glow on their face and in their heart.

Connor and Selma retired to their suite at two. Connor undressed and folded his suit over the back of a chair.

"Selly you did great. There wasn't a single thing that I'd change. The whole evening was just magic, don't you think?"

Selma had removed her dress, let her hair down and was standing at the foot of the bed in a bra and panty hose, her high heels had disappeared hours ago.

"It was exactly what I imagined, what I wanted. I'm pleased that you're happy too."

Connor sat on the bed; he was wearing only his boxer shorts. "This is really out of character for me, but would you mind if we waited until the morning? For sex I mean. I'm shot, not sure I could even get it up. I know everyone makes love on their wedding night but do you think we could wait? I mean, it's only been about forty eight hours since the last time."

Selma wiggled out of her panty hose and dropped her bra on the floor. She moved to the bed and stood directly in front of Connor. Her scent flowed over him: the light perfume, the shampoo in her hair, the sweat from the hours of dancing and the faint animal smell from her vagina inches from his face. He reached behind and massaged her ass and then pulled her down on top of him.

"What time does our plane leave tomorrow?"

She licked his lips with her tongue. "Not till the afternoon, there's plenty of time in the morning for more."

chapter

TWENTY-THREE

"You really like my office? You're not just saying you do?"

Connor nodded. "I like everything: wall paper, carpet, paintings. She did a great job. The furniture's attractive and comfortable too. What I really like is your conservatory. Those steel arches are like sculpture. The blued steel makes them look even more like art. You did a super job designing it. Have you decided what kinds of plants you're going to get?"

"I thought mostly herbs; maybe a lime tree. I like to cook with fresh lime."

Connor turned to her. "No flowers?"

She shook her head. "I like flowers, but I don't know much about them. The guy from the nursery is coming on Friday. I think I'll let him figure out what to do with the flowers and the bushes and plants for outside too; unless you want to get involved?"

Connor chuckled. "The only flowers I know about are the streets you named in my parent's development. I don't know a peony from a pansy. You and the nursery guy decide…Speaking of plants, we'll need to get a lawnmower. Grass will start growing in another month or so. Be nice to get a riding-mower; lots of grass on this big lot."

"I thought maybe a lawn service; unless you really like cutting grass?"

"You're kidding? We can afford a lawn service?"

"It's not that expensive. I can get the same company that does the model to take care of us; unless you enjoy riding around in circles?"

"I never even considered a lawn service." He put his arm around her shoulders and pulled her close. "I can find other ways to amuse myself."

They walked from Selma's office to the dining room. "How about in here. Anything you'd want to change?"

Connor bobbed his head from side to side. "What about those pictures? What do you think they're supposed to be?"

Selma stepped back and considered the larger of the two. It was black and white, about four feet by three feet and in a chrome frame. "Tina said that they're photographs; originals by some well known photographer. I'm not sure what they are? Machines?"

"Maybe cabinets, steel cabinets, or a workbench? I don't know... What do you think?"

"Sounds like you're not all that thrilled with them; me either; kinda strange for a dining room." Selma made a note on the yellow legal pad she had in hand. "Back they go."

"Maybe we could put that print of the whales you bought in Maui over here where the smaller photo is?"

"Umm, that might work. When it gets here I'll give it to Tina. She can have it framed. Maybe she can find something that will compliment the whales for the big wall?" She made another note on the pad.

"How about the table and chairs? Do you like the chrome and glass look?"

He sat at the head of the table. "Actually they're quite comfortable. Not bad."

Selma shrugged. "I don't think we're going about this the best way. I get the feeling that you're holding back. You shouldn't, you know. I gave Tina some ideas about what I thought I could live with but she made the choices not me. The deal is that everything here is on approval and we can replace anything we don't like. Say what you think, you won't hurt my feelings."

Connor took her hand. "Selly it doesn't much matter to me. The only furniture I ever bought was a used desk and a bed at Goodwill. You have good taste; I'm happy with what pleases you."

"I want your opinions. You're going to have to live with this stuff too."

"Okay, I got a great idea. Let's play rock, paper, scissors."

Selma frowned, "What?"

"I'm serious. We'll pick a chair or lamp and then count to three. On three we both have to hold out a hand with zero to five fingers. Zero's a fist and that's the worst. If the total score is eight or more we agree. If it's less than eight, we talk about it then re-vote. Give it a try?"

"Connor it's a nutty idea but it just might work. Let's experiment with these chrome and leather chairs. Ready, go."

They shook their fists in the air three times and on the third count each held out four fingers.

"No re-vote needed," Selma said. "Let's try the table."

The table, side-board and the two floor lamps all got eights.

They moved on to the living room. The furniture and lamps scored well but the three paintings got double fisted.

"Connor, you're a genius. This is an absolutely brilliant system."

"Maybe I could get a patent? *The Sullivan Decision System,* I'll license it, Congress could use it; corporations. I'll be rich and famous."

Selma shook her head. "Maybe you've peaked too early in your brilliant career?"

He smacked her rear. "Where there's one great idea, there's likely to be more. Stick around."

She kissed him on the cheek. "I intend to!"

Connor insisted that Selma be the exclusive decision maker for the kitchen…She agreed.

Selma opened the door to the basement rec-room. She switched on the lights. "No flashlight needed," she said.

Connor looked down the stairs. "What tender memories, our first grope."

When they reached the bottom of the stairs Connor was surprised to discover that it was finished exactly as Selma had described to him five months ago. The space had been divided in two by a paneled partition: rec-room on the left and utilities on the right.

"Selly this is fantastic! I love it. Just like you said, it's totally masculine." He flopped on the leather couch, "Comfortable too."

She turned on the built-in TV. "The latest RCA color…21 inches. All the stations come in clear as a bell."

"Fantastic, I may never leave here."

She grinned, "You won't have to." She pointed at the far wall. "That's a wet bar and then over here a bathroom with a shower." She opened one of the two doors in the partition. The couch folds out into a double bed; in case we have overnight guests."

Connor bounced up from the couch and inspected the bathroom.

Selma opened the other door and turned on the lights. "Through here's the heater/AC unit, the washer and dryer, and," She paused, "your wine cellar."

"Wine cellar?"

"You know; the one I almost sacrificed my life for."

Connor stepped through the door. The floor was ceramic tile. The space had been divided in two with the utilities behind a sliding door on the left. The wine cellar stretched across the front. The outside wall was paneled in dark walnut with a carved walnut door in the center. The door had a bright brass lock-set and the protruding key was adorned with a long tassel. In the center of the door, deeply carved were the Latin words: *In Vino Veritas.*

Connor's intake of breath was audible. "You designed this yourself?"

"Dad did, he designed and built it. It was a labor of love."

Connor lowered his head so that his chin rested on his chest. He shook his head. " I'm…I'm speechless."

Selma opened the door and turned on the lights. "This is the best part," she put her arm behind his back and gently pushed him through the door.

The walls were covered with custom-made bottle racks; the temperature was in the mid-fifties. A table with two metal bar stools stood in the corner; a Tiffany style chandelier hung over the table softly illuminating the racks and bottles.

"Dad says that it'll hold four hundred bottles. He's put in six cases to get you started…Papa paid for the cellar along with the rest of the house, but Dad bought the wine. I'm sure it's great stuff."

After ten minutes Selma lost patience. "Com'on. We've got lots more stuff to vote on. I'll bring down a sleeping bag and you can stay here all night and memorize the names of the bottles." She moved behind him and pushed him out the door.

Connor closed the big walnut door and then grabbed Selma in a bear hug. "I think that's the nicest thing anyone ever did for me in my whole life! Mere words cannot express the joy that's in my heart and shortly to be in my mouth."

"Dad's the one you need to thank. I just put the bug in his ear. Like I said this morning, your Mom and Dad are coming over at 6:30 along with Jack and Syd. You can thank him then. We're having dinner at Lucio's but not till 8:00, so you guys can hang out in the cellar for a while."

Upstairs, Connor slid onto a bar stool behind the kitchen counter. He patted the seat of the next stool. "Sit down Little Flower. We need to have a serious conversation."

She closed the cellar door, "Serious good or serious bad?"

"Trust me," he said and patted the seat again.

Selma hoisted herself onto the stool. Connor swiveled to face her and put his hands over hers.

"I just wanted to tell you how much I've enjoyed the first three weeks of being married; especially being married to you. Hawaii was perfect; it was like we checked out of reality for a while so I could learn even more about what a special woman you are. If I knew that growing up could be this much fun I think I could have more gracefully accepted the inevitable a few years ago." He stroked her cheek with his fingers. "Thanks for being my teacher. I promise that I'll do my best not to flunk out this time." He pushed her hair from her face and gently kissed her. A single tear spilled from the corner of her eye and dropped to their joined lips.

She tilted her head and took his hand, "Okay, what's the punch line?"

"Punch line?"

"Umm…You seldom say something sweet and beautiful without a punch line at the end. Know what I mean?"

He smiled, "I think I do. Perhaps if I didn't feel embarrassed telling you how I care for you I wouldn't need a punch line?"

She nodded, "That's a double negative. But something like that."

He squeezed her hand leaned forward and kissed her cheek. "No punch line."

She slid off the stool. "Alright Silver-Tongued-Devil, let's finish with the house. I want to have a nice long soak in my giant, new tub before we have to get dressed."

"Shall we go upstairs next or do our bedroom?"

"There's no reason to go upstairs; nothing there."

"I don't understand? I thought you said that everything was finished?"

"It is all finished: carpet's in, walls are in white primer, venetian blinds installed. The bathroom is all complete but there's only a fold out bed in the nursery."

Connor scratched his head. "You didn't want Tina to do it?"

"Nothing to do with Tina; there's no way I'm going to set up a nursery until I'm sure our baby is on the way.—Extremely bad luck!"

"This a Jewish thing?"

She shook her head. "No, just common sense. What if it takes a long while for me to get pregnant? I don't think I'd feel too comfortable knowing that all the baby stuff was sitting there. How about if I can't get pregnant? We'd have to move all of the baby furniture out; could be pretty traumatic."

"I see your point…Okay, let's check out the bedroom."

Selma stopped in front of the wide double doors. "Before we go in I need to tell you a couple things. Unlike the rest of the house, I picked out most of the stuff in our bedroom. I went to VanSkyler's with Tina. I've seen all of the furniture and decorations but I haven't seen the finished room yet; the curtains, carpets. The other thing that I want to tell you is that this is going to be a bit unusual, so if you don't like it, you have to say so. It would be terrible if you had to spend a lot of your life in a room you hated. Promise me you'll be honest?"

He reached for the door handle. "As long as there are mirrors on the ceiling and a big, brass trapeze, I'll love it."

"Connor, Promise?"

"Rock, scissors, paper never lie."

Selma opened the doors and they stepped inside. She focused on Connor's face. He smiled, "It's spectacular! I love it!"

She pointed to the huge Chinese screen that was attached to the wall as a headboard over the king-size bed. "You okay with that? All the little figures and the horses and dragons and stuff; won't give you nightmares?"

He moved closer to inspect. "It's fascinating…Is it old?"

She nodded, "Early nineteenth century."

"It wasn't made to be on the wall, was it?"

"No, it's a floor screen. I thought that it would make an interesting headboard. How about the walls? Can you live with the color?"

He nodded, "What would you call it; pinkish apricot?"

She shrugged. "Tina thought it went well with the screen. Do you like the cream wainscoting?"

"Perfect."

"How about our carved Chinese chests? They're old too. Tina said that they're wedding chests. In the old days in China rich people would have a pair made when they married. The carvings are Buddhist good-luck symbols."

"Selma they're fantastic." He opened the front panels of one chest. "I think this one's mine. It's got jockey shorts in it!"

Selma laughed, "Mom brought all your stuff over last week."

"No more messing around. I call for a vote."

On the count of three, Connor held up both hands and ten fingers. Selma squealed with delight and jumped into his arms, "Truth? You're really sure?"

"Absolute truth, I love it."

Connor sat on the edge of the big bed and bounced up and down. "I don't know about this bed though. I think we're going to have to test it out before we vote; feels a little soft. Probably won't get that trampoline push-back effect you like."

She shook her head, reached behind her neck and started to un-zip her pale green velvet jump-suit. "Why don't you go out to the ga-rage and bring in the suitcases while I turn down the bed?"

"Alright, but don't take your jump-suit off. Undressing you is my favorite part. I love finding all of those fun things under your clothes."

She grinned, "It's a good thing for you that I'm a nymphomaniac; otherwise, this might be a pretty short marriage."

Forty minutes later the bed got their approval.

"Shame about the mirrors," Connor teased.

chapter

TWENTY-FOUR

Selma was in her fourth month. She had been miserable for the entire third month with constant bouts of morning sickness that lasted most of the day. Miraculously, as she entered the fourth month the morning sickness disappeared completely. Except for her gradually expanding abdomen and some occasional cramps in her legs, she was feeling quite normal.

When she counted backward from her October due date, it was probable that the baby was conceived on their honeymoon in Hawaii. She hoped that the exact spot had been on the beach blanket next to the waterfall in the national park.

Even though Connor had been preoccupied with the grand opening at Sunny Slope Farms, he had been considerate and responsive to her needs. Connor had hired and trained two new sales people to help with the crowds and despite the heavy traffic through the models he had actually been able to come home earlier most days.

Jac Simensen

The Captain announced that the big TWA 707 was on schedule for the planned seven-forty landing at London's Heathrow, they had about an hour and a half to go. Connor had been sleeping for the past five hours. After he finished what he said was an excellent dinner of lamb chops and roast potatoes with several glasses of quality French Bordeaux, he pulled the blanket up to his chin and almost immediately started to softly snore. Although she felt well, Selma decided to stick with bread, salad and strawberry ice cream for dessert. She finished the Doctor Spock parenting book she had started a few days ago, the A to Z Guide to London and did three crosswords. She envied Connor; she had never been able to sleep on airplanes. The wide first class seats were comfortable enough and the forward cabin was reasonably quiet, never-the-less, she didn't sleep at all.

Selma went over Emma's directions to the French Horn Hotel in Sonning-on-Thames. It was only a short drive west from the airport on the M4 Motorway, probably forty-five minutes. She was looking forward to driving in the UK again. After graduation from Temple she and two girlfriends cruised to London and spent two weeks driving around the country before they continued on to Paris and Rome. Selma quickly became the permanent driver; the other girls were terrified of driving on the left side of the road. Selma discovered that the trick was to concentrate on keeping the driver's side of the car in the center of the road.

The stewardess bent down toward Selma. "Mrs. Sullivan, do you think that your husband will want some breakfast? I'll be serving in a few minutes."

Selma glanced at Connor. "He's not one to turn down breakfast, it's his favorite meal."

The stewardess smiled. "We have scrambled eggs or an omelet with bacon, sausage and toast or a continental breakfast with fresh fruit. If you'd prefer, I can get you some more ice cream."

The Doctor Spock book had triggered an earlier conversation about pregnancy and children. The stewardess had recently married and was looking forward to starting a family in another year.

"I think I've had enough ice cream, the continental would be perfect for me. I'm sure that Connor will want the whole works, rye toast if you have it."

"Rye toast it is. You might want to avoid the rush to use the restroom before I start serving. Everyone usually wants to freshen up and brush their teeth at exactly the time we serve breakfast."

Selma thanked her; the service in first class had been friendly and attentive. She took the toothbrush and toothpaste from the TWA amenity kit and headed for the toilet.

The distance from the arrival gate to the immigration hall seemed miles. Connor was fresh and rested and Selma felt good too. The number of people in the arrivals hall was overwhelming.

They followed the signs to the area posted for arrivals from North America. The section closest to the entrance of the massive hall was called the Blue Zone. Most of the people in the lines there were Asian or African. Connor starred at the saris, tunics, amazing head dress and multi-colored robes.

They got in the long twisting line in the next section. Unlike the line in the Blue Zone, the North American arrivals line moved along at a steady pace.

Connor turned to Selma. "I wonder why there are so many people here at this time of morning? It looks like a small city."

"I read in the A-to-Z guide that the British won't allow the airlines to land at Heathrow during the night, there are too many houses nearby so most of the overnight, intercontinental flights land within the first few hours after daylight."

"That makes sense. Look at all of those people, the saris and robes and the children, amazing!"

Their honeymoon trip to San Francisco and on to Hawaii had been Connor's first time in an airplane. This was his first trip out of the United States.

Despite the crowds, the system worked well and Connor and Selma were through passport control, baggage collection, and customs, on and off the Hertz bus and in their rental car in an hour and a half.

Jac Simensen

Connor had Emma's directions in his lap and was navigating. "Wow, they drive really fast here."

"The speed limit's seventy but most people are doing eighty plus. When you're going the other way toward London in the morning you're lucky to be averaging twenty. We're going away from the traffic."

Connor grinned. "The cars are so tiny, it's a wonder they can go as fast as they're going. Look, there's an E-Type like mine, but blue. Looks silly to see the steering wheel on the other side doesn't it? Does it feel strange to be shifting with your left hand?"

She shook her head. "Not really, I don't think about it."

"You'll have to give me a chance to drive later; not here though, not on a highway."

"Okay whenever you're ready." She said.

Emma's directions were perfect. They arrived at the hotel without a single misstep. The sign outside the hotel had no words, just a golden French horn painted on a black background.

Connor pointed ahead. "See the bridge? That must be the Thames; pretty narrow here, not like the pictures I've seen of the wide river in London."

"We're quite a ways upstream from London. This is the country not the city."

The hotel staff was warm, efficient and accustomed to welcoming weary travelers coming from overnight flights. Selma and Connor were quickly settled in their suite.

"Connor, check out this four poster bed, it must be three feet off the ground."

Connor opened the double doors that led to a tiny balcony overlooking the river and the manicured lawn. "Selma, you've got to see this, it's fantastic! Just like the pictures in *Wind in the Willows*; the river meandering past all the grand old houses. The manicured lawns flowing right down to the water's edge; just like *Toad Hall*! Look at the flowers and bushes. They have tables in the garden. Let's see if we can have lunch outside today. What time did Emma say they were coming to pick us up?"

Selma took Emma's letter out of her purse and scanned through the pages. "She's written 'half five.' Is that five-thirty or two-thirty? Must be five-thirty, two-thirty would be too early don't you think?"

She handed the letter to Connor and pointed to the time.

"Five-thirty makes more sense than two-thirty, must be five-thirty. She says to call her when we get in. We probably should do that now."

Selma looked at the clunky, old fashioned phone. "There's no dial. I guess you have to get the operator to place the call. What's the number?"

She picked up the phone and the hotel operator answered. "Hi, this is Selma Sullivan in Suite two; I'd like to make a local call please, yes in Sonning. The number I have is three-three-seven. Yes, that's right Dulforth." Selma paused. "Oh great, please tell her we'll be right down." She replaced the heavy hand set on the clunky phone.

"Emma's downstairs, she brought some flowers for the dining room, apparently dinner's here tonight after the rehearsal. I said that we'd come down to meet her. You go; I want to brush my teeth first. I'll just be a few minutes. I'm going to need to sleep for a while so let's not agree to go anywhere today, okay?"

He smacked her rear as he went to the door. "Sure, probably be best if we both got a little sleep and then we can try out Henry the Eighth's bed."

Emma was standing in the lounge in front of the fireplace. "Connor, how lovely to see you again." She embraced him and kissed him lightly first on one cheek and then the other. Her light brown hair was pulled back in a long pony tail and she was dressed in worn jeans, short boots and a baggy sweater. Neil was right; she looked like a young girl.

"Don't look at me, I'm a mess. I've been out in the garden all morning cutting flowers for the dinner tonight and the church tomorrow. Is Selma sleeping? Did she make it through the flight in one piece?"

She motioned for Connor to sit.

"Selma's fine, she'll be down in a minute. Two weeks after you guys called the morning sickness just went away. She's pretty much back to normal except that she eats like a horse."

Emma patted his arm. "I'm so pleased that she could make the trip. Neil was concerned that you might not be able to be his best man. I think he's getting last minute jitters, I'm glad you're here to shore him up."

Selma came into the lounge. Emma repeated the embrace and kisses. "Selma you are positively radiant. Your skin is just glowing, you look so healthy. Connor says that you're not having the morning sickness anymore."

Selma smiled. "At the moment I feel great." She patted her tummy. "I'm starting to get really fat. Nothing I own fits anymore, but I feel great. How about you, is everything going as planned for tomorrow?"

Emma shrugged. "I'm really relaxed about the whole thing. I learned from you, from your lovely wedding that what matters is that Neil and I have fun and enjoy ourselves. Unfortunately, we have to do everything the traditional way. My mother's family are pompous old gits who would hound my poor father until he died if we didn't do the traditional church service with all the trimmings. But look, I know that you need to get some sleep so let me quickly go over the schedule with you okay?"

Selma nodded. "I am going to need a nap soon, I'm afraid that I never sleep on planes. Connor, on the other hand, can sleep anywhere, I'm very envious."

Emma shook her head. "I know the feeling. Neil went on a pub crawl with my brother and a few friends last night; must have been quite a pissup. When I left this morning and looked in on him he was face down in bed fully dressed and sawing wood in high fidelity. I need to get back and make sure he's still breathing.

Right, here's the plan. Neil and I will come by at half-past-five and then we can all have a drink in the garden."

Connor smiled, "The garden's something out of a picture book."

"If the weather is fine and Selma's up for it, I thought that we'd walk down to the church. Saint Andrew's is over the bridge and down a quarter mile."

Selma sat back in her chair. "That sounds like fun, I'd like to walk."

"You'll have the opportunity to meet the Vicar, Father and the rest of the wedding party. There's only a few of us. My friend Jacqui and

Gillian and Annabelle, my cousins are the bridesmaids and my brother Thomas and Neil's friend Peter are the other two groom's men. I don't think that the rehearsal should take more than a half hour. The plan is to walk back to the hotel for drinks and then dinner at eight. If you like duck, it's the specialty here. They roast the ducks on spits right there in the fireplace." She pointed across the room to a large brick fireplace. "We should have you tucked up safely in bed by ten or so."

Selma walked to the fireplace where a small but hot fire had been lit. "Roast duck is one of my favorites. I've never seen it done on an open fire before."

Emma joined her. "You won't be disappointed. I've been coming here for special occasions ever since I was a little girl. Before I leave, I'll tell Richard that several of us will be having duck. When we come back from the church you'll see them going round on the spits in front of the fire. It's lovely ambiance."

Connor joined them at the fireside. "The wedding's at two tomorrow, isn't it?"

Emma nodded. "That's right. The woman from the shop will be at the hotel at ten-thirty with your hired suit. She said that she can make any necessary alterations in her van in the car park if there's a problem with the fit. Neil will pick you both up at one. The reception and dinner is at Father's house in the garden; there's a marquee if the weather turns. Selma, you can ride to the house with the rest of the wedding party and there will be a car to bring you both back here whenever you get tired. Connor, Neil did tell you about the best man's speech, didn't he?"

Connor grinned from ear to ear. "I've been writing it for the last week. My only problem is making sure it's not too long, I've known Neil since forever and have a lot of seedy, lurid details to draw from."

The women both laughed.

Selma gave Emma a hug. "I'm sure that it will be a very special wedding. I'm so very happy that you invited us to be part of it."

Selma woke at four. Connor wasn't in bed. She felt rested but was a bit disoriented; she knew it must be jet lag. Was it eleven or ten in the morning at home? She couldn't remember if the time difference was five hours or six. She pulled on the terry robe with the hotel logo, a bright yellow French horn and peered out through the double doors to the garden and water below.

There was Connor walking along the river bank and feeding bread crusts to an entourage of six pure white swans. She smiled and watched him for several minutes. There was a part of Connor that was still a curious, earnest, little boy; it was her favorite part. Connor gazed down the length of the river, no doubt waiting for Mr. Toad and the other river denizens to arrive, messing about in boats.

She wandered from the bedroom to the sitting room. On the table sat a glass and small pitcher of what looked like lemonade. On a silver tray a selection of tea sandwiches, scones and cookies had been nicely arranged. There was a linen napkin, cutlery and a small jar of strawberry jam. Next to the tray was a note on the hotel stationary.

"Woke at two, couldn't sleep any more, too excited! Decided to go for a walk. I had 'tea' in the garden. The manager suggested that he put together something for you in case you were peckish when you woke. (I guess that means hungry.) Be back by four to wake you in case you're still sleeping…..Hope your dreams were sweet…C

Emma was on her second gin and tonic. She was clearly relaxed and happy. "After Sydney we're going up to Cairns, to the Great Barrier Reef. We're there for two weeks, diving, snorkeling and boating."

Neil was still hung over and drinking club soda with lemon. "I don't think that Em's told you the really exciting news yet have you Em?"

"You mean about Florida?" she said.

Neil nodded. "Connor and Selma, we're going to be your neighbors. Well almost your neighbors. After our honeymoon we're flying to Tampa, that's where we're going to be living."

Connor almost dropped his wine glass. "Florida? You're joking! Florida with all of the wrinkloids?"

"Wrinkloids?" Emma asked.

"Yeah, you know the old, old wrinkly crowd; Q-Tips, ancient ones."

Emma laughed. "Wrinkloids, I haven't heard that before."

Neil waved his hands in the air. "No, you don't understand, we fell into this sweet deal. You've heard of Jamie Trevors the golfer?"

Connor nodded. "Sure, I've heard of him; he died recently didn't he? Small plane crash?"

Neil nodded his head. "Emma's father knew Jamie quite well. Jamie was about to retire. He had put a lot of effort and money into building a golf course community east of Tampa. He bought the land for next to nothing years ago. His plan was to build two golf courses and about two hundred fifty houses. He had the architects do all the plans, got the local politicians on board and had the first phase of the financing nailed down. Then he died; poof, just like that."

"How sad" Selma said.

Neil nodded. "It was. Trevor, that's Emma's Dad, says that Jamie was a real gentleman. Of course I never met him. Anyway, to make a long story short, Gaynor, Jamie's widow, she's Welsh, Trevor and Emma and I are going into a three way partnership to finish the golf courses and the houses. So Em and I will be Florida residents, wrinkloids, in about four weeks. If this development goes well, we plan to build others in Florida. Land there is really inexpensive and the northerners are still coming in droves."

Selma put her glass on the table. "That's really exciting. Is Emma's father moving as well?"

Emma shook her head. "Father's got a lot of things going right now. He's bought a cottage near the development and will probably spend a week or two each month in Florida for now. But who knows, if things go really well?"

Neil looked at his watch. "Speaking of Father, we better get going, it's six-forty and Trevor doesn't like to be kept waiting."

———————

Selma was surprised at the small scale of the wedding and reception. There were fewer than sixty guests at the wedding and not many more at the reception where there was no band, no music and no dancing.

Neil told Connor that there had been some sort of a family schism after Emma's mother's death that had distanced many of their Mother's family from Trevor; Emma hadn't told Neil the details.

The food was excellent, the wine superb and the weather mild. Connor's best man speech brought much laughter and applause from Neil, Emma, Trevor and the younger members of the party, but fell flat with most of the others.

"The English are really odd, aren't they?" Connor asked.

Selma was unpacking their suitcases for the second time in two days. "I guess that every country has their share of odd balls. I really like Emma, and Trevor was so kind to both of us, he went way out of his way to make us welcome. I thought that Emma's brother Thomas was funny; a little shy but really quite witty. That Jacqui though, Emma's maid of honor, was a true witch. It seemed that she had memorized all of the anti-American jokes she could find. I try hard not to use the word hate but I must say that I disliked her intensely. No, maybe I hated her."

Connor laughed. "It was fun. I loved the French Horn: the countryside, the river, the church, the food, the wine, the scenery. Even the weather was good. If they could get rid of the old farts with their noses in the air they'd have a pretty decent country."

"That's asking a lot; those noses have been in the air for centuries."

He turned away from the window and sat on the bed. "Okay boss, what's on for the day?"

She tilted her head to the side. "I picked this hotel from the list of London hotels because we could walk almost everywhere. Since today's Sunday lots of things are closed. My suggestion is that we walk up to Covent Garden Market first and then have a roast beef dinner at 'Simpsons in the Strand.' I read that Simpsons is a must do when in London. Then we can walk back here have a night cap and get a good night's sleep. Tomorrow's the Tower of London and Westminster Abbey and then theatre at night; I asked the concierge to find a good musical for us. Tuesday I thought that we could take the train out to Windsor and see the Castle; it's supposed to be spectacular. We'll be back in time for dinner at a place that Trevor recommended at a place nearby in Sheppard's Market, supposed to have an outstanding wine list. Then, Wednesday morning we're on our way home. That's the Selma Sullivan if this is Sunday it must be London tour. Are you up for it?"

He smiled. "As long as you two feel well and have the energy I'm happy to tag along."

Selma sat in his lap and put her arms around his neck. "We two feel just great. Let's go, there's a lot to see in this city and such little time."

Connor kissed her cheek. "Had we but world enough and time, your coyness lady were no crime."

She ran her fingers through his hair. "Is that Shakespeare?"

Connor started to unbutton her blouse. "An English guy named Marvell, Andrew Marvell. He emigrated to the US and started up Marvell Comic Books: made a fortune."

She smiled and kissed him full on the lips. "I guess Covent Garden will still be here the next time we come over."

chapter

TWENTY-FIVE

Connor was sick. He had a fever and was sweating copiously. He had moved to the fold-out bed in the nursery four nights earlier to give Selma the opportunity to sleep better on her own. She was two days past her due date and getting more uncomfortable each day.

Connor was hallucinating; he was dreaming non-stop and in vibrant color. The leering mayor of Blackwood was digging a hole with his shovel at Sunny Slope, his big, red nose inflating to huge proportions and then bursting, blood flying everywhere. The lava fields, waterfalls, and lush tropical foliage of the Big Island all passed through Connor's mind in a rotating collage. He heard Selma's laughter as they body surfed one moment and then snorkeled in schools of colorful reef fish the next. He howled as an unexpected wave tore away Selma's bikini top and left her semi-nude and frantically searching in the water for her bra.

When he awoke and was fully conscious he realized that he was shivering, freezing and sweating at the same time. He looked at the clock; it was 4:00 a.m. He felt an urgent need to get to the toilet and at the same time knew that he was about to vomit. He stumbled to the bathroom, sat on the toilet, grabbed the plastic wastebasket and relieved both ends at once. After a few minutes and a repeat performance Connor felt somewhat better. He put the reeking wastebasket outside of the door and drew a bath; he kept the water temperature as high as he thought he could tolerate.

He soaked, motionless in the hot bath for ten minutes. The shivering was gone and he was feeling more in control of his bodily functions. Sweat poured across his head and face and dripped from his ears and chin into the bath. He found it a struggle to get out of the bathtub, he was weak, dizzy and had trouble standing.

Connor wrapped himself in a large bath towel and cautiously tiptoed down the stairs and into the master bedroom. Selma was sleeping on her back with only a sheet to cover her. She had gained twenty-three pounds and had a seriously extended abdomen. Her cheeks had filled out and Connor thought that she looked like a cherub. He quietly opened the door to his closet put on a fresh set of pajamas and then pulled sweatpants and a woolen ski sweater over them. He moved to the en suite bath, took a hefty swig of Pepto from the bottle and then exited to the kitchen.

It was almost five. Ellie would be waking in a half hour. He warmed a cup of milk and poured in a generous shot of brandy. He assessed the condition of his stomach, it seemed stable. He stood at the sink and took a small sip of the milk and brandy. It burned his irritated throat. He finished the concoction but stayed at the sink in case it came back up.

He decided that he couldn't wait any longer, grabbed the kitchen wall phone and called his mother.

She answered on the second ring. "Connor, is it you?"

"Yeah, it's me."

"Are you home or at the hospital?"

"I'm home mom. Selma is okay, she hasn't started labor or anything." Connor could sense her puzzlement.

"She hasn't?"

"Mom it's me, I've got the flu. Big time, fever, sweats and going at both ends."

"You're sure it's the flu?"

Connor could hear her relaying the conversation to Con. "No, it's Connor, he's got the flu."

"Mom, I think that I need to get Selma out of this house before she gets it too."

"Have you called her doctor?"

"No, do you think that's what I should do?"

"Do you have his number?"

"No, but it must be in Selma's phone book."

"Connor, call her doctor."

"Gotta go mom, nature is calling and loudly. Bye." Connor ran for the powder room. The milk and brandy hadn't been a good idea.

The woman at the answering service was calm and professional. Connor explained the situation; the woman asked a few questions and then told Connor she or the doctor would call back shortly.

Five minutes later the phone rang. "Mr. Sullivan, this is Doctor Stevens, I'm Doctor Kumar's associate, Doctor Kumar's delivering a baby at the moment."

"Thanks for calling back so quickly."

"I don't have your wife's information so I need to ask you a few questions. She's due to deliver soon?"

"She's two days past her due date. It was Wednesday."

"Is it you who has the flu or your wife?"

"It's me."

"Has your wife had any flu symptoms?"

"Not as of last night, she's asleep, I haven't woken her."

"At which hospital is your wife delivering?"

"Truman Memorial, in Stratford."

"How old is she?"

"Thirty one."

"Do you have any other children?"

"No, this one's our first."

"Just a minute Mr. Sullivan," Connor could hear a muted conversation in the background.

"Mr. Sullivan I'm going to make a judgment call on the side of safety. I think that it would be best if we send your wife to the hospital now. I'm going to call the hospital and tell them to expect Mrs. Sullivan to check in today. I don't think that there's any need to wake her now, why don't you plan on getting her in by noon. Can you have someone bring her?"

"No problem, my mother's nearby."

"Okay. Make sure that you get to a doctor yourself as soon as you can. Drink lots of fluids, the diarrhea and vomiting will dehydrate your system quickly."

"Thanks for your help Doctor Stevens."

"Goodbye Mr. Sullivan."

Connor called Ellie. Ellie said that she would come and take Selma to the hospital. She also volunteered to call Dr. Price, the Sullivan's long time physician, to make an afternoon appointment for Connor.

"I should be back from taking Selma to the hospital by one or one-thirty. I'll make your appointment after two thirty so I can drive you. How do you feel now?"

Connor groaned, "Dreadful, I'm starting to shiver again. I need to take a hot shower and then cover up in bed and sweat it out."

Ellie knew he was feeling really bad, Connor never complained when he was sick, he always went off by himself and slept.

"Connor, maybe I should come over now?"

"I don't think so Mom. Selma hasn't been getting up much before nine lately and I'm just going to dive back in bed and sleep, ten's fine. Thanks; love ya, bye."

Connor's teeth were chattering. He took the yellow pad Selma kept next to the phone and wrote a note.

'Selma—I have the flu and am feeling really poorly. Please DO NOT come upstairs it's critical that you don't get the flu! It's contagious!

I called Doctor Stevens, he said that you need to go into the hospital now so that they can watch you and make sure that you haven't got the flu. He made arrangements for you to be admitted at noon today. Mom is coming over at ten to help you get ready and to drive you in….Please, please believe me, you have to do this!'

If you holler before you leave, I'll come to the top of the stairs and say goodbye. I'll talk to you on the phone at the hospital later today and come see you when the Doctor says I'm no longer toxic......Please, this one time, do exactly as I say......All my love, Connor.'

Connor tore off a piece of Scotch Tape and taped the note to the inside of the bedroom door where she'd see it as soon as she got up. He dragged himself up the stairs, stood under a hot shower for as long as he could manage, pulled his clothes back on, got a heavy quilt from the hall closet and fell into bed. He was drenched in sweat and asleep a few minutes after he hit the bed.

Selma woke at 9:30 and headed straight for the toilet. She calculated that this was the fourth time she had to urinate since midnight. She shook her head. "I guess that I'm peeing for two as well as eating for two."

She washed her hands and face, pulled her hair back into a pony tail and brushed her teeth. She struggled to her closet to get Connor's robe; her robe had ceased to cover her belly. She was starving and lusted for oatmeal with a banana, honey and vanilla ice cream. Connor would have left for work by now and she would have a leisurely breakfast and read the paper before thinking about showering and dressing.

She patted her abdomen, "Okay kiddo, I know you're comfortable in there but it's time for you to meet your mom and dad and get started with your little life. Today's a great day to be born, got that Chris?"

Selma was positive her baby was a boy. He felt like a boy, he was active like a boy, she knew it was a boy. When they were sure that she was pregnant, they agreed that Selma would pick the name for a boy and Connor for a girl. Selma had quickly decided on Christopher Benjamin. Connor liked her choice. He either hadn't decided on, or wouldn't tell her his name for a girl.

Selma saw Connor's note. She smiled. It was kind of Connor not to wake her, he had been so thoughtful and accommodating throughout her entire pregnancy. She pulled the note away from the door and carried it to the kitchen counter. She looked on the kitchen table for the newspaper, it wasn't there. She was puzzled. For the last few weeks Connor had been bringing the paper in and leaving it on the table for her. She trudged to the front door; there was the paper on the door step. She pushed it with her foot so that it stood up against the door sill. She bent and could just grasp it with the tips if her fingers. She stood and was out of breath.

Back in the kitchen she dropped the paper on the counter on top of Connor's note and went to the pantry for the oatmeal. When she opened the pantry door she heard an unexpected noise. She turned her head toward the stairs. It sounded like Connor coughing; no not coughing, retching.

"Connor!" She called. "Are you sick? Are you okay?"

Connor heard her call but he couldn't reply; he was too busy spitting up more yellow-green mucus. He pulled a wad of tissue from the toilet roll, wiped his mouth, wiped the rim of the toilet bowel and flushed. He was just rinsing out his mouth when he heard Selma open the nursery door.

"Connor, are you alright?"

He closed the bathroom door all but a slit. "Selma! You can't come in here! I have the flu, I'm contagious!"

He heard her enter the room and he shut the door. "Selma, go away. I don't want you to get sick. Didn't you read my note?"

She knocked on the door. "Connor, you're sick, let me in."

He locked the door. "Go down stairs right now and read my note, it's on the inside of the bedroom door. I have the flu!"

Selma was confused and upset. She was on the third stair from the top when the toe of her slipper jammed against the carpeted stair tread. She wasn't holding onto the rail and started to tumble forward. She saw the bottom of the staircase twisting toward her. As her body turned she reached out reflexively and caught the stair rail with her left hand. Her body pivoted and she found herself standing upright facing the opposite direction. She had accomplished a perfect pirouette to the next stair down. To her surprise, she found that she was calm. She descended to the first floor and went to the kitchen.

The phone rang, "Selma, its Mom. Are you okay? Is Connor alright?"

Selma took the phone from her ear and stared at it.

Ellie called out, "Selma! Selma!" Selma put the phone back to her ear and started to sob. "I'm, I'm okay, but Connor is really sick and he's locked himself in the bathroom and he won't come out and I almost fell and I don't know what's happening."

"Selma, sit down and stay quiet, I'm on my way."

Ellie hung up. Selma saw Connor's yellow note sticking out from under the newspaper. She read it and then read it again. She pulled some paper towels from the roll on the counter and wiped away her tears. She walked to the bottom of the stairs and called. "Connor, Connor, I read your note. I understand. Mom will be here in ten minutes."

The nursery door opened and a sad looking Connor wrapped in a thick quilt came out and sat on the landing his back against the wall.

"I read the note," Selma called to him. "I understand."

Connor's hand emerged from the quilt and waved to her. "I'm sorry I scared you, I thought that you would see the note on the door when you got up."

She nodded, "I did, I did see it. I took it down and put it on the counter but before I could read it I heard you getting sick and went upstairs."

"Connor shook his head. "Oh, that's what happened."

"This flu is really bad?"

Connor nodded, "I had it once before, you feel like you're gonna die. But in a day or two it goes away and you're back to normal. You're the one we need to focus on, it's really important you don't get the flu. It could be a disaster."

Selma sat on the second step. "I feel just fine, I'm okay."

Connor groaned. "I felt just fine when I went to bed last night and look at the gurgling mess I am now. Selma, imagine if you came down with the flu when you were in labor, if they told you to push and you had diarrhea the result could be pretty disgusting."

Selma laughed, "Okay, you made your point. I'll stay down here. You are going to be all right?"

She saw the top of the quilt nod. "Mom's taking me to the Doctor this afternoon, he'll give me a shot and by tomorrow morning I'll be nearly human. See if you two can postpone the grand entry until to-morrow. Maybe if I wear a mask and gown they'll let me in to see you."

Selma shook her head. "Sorry, crossing my legs won't work. I think Christopher is getting quite curious to see what his crazy father looks like. I don't think it's going to be too much longer."

The front door opened and closed; Ellie called out. "Hello, anyone alive in here?"

Selma replied, "We're here Mom, on the stairs."

Selma waved to Connor. "Love you baby. We'll see you as soon as you can make it, both of us. Don't worry we'll be fine. Love you. Go back to bed and sleep as long as you can. Love you."

Connor returned her wave. His salty tears behind the quilt contributed to his overall state of dehydration. "I Love you Selly, I'll see you as soon as I can. Love ya."

Ellie took over. Selma was washed and fed and whisked away to the hospital.

When Ellie returned Connor feasted on ginger ale and fat free chicken broth. He got a shot from Doctor Price and then returned home to sleep in a freshly made up bed in the master bedroom. Ellie sprayed Lysol on every visible surface in the nursery and bathroom.

At 4:30, Ellie returned to the hospital to make sure that Selma was being properly looked after.

At 5:30, Con joined her and stayed with Selma while Ellie drove back to Cherry Hill and prepared another gourmet meal for Connor; this time with the added feature of Saltine Crackers.

Con called at 6:45; Selma's water had broken and she was having contractions. Connor was sleeping. Con and Ellie agreed that he would stay with Selma and she with Connor.

Con called at 9:50. The Sullivan's had a grandchild and Connor and Selma a daughter! She had all her parts and a mass of reddish brown curls. Mother and daughter were both well. The beautiful, eight pound four ounce little girl looked just like Selma. Con was ecstatic, maybe even giddy.

Ellie woke Connor. "Selma is going to be calling in fifteen minutes. She's happy and quite a few pounds lighter. You have a beautiful, healthy little girl."

Connor bounded out of the bed, "Oh my God! I've got to go. I've got to see them!"

Ellie grabbed his arm. "Sit down Connor, you're not going anywhere. Dr. Price told you that the hospital is off limits until your fever is gone and you can hold down some real food. You're staying here with me. Your Dad is with Selma and she's doing fine—maybe tomorrow night."

Connor smiled, "A girl you said, I knew it! I knew it was going to be a girl as soon as I thought up her name." He hugged his mother. "They're okay? They're both okay?"

"Your Dad says that they're both perfect. He said the baby looks like a miniature Selma. She's over eight pounds, a big healthy girl. Now get yourself together, Selma will be calling in a few minutes. Make sure that you tell her you're feeling better she's worried about you."

Connor kissed her cheek. "Feeling better? I'm perfect. No more flu, I'm completely recovered. A little girl, a little girl!"

Selma spoke first. "Connor are you all right?"

"Selma you did it, you're okay right? Our daughter's okay too? Selma you did it all by yourself without me!"

"Well not exactly without you. Dad's here, he's been taking good care of me. Wait till you see our baby, she's perfect, she doesn't have my nose! She's beautiful!"

"Oh Selma I'm so happy for you, for me, for all of us."

"Connor you're better?"

"Don't think about me, I'm fine, the Doctor gave me a shot and Mom's been feeding me, they're going to let me see you tomorrow, I'll see you both tomorrow."

"Connor I'm exhausted. I have to sleep. One thing though, what's her name? What's our daughter's name?"

"I don't want to tell you now, not on the phone. I'll tell you both tomorrow when I see you."

"Connor you need to tell me now. The nurses are writing down Baby Sullivan on all the forms. She needs a name."

Connor grinned. "Okay, I'll tell you." He buzzed his lips to simulate a drum roll—"Bathsheba Eleanor Sullivan."

"What! You're not really serious! How about we settle for Eleanor Bathsheba instead?"

"You have to trust me on this one. It's Bathsheba Eleanor Sullivan. I decided on that name a long time ago. You can call her Sheba of course."

"Good night Connor, I'm so tired. I love you and I'll see you tomorrow. Sheba huh, you're sure?"

"I love you Selma and I'm sure."

chapter

TWENTY-SIX

"She's asleep. I'm not sure how long she'll stay that way. These new teeth coming in seem to be bothering her a lot."

"I'll go up and check in a while. Don't worry, I won't wake her. If she wakes during the night I can play with her then."

Selma patted his arm, "I'm sorry I know how much it means to you to have some time with her when you get home. When you're this late it's difficult to keep her up, she needs a fairly regular schedule; babies do."

Connor opened a bottle of wine then pulled a chair out from the table. "Sit down for a minute; there are some things we need to talk about."

"Good things?" she asked somewhat apprehensively.

Connor passed her a glass. "Great things!" He lifted his glass and clinked with her. "The meeting with Jack went really well."

She nodded. "Oh that's where you were tonight. I know, you told me, I just forgot."

Connor thought that Selma appeared on edge and distracted. "Are you okay? You seem kind of nervous tonight; everything all right?"

Selma put her hand on his. "I'm okay. I just have a lot on my mind. The baby's' teething is making her cranky. She's always so bright and happy, I'm not used to seeing her cranky."

"Jack is really pleased with everything I'm doing. He said that my new hires are 'excellent, professional sales people.' He liked the newspaper ads we did last month and he is blown away with our sales figures."

Selma smiled. "That's wonderful Connor, I'm so happy for you, you've worked hard."

"Jack agreed to the bonuses I proposed for Randy and Karen, he approved the newspaper ads we're running weekend after next and he's giving me another performance bonus. We sold twenty-eight units last quarter that brings the total since we opened Sunny Slope to one-hundred-and- nine! We have a six month backlog and Jack's having trouble building houses fast enough. Not bad, huh?"

"I'm proud of you, Sheba is too."

Connor angled his chair away from the table to face her. "I told Jack about my idea to open our own brokerage when I can get a broker's license in two years. He asked a lot of questions but in the end he was enthusiastically behind the idea. He gave me the go ahead to develop a business plan. He thought that maybe we could find a retired broker to front us and get going sooner."

Selma frowned, "I don't understand why you need to get a broker's license? Didn't you already get your license, wasn't that what the school you went to was all about?"

Connor shook his head. "I got my real estate sales license that means I can legally sell property, draw up documents and handle closings. A broker's license means that you can set up your own agency, hire sales people, take listings, and run your own show. You know, 'The Sullivan Real Estate Agency' with an office, maybe two, signs in people's front yards and ads in the paper. Jack would be an equal partner; he'd put up the capital to get started and we'd sell all of his future developments through the agency. Also, we'd take on re-sales, and even new construction for other builders. With the growth in this part of the world we stand to make a fortune!"

Selma put her palms on the table. "Sounds like a lot of work. Do you really want to work that hard? You don't have to, you know."

Connor grinned, "That brings me to my second topic."

"I told you that I've been talking with Neil and Emma about the golf course development near Tampa they're building. Remember I showed you the plot maps that Emma sent last month?"

Selma nodded.

"Emma called today; she's the brains behind this whole project of course. She and Neil want us to come down and visit with them. They're going to be meeting with the banks and want to get my input on their sales promotion plans and sales projections. I told Emma that I don't know anything about Florida real estate but she said that I know a heck of a lot more about selling houses than either one of them. Actually, when you think of it, their project is just about the same size in numbers of units as Sunny Slope. I think maybe I could help. She wants to send us first class plane tickets, to put us up in a posh seaside hotel and rent us a car; all of us, Sheba too. I have two weeks' vacation coming to me this year and I asked Jack if it would be okay to take next week off, that way I could go to the meetings with them at the end of the week. Jack said fine with him as long as I made sure to come back."

"What do you think? Wouldn't it be great to get away for a while? Not counting the five days in England, we haven't had a real vacation since our honeymoon. We could get Sheba all slathered up in sunscreen and take her to the beach and maybe do some boating or fishing, spend some time relaxing together?"

Selma sighed and sat back in her chair. "Connor I don't know, this is so sudden. I have appointments, meetings. I'm supposed to do the mid-year review with the accountants next Thursday, Mom is set up to take care of Sheba. And Sheba's teething; she'll be cranky and cry all the way on the plane. I don't know."

"Selly, Sheba is going to be cranky whether we're home or in Florida. I know that your organizations and the Trust are important to you. I'd be the last person to say anything disparaging about what you do; but don't you think that you could change some dates around, just this once? I think that this would be a good thing for all of us."

"Let me think about it, I'll need to make some calls tomorrow."

Connor patted her hand. "Good, make some calls and we can let Emma and Neil know tomorrow night, okay?"

"I don't know Connor, I'll see."

Connor stood and walked to the baby's high chair where he had dropped his jacket and tie. He fished inside the coat and pulled out an envelope. He put the envelope on the table, massaged Selma's shoulders for a few minutes and then returned to his seat. He reached across the table and took her hand.

"Baby, I want to give your father his money back."

Selma's head jerked around. "What? What money?"

Connor flashed his best smile. "The dowry, I want to give him his money back. I spent some of the first year's payment but I was able to replace it with my last bonus. I haven't spent any of the money from this year's payment; altogether, it comes to $51,250. What Jack pays me more than covers my personal expenses and I don't think there's any room left in Sheba's closet for more stuffed animals. I can't pay Papa back for the Jag, or the tickets right now, but he won't have to buy any cars for me in the future."

Connor squeezed her hand. "Selly, if I can get this brokerage going you won't need to pay for our expenses anymore. I believe I can start generating a lot of cash in a few years and then you can retire: if and when you want of course."

Selma was shocked. She felt her throat tighten and her skin grow cold.

"Look, I wrote this letter to Papa thanking him for the dowry and explaining why I want to give the money back. I've put a check with it and I'm going to send it to him tomorrow. I'd like you to read it first. I think that he'll really be surprised, don't you?"

Selma closed her eyes and lowered her head. "Amazed," she mouthed, "amazed."

Selma stared at the floor for nearly a minute before she looked up. "Connor, you can't give Papa the money back, there was no dowry. He never paid you any money. Papa gave us this house as a wedding present, he paid for our wedding and he gave you the sports tickets. That's it, that's all. There was no dowry."

Connor smiled. "Come on, you're kidding? I got twenty-five thousand deposited in my bank account last year and I got another twenty-seven this year."

Selma clasped her hands together and sighed. "That money came from me. I paid for the car and the honeymoon as well. Papa gave us the house and paid for the wedding, that's it."

Connor stood and put his hands on the back of the chair. "Selma you're confusing me. That night at the Art Museum you told me that your father was willing to pay a dowry to someone who would marry you, you told me all the details: the money, car, everything. Did I get that wrong?"

She was feeling nauseous. "No you got it right…That night I also said I told Papa I wouldn't accept him paying out a dowry. Then I said that if you were interested in marrying me that it might be different, that maybe it would be okay."

Connor started to pace. "Selma, this is crazy! You paid for everything; you gave me the money, the car? This is crazy!"

Selma felt hot tears welling up inside, she didn't want to cry; she needed all of her strength to explain her actions. "Connor I loved you. I thought that the dowry was the only chance I had to gain some time with you, time to try and make you love me."

Connor felt a flash of uncontrolled temper shoot up his spine. "With lies? Win my love with lies?"

As hard as she tried Selma couldn't hold back her tears. "Connor you have to believe that it wasn't like that, it just happened. I told Papa no dowry and then realized that the dowry might be the only way for me to win your love. I didn't plan to deceive you, I didn't plan on lying to you, things just happened."

Connor stopped pacing and intently stared at her. "And did you ever think of telling me the truth or were you planning on letting this deception go on forever?"

Selma took a napkin from the table and blotted her eyes. "I almost told you on our honeymoon but then I lost the courage. Since

Sheba's birth I've been so confused, so different. I tried to tell you several times but I never could. I'm sorry, I'm so sorry."

Connor shook his head and started to pace again. "So the money didn't come from your father. Where did you get it?" He took the check from the envelope on the table and held it in front of her. "Fifty two thousand's a lot of money. Do your father and brother pay you that much extra?"

Selma regained some measure of control. "Connor please sit down, I need to tell you everything. No more secrets, no more lies."

Connor stared at her and then sat. "Secrets, lies? What do you mean?"

"Connor, you and I are wealthy, very wealthy. I told you about my Grandmother's apartment buildings."

Connor nodded, "Yes, I remember."

"When Grandmother came to live with us she had something less than one million dollars in assets. She took that money and created a Trust fund administered by an accounting firm in town. Grandmother set up the Trust so that the principal would never be spent; it would come to me on my twenty-first birthday. She arranged that the interest on the Trust's investments would be paid to her charities. The way she set up the Trust there was a cap on how much would be paid out each year. Because of the cap, each year the Trust generated a lot more interest then it paid out and that surplus rolled over into the principal. The increased principal earned even more interest. Grandmother spent very little of the returns. Papa paid for all of her living expenses, and her personal needs were few, mostly gifts to family and friends. This went on for all the years Grandmother lived with us."

"When she died the Trust continued on unchanged. When I turned eighteen, Mr. Goldstein asked me to come to his office to discuss the state of the Trust. I was flabbergasted to discover that over sixteen years the principal had grown to seven million dollars. When I took legal control at twenty-one the principal had grown to over eight million."

"I made some changes. I increased the payout to Grandmother's charities and added some new ones. I set up college funds for all of Jacob and Morty's children and I set up quarterly payments to myself.

Even with that, the Trust still isn't in balance. The principal is still growing by nearly a hundred thousand a year. That's above what I take for myself, for us.

The way things stand right now, there's about a hundred eighty thousand available to us each year, that's without changing any of the payments to charity. Besides that, the eight million plus in principal and the interest that currently goes to charity belongs to us as well. There's nothing legally binding us to continue those contributions, although I expect we will. We are very wealthy people; you, me and Sheba. That's where the dowry payments came from, that's where the Jaguar came from, and that's where the honeymoon came from."

Connor put his head in his hands. After a while he looked up. "Anything else; gold mines in Africa, The Hope Diamond?"

Selma felt curiously calm. There was one more thing she needed to tell him, but she couldn't do it, not now. She shook her head, "No, nothing."

Connor was in total confusion. Selma had lied to him. Lied about the dowry and lied about the Trust. His emotions were raging. His sense of reason kept telling him that he loved his wife and daughter… His emotions won.

In what was almost a whisper, Connor said, "Do you know why I saved up the money to repay your father, why I wrote the letter and the check?"

Selma's flat voice reflected her mental state. "I think I do. You wanted me and Papa and everyone else to know that you're successful and will be even more successful in the future."

"Got that right," He began to pace again. "That's where I started. I wanted everyone to be proud of me. But then you know what happened? I decided to tell you that I've grown up. I wanted to show you that I didn't need your father's money or cars or tickets or houses. I don't need anything but you and our baby."

He turned away and stared out of the window into the night… "I'm confused. It's like we're in the middle of a chess game and all of the rules have been changed. I don't know where I'm allowed to move, what I think, I don't know how I feel…I need to get away by myself for a while…I'm going to drive down to Tampa…Now, tonight."

Jac Simensen

Selma stood. "Do you think that's wise? It's nine-thirty, you're up-set. Please don't go now. You could go tomorrow, maybe fly?"

"I need to think. I need to be alone. I'll stay in a motel off the Turnpike tonight."

Selma sat at the top of the stairs outside Sheba's bedroom. She listened to the raspy exhaust tones of the XKE as Connor and the car receded into the night.

She forced herself to stand and tiptoed into the baby's room. Sheba was lying on her side, sound asleep. Selma returned to the kitchen. She dumped the half-full glasses of wine into the sink.

She picked up Connor's check from the table and started to put it back into the envelope when she realized that she hadn't read the letter. She sat and unfolded the single sheet.

Dear Papa,

Enclosed is a check covering the two dowry payments you de-posited in my bank account. Sorry, but I'm not yet able to repay you for my car but I will soon. I don't expect you to pay for any future cars.

Please don't take any offense to my returning this money. I un-derstand that you offered the dowry to me with the very best of intentions; to make your daughter happy. I think that I can confidently say that the dowry accomplished its purpose and that our Selma is happy in her new life and secure in my love.

I'm a very different person today than I was two years ago when I met Selma. As you know I've been pretty successful at my job. That's good and I'm proud that I'm no longer a first class screw-up. The important thing is that my life now has a center and it's no longer me. My life revolves around my two girls. I love my wife and my sweet baby daughter with all my heart. My real job is to care for them and protect them for the rest of my life.

I'm looking forward to the beginning of football season and our Sunday's together at Franklin Field.

I don't see any reason why you or I ever need to mention the dowry again.

Your Grateful, Number Three Son,
Connor

Selma dropped the letter, it drifted to the floor. She started to laugh; and then she began to cry.

chapter

TWENTY-SEVEN

The sun had just risen, revealing the prospect of a cloudy, over-cast day. Connor pulled up in front of the garage. He pushed the re-mote and the big door rumbled upward. He looked at his face in the mirror on the sun visor; not pretty. He had a two-day beard and his eyes were red and hollowed out from non-stop driving. Selma's car was gone. He left the Jag outside and entered the house through the garage. He looked on the kitchen counter for a note, there wasn't any.

"Selma," he called. No reply. He bounded up the stairs to the ba-by's room. The blankets in the baby's crib were neatly folded. Sheba's teddy bear and skunk were next to the pillow, awaiting her return. Connor wandered from room to room. Everything looked as usual but there was no Selma, no baby, and no note. Connor walked out to the mailbox. There was no mail so apparently they hadn't been gone for long.

Connor's stomach hurt. He hadn't had anything besides Twinkies, Fig Newton's and coffee for the last day and a half. He had a headache and his rear was sore from sitting.

He showered, shaved, dressed and went to the kitchen to make a sandwich. He was hungry but felt nauseous at the same time. He made a Swiss cheese on rye and poured a glass of iced tea. The first bite tasted dry and he had trouble swallowing, but the remainder of the sandwich went down easily and cured the nausea.

He needed to see Selma. He needed to see the baby. He needed to see them right away.

He walked to the pantry and opened the door. Selma kept a calendar on the back of the door where she noted their appointments. He ran his finger across the dates to the nineteenth. Selma had written, 'Dr. Beegan—10:30.' He was puzzled. Dr. Beegan; Neil Lionel's mother? Beegan was an unusual name, surely it must be her? He saw that two days before on the seventeenth there was another entry in Selma's distinct writing. 'Dr. Corley—Pre-op exam, 9:50.' Connor narrowed his eyes. Pre-op exam, what was going on?

Connor called Ellie, she answered on the third ring. "Mom, it's me. Are Selma and the baby with you?"

"Connor, where are you?"

"I'm home and Selma and Sheba aren't here, do you know where they are? Selma's written something on the calendar about an appointment with Dr. Beegan. Do you know what's going on?"

Connor heard Ellie take a deep breath. "Connor, the baby's here with me. Selma's in the hospital. She's okay but having some surgery. They should send her home tomorrow. Come over now and I'll explain. Look in the pantry and see if there's any of that peach jam that the baby loves, I forgot to get some."

Connor felt the nausea return. "What's wrong with Selma? I need to know, now."

"Selma's okay, she's not in any danger. Don't drive fast and bring the peach jam."

Connor was about to object when he heard a dial tone. Ellie had hung up.

What in hell was going on, Selma in the hospital having surgery? Connor's head was pounding; he went into the bathroom and took three aspirin. He saw his face in the mirror. He looked better without the stubble but his eyes were still badly bloodshot. He dropped in some Murine; there was an initial sting followed by comfort. He went back to the kitchen, grabbed his keys and started to exit to the garage. "Woops, peach jam," he said aloud.

Connor's mind raced. Surgery, what kind of surgery? Dr. Beegan, why Dr. Beegan? Connor remembered that Billy worked at the Veteran's Administration Hospital in Philly. He thought that he could recall his mother telling him that Billy was an expert in repairing soldiers disfiguring combat damage from bullet and shrapnel wounds and burns. Burns! That must be it; Selma had burnt herself and was getting some kind of skin graft. No, that didn't make sense. On the calendar she had marked 'Pre-op exam' and that was for the day before yesterday. People didn't have advance Pre-op exams for emergency surgery. Thank God, probably not a burn.

Connor's pulse was pounding; he looked at the speedometer, he was doing fifty-five in a thirty zone. He slowed; this was not the time to get stopped for speeding. He was close now, only a few miles from his old home. A large black dog shot out from between two parked cars. Connor slammed on the brakes and steered to the right, the dog flashed by uninjured and the Jag managed to hold to a true track and allow Connor to regain control. Connor shivered. Thank God for disc brakes, he thought.

Connor pulled into the drive and jumped from the car. He was nearly to the side door when he remembered the jam. "Damn!"

Ellie was standing in the kitchen with Sheba in her arms. "It's Daddy!" She cried as Connor entered.

Sheba turned her gaze to Connor and extended her arms. "Daaa," she called excitedly, "Daaa." Sheba was in a growth spurt. In the seven days since Connor had seen her, he thought she must have grown an inch. Her hair fell onto her forehead and framed her small face in large, reddish brown curls.

Connor took the baby from his mother and held her aloft. Sheba smiled and giggled as Connor pumped her up and down in the air. He kissed her on the nose and held her close to his chest.

"Mom, what in hell is going on? What's wrong with Selma? Why is she in the hospital?"

Ellie gently removed the baby from his arms. "Connor you need to calm down and sit down while I take care of this starving baby. Did you bring the peach jam?"

Connor pointed to the jar he had set on the counter. Ellie plopped Sheba into her highchair, adjusted the tray and tied a bib around her neck. "Connor get the box of teething biscuits on the counter and the jam, please."

Connor opened the jam jar and took two biscuits from the box. "Two enough?"

Ellie nodded. "Now get us some coffee and we'll talk in just a minute." Ellie spread the jam on the biscuits and placed one on Sheba's tray. "If you give her two, she always throws the second one on the floor. She's got a new tooth coming in, had a bit of a fever last night, nothing to be concerned about."

The baby licked the jam from the biscuit and gurgled a long, incomprehensible infant sentence.

Connor poured two cups of coffee and sat at the table next to the high chair. He ran his fingers along Sheba's chubby toes. Ellie sat on the other side of the highchair. She looked at Connor and shook her head.

Ellie patted Connor's hand and put the second biscuit on the highchair tray. "It's going to take me a few minutes to tell you the whole story. Understand, Selma's in no danger, she'll be fine and home tomorrow or the next day."

Sheba banged the biscuit on the tray and babbled in Ellie's direction.

"She's a smart little girl. Last night she stood up by herself…Okay, let me tell you what's been happening. Have you ever heard the expression *Baby Blues*?"

Connor shook his head.

"Well after their babies are born, a lot of women feel really down and depressed. It's actually quite common. Some women are depressed for a day or two or a week and a few for longer. Selma's been down for months."

Connor interrupted. "Are you sure? She didn't seem particularly down to me."

Ellie smiled. "That girl is so strong-willed that she's been keeping it bottled up inside of her. I only got to see what was wrong with her after you left for Florida. She and I have done a lot of talking this past week."

Connor lowered his head. "Mom, it was so stupid of me to rush off that way, I really screwed up didn't I?"

Ellie patted his hand. "Let's stick with Selma; we'll talk about my idiot son later."

Sheba banged her tiny fist on the tray.

"Can you get another biscuit daddy? We're so hungry today aren't we?"

She turned back to Connor. "Remember when you were taking that course for your real estate license right after Selma and Sheba came home from the hospital?"

Connor put the box of biscuits next to Ellie. "Yeah, I had already started the course and Reba was staying at the house then, so it seemed alright to finish. Selma said she was happy for me to finish. Was there a problem?"

Ellie nodded. "There was, but it wasn't your fault. Do you remember the story Selma told you about how her father started to fool around with other women right after she was born and how he took a mistress?"

Connor sat back in his chair. "I promised Selma not to tell anyone about that, I took a pinky promise!"

Ellie laughed loudly. Sheba pointed to Ellie and laughed in imitation. "It's okay; I made a pinky promise as well." Ellie spread more jam on the baby's biscuit and handed it back to her.

"Because of her depression Selma was convinced that you were fooling around with other women. She said that when you came home at night that she would search all over your jacket and shirt looking for hairs or lipstick. She was so paranoid that she even inspected your underwear!"

Connor bit his lip. "Good God, I never knew, I never imagined. I wasn't you know; I mean screwing around with other women."

"Yes, I know, I know you very well."

"So for the last ten months, Selma's been stewing in her blues afraid that she would lose you, terrified that you would go off with someone more attractive. You know that she really loves you don't you?"

Connor lowered his head into his hands. "Yes, I know she really loves me."

He looked up, played with Sheba's hair and pushed a ringlet behind her ear. Sheba grabbed his finger and tried to pull it to her mouth. "No, you don't want to eat fingers, they're tough and nasty." He picked up the biscuit from the tray and put it in her hand. She looked for jam and seeing none extended the biscuit toward Ellie.

"See what I mean, see how smart she is?" Ellie spread more jam on the biscuit.

"Two months ago Selma went to see her Aunt Sally. Selma told Sally that she wanted a nose job. Sally tried to change her mind, she told Selma that rhinoplasty on mature people was more problematic than on adolescents. Selma was adamant, she begged Sally to help her find the absolute best specialist to do the procedure. Sally told her that there was only one person she would consider; my old friend, Doctor Billy Beegan."

Connor turned his head. "I had no idea that Neil's mom did nose jobs."

"She doesn't. After her brother Lionel died during the war Billy decided to specialize in restorative surgery for facial wounds, mostly combat injuries. Most of her work is for the Veterans Administration, she flies all over the country to VA Hospitals to work on the faces of war-scarred veterans. She doesn't make nearly the kind of money working for the VA that she would in private practice, but since her parents left her a fortune, money was never her concern. Billy does only restorative surgery, not cosmetic surgery but she made an exception for Selma. With Billy's heavy case load, she told Selma that it would take a while to schedule and that she could only give Selma a few days notice when they were ready to go. Billy's office called her the day after you went to Florida."

Connor smacked his fist on the table. Sheba was startled and looked like she might cry. Connor stroked her head and let her grip his thumb.

"Mom, why didn't she tell me? Why didn't she say something?"

Ellie shook her head, "I don't know I really don't. After you left and Billy's office called, Selma and the baby came to see me, just dropped by. Selma was nearly hysterical. The dam was ready to burst. Ever since her grandmother died she's been holding a lot inside; over twenty year's worth. Most of our conversations will stay between me and Selma. I'll tell you this though. Selma is one fine woman. She loves you and Sheba with all her heart….Know this Connor Sullivan; you couldn't do any better than Selma, in fact I'm not sure that you deserve her."

Connor put his head on the table.

Ellie wiped Sheba's hands and face with the clean side of the bib and lifted her from the highchair. "I'm going to put this baby in for her nap. I'll be back in a few minutes."

When Ellie returned, Connor was standing in front of the kitchen window looking out at the bird feeder. "There's a pair of cardinals at the feeder. Cardinals were Grandpa Jakes favorites. He used to buy special seeds to attract them. I remember once sitting with him watching the cardinals feed during a snow storm; their red bodies, black masks and yellow beaks dancing between the snow flakes."

Ellie stroked the back of Connor's head. "Sunflower seeds, that's what he bought. I still buy them."

Connor continued to stare at the feeder. "She didn't need to do this you know. I'm not gonna love her more because she has a pretty, new nose. It doesn't matter to me anymore."

Ellie shrugged. "Maybe this doesn't have anything to do with you."

Connor turned toward her. "What? I don't understand?"

"Connor maybe this isn't about anyone but Selma. Think about it; ever since Selma can remember she's been told that she's flawed. Her grandmother told her she would never find a husband, that's why she wanted to make sure Selma had enough money to take care of herself. Others gave her the same message, but with their actions toward her instead of words. She looks at you, the man she adores; she sees a handsome face, a captivating smile. She looks at Sheba and she sees herself, her own face, but perfect, unflawed."

Connor closed his eyes and lowered his head. "Mom, where is she? I need to go to her now."

"She's at Jefferson; Reba took her in this morning. The surgery's scheduled for twelve-thirty."

Connor hugged his mother and headed for the door. "I have to go, probably too late to see her before she goes into the operating room but I want to be there when she wakes up."

Ellie called after him. "Don't be too hard on yourself, everything is going to turn out fine, I know it will."

———

Connor was approaching the Ben Franklin Bridge when he noticed that the gas gauge was in the red…'Reserve Fuel,' it read. He'd never seen the gauge that low and had no idea how many miles the Jag could still travel before it hit the bottom of the tank. He was coming up on the last gas station before the bridge and had to make a decision fast, he was pretty sure that there were no gas stations near the bridge on the Philadelphia side; he kept driving.

He crossed the bridge and wound his way toward Spruce Street. The mid-day traffic wasn't particularly heavy. As he turned onto South Eleventh Street he began to see signs for all the different buildings and branches of the hospital; he had forgotten what a huge facility Jefferson was. He started to panic, he had no idea in which building he would find Selma. At the end of the block Connor saw a policeman. He pulled near the policeman and rolled down the window.

"Excuse me officer, my wife is having surgery, do you have any idea where they do the operations?"

The policeman approached the Jag; he was a very large, black man with a barrel chest and huge arms. The driver of the Yellow Cab behind the Jag started to blow his horn.

The policeman lowered his head and said to Connor. "Excuse me one minute sir, just stay there." The policeman crossed to the other side of the Jag and pointed to the taxi. "You, this is a Hospital Zone,

one more beep on that horn and I'll present you with a ticket for a fifty dollar fine."

The taxi driver slid down in his seat and looked the other way. The policeman returned to the Jaguar.

"Surgery, you said sir?"

"Yes, officer, that's right."

"She's having surgery at Jefferson?"

"Yes, at Jefferson."

"You go down two blocks and turn left then right away turn left into the underground parking garage. Go to the first floor and they'll direct you from there."

"Thanks officer, I appreciate your help."

———

Connor ignored the reserved sign and pulled into the first open parking slot. The gas gauge was at the bottom of Reserve Fuel. His fingers hurt from the intensity of his grip on the wheel, his pulse pounded in his ears and his head throbbed.

He switched off the ignition, closed his eyes and lowered his head…Sheba's smiling face danced before him…she was perfect, flawless.

It started at the back of his neck, spread to his face and then throughout his torso; a feeling of peace, of serenity. Connor went limp. His chin rested on his chest. He sat motionless for nearly five minutes.

A well dressed, elderly man tapped on Connor's window with the handle of his cane. "Are you alright? Do you need help?"

Connor broke from the trance and rolled down the window. The man repeated his questions.

"Thanks. I'm just fine."

The gentleman moved from the window and started to walk away. Connor opened the door and got out. "Thanks for your concern. Everything's just great."

The woman at the information desk sat so motionless that she could have been a mannequin. She wore a dark dress with a cheap-looking faux cameo at the throat, her glasses hung around her neck on a black cord.

"Excuse me ma'am, my wife is having surgery, can you tell me where I can find her room?"

The woman's head twitched as if she was awaking from sleep. She looked at Connor. "What, what did you say?"

Connor repeated his question.

"Surgery you said?" Connor nodded.

"Her name?"

"Sullivan, Selma Sullivan."

The woman looked at Connor for the first time. "Do you know her doctor's name?"

"Yes, it's Beegan, Dr. Billy Beegan."

The woman's whole demeanor instantly changed. "Oh, your wife is the one Dr. Beegan's come to see. How fortunate for you, for her. Dr. Beegan is the finest surgeon in Philadelphia. She seldom comes here anymore except for special cases. Your wife must be someone important."

Connor nodded. "She's very important to me. Dr. Beegan's family and my family have known each other for years."

The woman was not to be denied. "Well then that makes your wife someone important. Just a second, Mr. Sullivan." She picked up the phone and pressed a button. "Candice, can you come out to the front please? I have a gentleman who needs to be escorted to the Director's waiting room. Mmm, Dr. Beegan is operating on his wife." She hung up and turned to Connor. "Please have a seat Mr. Sullivan; Candice will be right out to take you to the surgical waiting room."

Connor thanked her and sat on a stiff leather chair. He had hardly eased himself into the chair when an attractive young woman with her hand outstretched appeared.

"Mr. Sullivan, I'm Candice Tyler. Can you please come with me?"

They passed through a door marked 'Private—Staff Only,' and after a few steps entered a small elevator. Connor noticed that Candice checked out his wedding ring. "It's your wife who's having surgery with Dr. Beegan, is that right?"

"Yes, Selma, Selma Sullivan."

The elevator stopped at the third floor. Candice stepped out. "Follow me please. They walked down one long hall and stopped at a door marked Private. Candice opened the door and motioned for Connor to enter. The room was large and filled with comfortable furniture. There was a TV and phones were placed on tables around the room. At the far end of the room were a bar and a small fridge.

"This is the Director's waiting room. We like to take very good care of Dr. Beegan when she's with us and her patient's families as well. There are sandwiches on the bar, soft drinks in the fridge and fresh coffee in the urn. Please help yourself. I think that you'll find everything you need. The rest room is behind that door. Please feel free to use the phone and switch on the TV if you wish. If you need anything press the red button at the bottom of the dial, which will connect you with Margaret, the Director's assistant. Margaret will be with you in a few minutes; she'll bring you up to date on the progress of your wife's procedure. I believe that you know Dr. Beegan?"

"Her son is my best friend, we grew up together."

Candice smiled. "Do you have any questions?"

"Is there any chance that I can see my wife before she goes into surgery?"

"Candice shook her head. You'll have to ask Margaret, she'll know your wife's status. Anything else?"

Connor extended his hand. "No, Miss Tyler, thank you."

She gave him a big smile. "My pleasure; I don't believe that anyone beside you will be using this room today."

Connor was quite hungry. He checked out the sandwiches. The bad news was that they were the little cocktail sandwiches that women had with tea; the good news was that there were lots of them.

The door opened and a small, slim woman entered, she was obviously of Asian ancestry. "Good Morning, Mr. Sullivan, or rather, Good Afternoon. I'm Margaret Owens and I'll be looking after you while you're here." They shook hands.

"You're English?" Connor asked.

"No, I'm from India. My husband worked for the State Department and when he returned home from an assignment he brought back some Asian art and me as well. I've been here in Philadelphia for twenty years, but the accent endures, British schooling you know."

Connor grinned. "Ah, I see."

Jac Simensen

"Actually Mr. Sullivan we were quite surprised to see you here. Your wife said that you were in Florida, on business."

Connor nodded. "Yes, I was, but I drove back last night."

"My, how long did that take? Florida's a good way off."

"It took about a day and a half."

She patted him on the arm. "I'm sure that your wife will be very pleased to see you when she wakes up. Shall we sit over here on the couch and I can tell you what to expect?" She and Connor moved away from the bar to the couch.

"Mrs. Owens, is there any possibility that I can see my wife before see goes into the OR?"

"I was sure that would be your first question so I called the holding area where Mrs. Sullivan is waiting before I came here. She's in a sterile environment where you could enter only if you were scrubbed, gowned and masked; unfortunately, there isn't enough time for that now."

Connor nodded. "I understand, thanks for checking."

Mrs. Owens looked down at the notepad in her hand. "I'm not part of the medical staff so I can't explain any aspect of the procedure, but I can keep you apprised of the progress."

Connor nodded. "I understand."

"The procedure should take an hour, perhaps a bit more. Doctor Corley will be assisting Doctor Beegan. Doctor Corley is a surgical staff member here at Jefferson, he and Doctor Beegan often work together. After the procedure is completed Mrs. Sullivan will be taken to the recovery area. When Doctor Beegan is satisfied that your wife's overall condition is stable, I'll bring Doctor Beegan here to talk with you.

When Mrs. Sullivan has settled in her room I'll take you to see her: its twelve-fifty now so I expect that will be about three. I'll come by to let you know when she's in the recovery area. Is there anything else I can do for you?"

Connor extended his hand. "Thank you Mrs. Owens you've been very kind, everyone has."

She took his hand. "If you need me my office is just two doors down on the right. Oh, if you leave this room would you please let me know so I'll know where to find you?"

244

Connor thanked her again and she left.

Connor picked up the phone and dialed Ellie; it rang ten times before he hung up. 'Probably doing something with the baby,' he thought.

He walked to the bar put several of the tiny sandwiches on a plate and opened a can of apple juice. He ate the first sandwich in one bite and drank the juice from the can. He ate several more sandwiches and finished the juice. He took the *Inquirer* from the rack and scanned the headlines. The stories were mostly about Vietnam. His eyes scanned the words but with little comprehension. He looked at his watch; it had been twenty minutes since he called Ellie. He picked up the phone on the bar and dialed again, this time she answered right away.

"Oh, hi, was that you a few minutes ago? I had the baby in the tub and couldn't leave her."

Connor told her where he was and what he knew about Selma.

"I've got some interesting news for you too. Just before you called, Billy phoned. She's there at the hospital and was just getting washed up. She talked with Emma in Florida last night and knew that you were probably here by now. I told her that you were on your way to the hospital. She wanted to know if it was alright for her to tell Selma that you were at the hospital. Emma must have told her something of the circumstances of your departure from Florida."

"Yeah, Em and I had several talks."

"Billy wanted to know if she should tell Selma that you were there, I told her yes, I hope that's okay?"

"That's great mom, I'm really happy she knows I'm here. Did Billy say anything else?"

"Only that she was sure that things would go well with the procedure."

"Okay Mom, thanks for calling. Woops, I called you. I think maybe I'll try and get a little sleep, I'm starting to get mentally frazzled."

"Okay, call me when you can."

"Right and give my littlest girl a kiss. Love ya."

"Love you too, bye,"

Connor took off his shoes and stretched out on the couch. 'They're probably just putting Selma under now,' he thought.

———————

Connor felt a sense of emptiness and loss; it was both a physical and mental sensation. The cold spread from his legs across his abdomen and into his chest. He was a child, frantically wandering the aisles in the tool department of a Sears store looking for his father; Connor was lost and alone and started to cry. He heard Selma calling to him; it wasn't a cry for help but more an erotic call for his attention. She was in the blue French negligee and was smiling, standing in a forest with the wind blowing her hair out behind her. He ran toward her, she sneezed and covered her mouth with her hands. When she moved her hands from her face they were bloody, blood flowed from her nose and mouth and dripped onto her breasts. Connor screamed and sat straight up.

Mrs. Owens was kneeling next to the sofa rubbing on his arm. "Mr. Sullivan, wake up, Mr. Sullivan!"

Connor focused on Mrs. Owens anxious face. "I'm sorry; I was having a bad dream." With a shock Connor saw that Mrs. Owens appeared concerned. "Selma; is there anything wrong?"

She smiled. "Nothing's wrong, the procedure went well and Mrs. Sullivan is awake and in post-op recovery."

Connor's entire body went limp. "Thank God," he said. "Thank God."

Mrs. Owens stood up. "You gave me a fright Mr. Sullivan, you were screaming like the devil himself was chasing you."

Connor shifted on the sofa and sat up. "I think I was overly tired from all of the driving, I was having one bad dream after another. I'm sorry I frightened you."

"No matter," she said. "Your wife is just fine, that's what's important. Doctor Beegan is finishing the paperwork and will be up in a few minutes. As soon as they tell me that Mrs. Sullivan's back in her room and receiving guests I'll come and get you."

Connor stood. "Thanks Mrs. Owens, I'll just go clean up in the wash room."

"There's a disposable toothbrush and tooth paste in there and some mouth wash as well."

"Would you happen to have any aspirin?"

She shook her head. "Anacin, will that do?"

Connor smiled. "Sure, that's fine."

Mrs. Owens started for the door. "I'll leave it on the coffee table if you're still in the lavatory."

Connor hadn't seen Billy since Neil Lionel's wedding. She was wearing slacks, penny loafers and a University of Florida, Gators sweat shirt; she dropped her brown leather jacket on a chair.

"I have a message from Selma. She said to tell you that now she's as beautiful as you and Sheba!" Billy gave Connor a big hug.

"Connor I'm so pleased that you could be here. Ellie told me that you were on your way and I told Selma just before we sent her off to 'LaLa Land.' She went to sleep with a big smile on her face. I just left her in post-op; she's wide awake, fully conscious and talking. After they get her cleaned up and back in her room you can see her yourself."

Connor smiled broadly. "Billy we're so appreciative that you did this for Selma, all of us."

Billy put her hand on his shoulder. "Actually Doctor Corley did the difficult part, all the internal reshaping. I just made sure that her lovely skin was put back just so. Connor she's not going to be exactly beautiful for a few weeks. All the stress to tissue, bone and nerves results in considerable contusion and swelling. She's going to have some pretty colorful bruises and black eyes for a while. She's going to be mighty sore as well. The nurses will explain all about her care requirements tomorrow before they let you take her home."

Mrs. Owens opened the door. "Your car is here, Doctor Beegan."

Billy hugged Connor again and kissed him on the cheek. "Sorry, Connor I have to run. I'm doing two cleft palates in Miami tomorrow morning; turning a couple of sad little tykes into the beautiful children they were meant to be. Then, I get to go to Tampa and spend five relaxing days with my profligate son and his beautiful, intelligent wife. Big Neal's coming in for the weekend as well. It'll be only the second time we've all been together since their wedding." She picked up her jacket and headed for Mrs. Owens and the open door.

"Bye Connor, love to everyone and I hope to see your beautiful Bathsheba soon, Ellie's promised to get us all together before the year's out."

Connor waved. "Bye, Billy, thanks a million."

Mrs. Owens pointed at Connor. "Don't go anywhere; I'll be right back for you."

———

Connor was ecstatic. He called Ellie and gave her the positive news. She volunteered to help take care of Selma and Sheba for as long as necessary.

"And Connor, why don't you stop home and pick up some clothes and then come here for dinner and overnight. I'm afraid that Sheba has evicted you from your room, but the guest room's free. Be good for you to be with your daughter and family tonight, wouldn't it? I'll make meat cakes in brown gravy with lumpy mashed potatoes."

Connor grinned. "How could I ever resist your lumpy mashed potatoes?"

———

Mrs. Owens left Connor at the nurse's station with Nurse Kenisha Allen.

"Just you stay right here while I make sure that your little girl is ready for you." Kenisha waddled off towards Selma's room; she was almost half as wide as she was tall. After a minute or two she stuck her head out of the doorway. "Com'on honey." As Connor and Kenisha passed each other in the hall she tapped him on the arm. "Now don't you stay too long, this girl needs some rest; and no hanky-panky!" She laughed loudly at her own humor. Connor was taken back by Selma's room. It was like no hospital room he had seen; a private room with sea blue carpeting, chestnut paneling and birch, Swedish modern furniture. There was a long west facing window that filled the room with afternoon light. Selma was sitting up in a conventional hospital bed. She was wearing a pink nightgown Connor recognized. Her long, dark hair cascaded down the side of the pillows that were placed behind her back. She had an IV drip attached to her left hand and held an ice bag to her forehead. She had a phone in her right hand. She beamed at him and gave a wave with the ice bag when he entered. He noticed that she already had several bouquets of cut flowers.

"I've got to go, Connor's here. Yes, call when Dad gets home, I can talk to Sheba then. Okay, bye Mom, love ya too."

Selma put down the phone and held out her right hand. He took her hand in both of his and held it to his lips.

"Hi," she said, in her best husky voice.

"Hi yourself," he replied, he continued to hold her hand.

"I was so pleased that you were here during the operation. When Billy told me that she had talked with you and that you were here at the hospital it felt like you were right there with me."

Connor smiled at her. "I was with you; I'll always be with you."

She squeezed his hand. "How do I look? Doctor Corley gave me a mirror when I came too, before they put all of these bandages on and this plastic contraption over my nose. All I could tell was that I had a lot less nose and that what was still there was bright red, like Rudolph."

Connor grinned.

"So, how do I look?" She repeated.

He rubbed her arm with one hand while he held her hand with the other. "Truth?" he said.

"I think it would be alright if you lied, just this once."

"I can't see your new nose but I'm sure it must be perfect just like the rest of you. Your eye shadow is truly amazing, I've never seen so many intense shades of pink, green, yellow, blue and black around a woman's eyes before, remarkable."

Selma grinned, "That bad, huh? Kenisha put on the lip gloss. You met Kenisha, right?"

Connor nodded.

"She said that I needed to be beautiful for my husband, but she wouldn't give me a mirror."

"Billy said that you'd be pretty banged up and sore for a few weeks. They're going to teach me how to take care of you tomorrow morning before I take you home."

"Mom said that she'd bring Sheba home tomorrow afternoon and then hang out for a few days. That's good; I think I'm going to need help. They've got me all doped up with local anesthetic so I'm not feeling much now, but I'm sure that this isn't going to be fun when the local wears off. You know how painful it is when you bang your nose."

Connor grinned. "You've probably had more experience with hitting your nose than I have."

"Connor!" She threw the ice bag and hit him in the chest.

He laughed, "You have to understand, now that you have a beautiful new nose, nose jokes aren't off limits anymore."

"Connor, you are truly exasperating!"

He retrieved the ice bag and placed it back on her forehead.

She put her left hand over the bag. "When did you get back from Florida?"

"This morning, early…I washed up and changed at home and then went to my parents and had breakfast with my beautiful daughter."

"When did you find out about my operation, that I was in the hospital?"

"When I talked with my mother…I saw your notes on the calendar at home so I knew that something was up."

Selma lowered her head. "It must have been quite a shock. I really struggled to decide whether to call you in Florida. I wasn't sure when you were coming back, if you were coming back. I couldn't decide what to do. I'm so sorry; do you think that you'll be able to forgive me for the lies, all the things I did wrong?"

Connor squeezed her small hand. A tear spilled from his left eye and ran down his cheek and then another; tears of relief, of joy. "You didn't do anything wrong, there's nothing to excuse. I'm sorry that I stormed out on you. I acted like a selfish, spoiled jackass. If there's any forgiving to be done it should be me asking you."

Selma stroked the damp lines on his cheek. "So, are you asking?"

"What?"

She grinned impishly. "Are you asking for my forgiveness, selfish, spoiled, jackass?"

Connor grinned and they both burst into laughter.

Selma took a few tissues from the bedside box and passed them to Connor. He wiped his eyes and blew his nose. She stroked the side of his head. "So, we're okay?"

Connor placed his hand on hers. "We're not okay, we're great."

"No, I mean us, you and me, we're okay?"

"Well, let's see…I love you and I'm positive you love me and we both love our sweet little girl. Yeah, I think we're okay."

She bit her lip, "How about Florida, Neil Lionel's development, the golf course?"

"Not a big deal."

"You're not just saying that, you're positive?"

Connor nodded, "Positive."

"Okay," he said. "Here's the plan. First, we're gonna get you through the next couple of weeks of discomfort. Then we'll take your expensive new nose to the Caribbean and get it tanned. Emma told me about this exclusive place in the British Virgin Islands where she and her parents stayed when her mother was alive. We're going there for two weeks, maybe three, all of us, Sheba too. And then you're going to start working on my education."

"Education?" Selma asked.

"Uh huh, you're going to teach me the in's and out's of being seriously wealthy, that's a course I know I can ace; and, when we get back home, I think that I'll just spend the rest of my life taking care of my girls."

Selma grinned and held out her right hand with the little finger extended. "Pinky promise?" she asked.

Connor intertwined his finger with hers, "Pinky promise," he replied.